Praise for the Shay O'H...

Bingo Barge Murder

"A winner. This is the author's maiden voyage, but you would never know it without reading Ellen Hart's blurb on the back cover. Chandler introduces Shay O'Hanlon, co-owner of a Minneapolis coffee house. Shay makes the rapid transition from barista to sleuth when a good friend is accused of murder. What on earth is the connection among murder, bingo and barge? Pick this one up to find out. Let me assure you that you won't be taking a gamble on reading this delightful romp."
—*Mystery Lover's Review*

"*Bingo Barge Murder* is a solid first entry in the Shay O'Hanlon mystery series. Chandler writes with a wonderful sense of place, plenty of humor, and a crisp pace. The best part for me were the characters, which were so richly drawn that they felt like instant friends. This is a great read from the very first page!"
—Ellen Hart, author of the Jane Lawless Mystery Series

Hide and Snake Murder

"Fast paced and witty. It is peppered with wonderfully colorful characters, making it a strong second novel in the Shay O'Hanlon Caper Series."

–*Lambda Literary*

"*Hide and Snake Murder* takes us to the beginning and end of the Mississippi, New Orleans and Minneapolis, capturing the quirky charm of both cities. It's a rollicking read with an entertaining cast of funny and fascinating characters. You won't be able to turn the pages fast enough."

—J.M. Redmann, author of the Goldie award-winning novel *Water Mark: A Micky Knight Mystery*

Pickle in the Middle Murder

"If you only read one Twin Cities pickle-based murder mystery this year, make it Jessie Chandler's. Oh, and the dogs - Dawg and Bogey - only just manage not to steal the whole show. Great fun with a big heart: I loved it."

—Catriona McPherson, award-winning author of the Dandy Gilver Mystery Series

"Thrilling third Shay O'Hanlon Caper. Chandler keeps the suspense high."

—*Publisher's Weekly*

Chip Off the Ice Block Murder

"The wackiness and zaniness continues! In Book 4 of Chandler's award-winning Caper Series, Shay and her pals get into yet another big mess, and the results are amusing, suspenseful, and hilarious."
—Lori L. Lake, author of *Eight Dates*, *Like Lovers Do*, and The Gun Series

"Chandler's style is easy, her pace is fast and she's earning a growing reputation among lesbian and straight readers."
—Marianne Grossman, St. Paul Pioneer Press

"...buckle in for an icy, chuckle-inducing, fast-paced roller-coaster under the overcast skies of wintry Minnesota. Enjoy!"
—C-Spot Reviews

"It's all good fun from a whodunit and whydunit perspective, and the book ends with a new challenge for Shay, not a mystery per se, but one that will nonetheless have readers looking forward to the next in the series to see how it plays out."
—*Mysterious Reviews*

Early Praise for Operation Stop Hate

"From the gripping opening to the final, suspense-filled scene, Chandler has penned a page-turner that propels the reader down the rabbit hole into the center of one of today's most deeply disturbing crimes. With grit, humor and heart, Chandler has truly hit her stride in this compelling new mystery."
—Ellen Hart, author of the award-winning Jane Lawless series

In Operation Stop Hate, Jessie Chandler proves herself a gifted writer, as capable of handling intense drama as she is of navigating comic capers in her popular Shay O'Hanlon series. OSH hit me like a gutshot--timely, elegantly plotted, with characters who'll stick with me for a while.
—Jess Lourey, author of the Lefty-nominated Murder by Month Mysteries

Topical and compelling, Operation Stop Hate introduces a new heroine who readers will want to see more of. Chandler weaves current crisis and human drama that grabs hold of your throat and won't let go.
—Lori L. Lake, author of The Gun Series & The Public Eye Series

Also By Jessie Chandler

GOLDIE AWARD-WINNING AUTHOR

JESSIE CHANDLER

OPERATION STOP HATE

BOOK ONE IN THE OPERATION SERIES

Train Wreck XPRESS

Minneapolis, Minnesota

FIRST EDITION
First Printing 2015

Book format: Patty Schramm
Cover design: TreeHouse Studio
Production Editing: Lori L. Lake & Patty Schramm
Copyediting: Nann Dunn

Train Wreck XPress

Chandler, Jessie.
Operation Stop Hate: an Operation Series novel/Jessie Chandler.—
First Edition
ISBN 978-1-63304-801-0
1. Lesbians—Fiction. 2. Murder—Investigation—Fiction. 3. Minneapolis (Minn—Fiction). 4. Mystery Fiction. I. Title.
Train Wreck XPress
Minneapolis, Minnesota
trainwreckxpress.com
Printed in the United States of America

Dedication

For Lori L. Lake, teacher, cheerleader, and occasional whip-wielder. With this novel we come full circle, from terrified student with a ghastly manuscript to a theoretically semi-competent writer, and what I hope is a truly entertaining tale.
Thank you.

Acknowledgments

Wow. I wasn't sure Operation Stop Hate would live to see the light of day. For ten years this bad boy gathered dust languishing on my hard drive. Without the encouragement of Lori L. Lake and Patty Schramm, I would not have had the guts to tackle the seething mess of a manuscript and turn it into something I'm proud of and am excited to share.

Nann Dunn is a last minute trooper. With grace and patience, she took this manuscript and line-edited the hell out of it. So many thanks for the fast and thorough work, and for the love you put into all you do.

So many readers have had a hand helping me reimagine this story. DJ Schuette, Judy Kerr, Lori L. Lake, MB Panichi, Patricia Lopez, Patty Schramm, Ruta Skujins, and I don't know who I'm forgetting—my appreciation knows no bounds.

Brian Landon and the rest of the Hartless Murderers had my back when I started writing this book, and Brian still has my back now. It's been a great collaboration, and may we continue on another ten years.

Once Upon a Crime Bookstore and my beloved Pat and Gary. Steadfast booksellers, voracious readers, and loyal supporters, you are vital to the mystery community. And to me.

Still standing strong behind me is my wife, my love, and my inspiration. Betty Ann, your support of this always iffy endeavor is unwavering. Love you so much. Always forever.

To those of you who put up cold, hard cash to purchase books, read them, and love them—I adore you. Thank you for your support!

Prologue

The second gunshot came less than a minute after the first. The sharp blast faded, replaced by the frenetic sound of music drumming through Sony headphones. They covered the ears of a young man who moved with slow, deliberate steps down an empty hall. Blond curls brushed the collar of a black Carhartt jacket, and worn jeans hung loosely on his thin frame.

He peered carefully through the narrow, rectangular windows on each classroom door. Inside, students cowered alongside terrified teachers. As he systematically checked one room after another, he tonelessly hummed to the thumping rhythm in his ears. Halfway down the hall, he froze in front of one of the windows. After a moment, he raised a hand and tried the doorknob.

School protocol dictated that in the event of a threat involving potential or realized violence, the teacher's task was to lock down their classroom. The teacher within had followed directions.

The boy wrenched violently at the knob. The door shuddered under the onslaught.

He stepped back, aimed a black handgun between the knob and the doorjamb and pulled the trigger. The deafening report of the gunshot sent the still classroom into a blur of movement. Kids screamed, scrambling for cover. The teacher charged toward the now-splintered entry at the same time the shooter slammed the sole of his scuffed boot in the center of the door. It swung violently inward, into the woman. She bounced off the door and skidded across the floor.

The boy calmly stepped over the motionless teacher and scanned the room. He reached up and tugged his headphones off, leaving them slung around his neck, the pounding bass now clearly audible.

The shooter focused on a thin teen in jeans and an untucked, green flannel shirt. "Hunter."

A wide-eyed, longhaired girl who'd been standing near Hunter backed slowly away.

Hunter made a choking sound and his face blanched. He raised his hands. "No, Mike, please. What's—"

The gunshot shattered the air. Hunter spun as if a hand reached down from the ceiling and twirled him like a top. He crashed into the girl. Both went down in a flurry of arms and legs. The panicked shrieks of thirty terrified students reverberated through the classroom.

Mike exited without a backward glance, humming once again. Three doors down, he paused and tried the doorknob. This one turned. He pushed the door open.

A chubby man with a fringe of white hair stretched his arms protectively in front of a number of students who huddled like lambs behind him.

Mike looked past the teacher and locked eyes with another student with a buzz cut and an athlete's physique.

"Billy." Mike's voice was glacier cold. "Mr. H., please move."

"Mike," Mr. H. said, "this isn't what you—"

"Please, just move."

"You don't have to—"

"Move it!"

Mr. H. lunged toward Mike. Blood spewed as the report of the shot hammered through the room, the concussion almost a physical force in the enclosed space.

Kids yowled. They scrambled over desks and each other in an effort at self-preservation.

Mike calmly skirted the fallen Mr. H. He stopped in front of Billy, who was backed up against the windows that overlooked the parking lot.

"What are you doing?" Billy's voice sounded like someone had kneed him in the nuts.

"What am I doing?" Mike echoed faintly. He raised the gun. "You know what." Mike's body quaked and he shouted, "No more!"

"Please—"

"Shut up." Mike stepped closer. He pressed the barrel of the gun into Billy's sternum.

"Mike!" a voice shouted from the doorway. "Please, please don't."

He cast a glance back at a tall, plump girl who stood on the threshold. She breathed heavily, eyes wide. Like rats deserting a sinking ship, kids squeezed past her and ran down the hall. Mike let them go.

"No, Livy, not this time." Mike refocused on Billy. Over his shoulder he said, "Get out of here. You don't want to see this."

"Dude, come on." Olivia took a couple of steps inside the classroom. "It doesn't have to be like this. They're not worth it."

"Olivia, go!"

Billy's eyes flicked between Mike and Olivia. "Yeah, Mike, come on—"-

Mike dug the barrel harder into his chest, and Billy grunted in pain.

Mike's voice dropped, hardened. "Hunter and this asshole did something to Otis. To my goddamned dog. We had to put him to sleep last night."

"Oh, God," Olivia whispered on an exhale.

Billy said, "Come on, man. I swear I didn't—"

"Shut up, fucker. Paybacks are a bitch." More gently, he said, "Get out of here, Livy. Do it now."

Olivia backed away, stumbling over an upended desk. A thunderous blast chased her out the door. Glass shattered, the sound almost lost in the din of screams echoing in the hallway.

At last, nothing remained but the tinny beat of heavy metal rock music.

Chapter 1

Raindrops pounded the ground. I forcefully shook my head before stepping through the back door into my apartment, which was half of an ancient, two-story Northeast Minneapolis duplex. Built railroad-style, the apartments had a long hall that ran along the outermost wall, going through the unit from the front door straight to the back door. The kitchen, the living room, and a half-bath opened off the hallway. On the second floor, two bedrooms and a full bath were situated off of a duplicate hall.

I shrugged out of my wet jacket and hung it up. April showers might bring May flowers, but they didn't do much more than make me cranky. The week had been grueling, and I looked forward to an unexpected weekend off.

Mail injected through a slot in the door by the postal

carrier was strewn haphazardly across the foyer. I scooped up the envelopes and brought them into the kitchen.

At the table I flipped through the mail. Two credit card applications landed in a shred pile. A Target bill and a reminder that my teeth were overdue for cleaning went into another.

A pink envelope had the return address of one E. Knight. Eli was a redheaded Tasmanian devil, an ex who'd recently decided she no longer wished to hold that status. After what the tramp had pulled on me, that status wasn't about to change. Ever.

In the midst of an intense four-year relationship, I'd come home unexpectedly early one afternoon and walked into our bedroom to the shock of a lifetime.

Eli and a woman she worked with were sprawled in our bed, between our sheets, doing the horizontal mambo. After my brain caught up, I flashed the gun in my shoulder holster and sent them both packing, dressed in nothing but their birthday suits.

As they scrammed down the stairs and out the front door, I picked up the clothing they'd dropped and threw it out the bedroom window. The neighborhood gossiped for the next month about the two naked chicks scrambling around my front yard attempting to cover themselves while trying to gather their stuff.

That was nearly two years ago. Eventually, for whatever reason, Eli decided she wanted another go. Ever since I'd come home from an assignment in New Jersey last winter, she had been a pain in my ass. I figured sooner or later she'd knock it off, but five months had passed, and she hadn't let up. She'd recently taken over the helm of the advertising agency she worked for when we were together. The little womanizer had the gall to claim she'd slept up the ladder for me. For me? Yeah. Whatever. She was a certified nut job wrapped inside a power-hungry barracuda.

I gazed at the stack of pink envelopes on the table and then at four empty vases—vases that had held red roses before I pitched them directly into the trash—sitting on the kitchen counter between the refrigerator and the microwave. All the flowers had come in the last week. Maybe it was time to admit my ex had lost her mind.

I ripped the newest missive open and pulled out a single sheet of scented stationery. The smell brought unbidden memories of times best forgotten.

Cailin,

Why are you shutting me out? I'm finally at the top, and you're meant to be here with me. I'm the only one who knows how to love you, and you know it. Let me give you all of me. I love you, Cailin. I know you love me too.

Eli

I tucked the note back into the envelope and tossed it onto the growing pile of undying love. It was past time to call her on her bullshit, but I'd put off a confrontation hoping she would pull her own head out of her ass without help.

I threw the rest of the junk mail in the recycling bin and dialed Northstar Gallery.

"Northstar," a distracted-sounding voice answered. My heart thumped, like it did whenever I heard Alejandra—Alex to those she knew and loved—Rodriguez speak. My girl was always quick to make it clear she wasn't to be confused with the ex-Yankee baseball player. While she had bigger figurative balls than half the Yankees put together, she came by her strength naturally. Every night, when I lay down and held Alex to me, I thanked the gods and goddesses for bringing her to me.

My responsibilities as a special agent for a small branch of the Department of Homeland Security called the National Protection and Investigation Unit took up the majority of my life. The Federal Government wasn't creative enough to come up with a new set of job titles for the NPIU, so we were stuck with the same ones the Feebs used. Beyond that, though, were some major differences. The NPIU had three main goals. The first was to assess, track, and stop homegrown terror plots by analyzing and acting on information gathered by a number of agencies at all levels of government. Information collection proved exceptionally tricky. Just ask those folks at the National Security Agency.

Currently, the NSA was under fire for overreach in their efforts to collect international intelligence. I didn't know how the mess would end, but no matter which way it went, the reputation of the United States had taken a serious hit. I was glad I worked mainly on this side of the pond.

The second mandate was to be available to any agency who requested our assistance, terror-related or not, so long as imminent danger to the American public was established.

The last, and in my opinion, most critical mandate was to improve cooperation—sharing of vital information between city, state, and the federal agencies in an attempt to bridge the negative attitudes departments often held against each other.

The pervasive cooperation problem reminded me of a pack of dogs fighting to mark their territory by seeing who could lift their leg higher. The truth of the matter was, all too often, no one was getting any relief.

I'd been caught in one of those leg-lifting battles last September. Two of us had been sent to New Jersey to help the ever-shorthanded East Coast Bureau investigate a threat involving the Holland tunnel. The bright spot out of that mess was Alex. We'd begun dating, and she allowed herself to be dragged to Minneapolis when the assignment ended. I was still shocked she was here.

Alex cleared her throat and repeated, "Northstar."

"Hey."

"Hey, yourself." I heard the smile in her smoky voice. "What's up?"

"Aside from being whiny from loneliness, I figured you'd like to know I got another letter."

Alex let out an exasperated sigh. "What did it say this time?"

"Same shit, different day."

"Jesus Christ. What'll it take for her to get the hint? Get a restraining order. Shoot her. Something."

Alex was only half-kidding. Eli had been incessant

since we'd come home. She had an obsessive streak, but in the past she eventually grew bored with whatever her current obsession was and would fixate on a new one. Why she wasn't doing that this time was beyond me.

In the deepest recesses of my gut, a part of me felt wholly inadequate because I couldn't find a way to successfully rein in my ex-lover. The chats I'd already had with her had no impact. Maybe a restraining order wasn't a terrible plan, but the idea that someone who worked in law enforcement couldn't take care of their own shit was pathetic. I needed to be firmer. On occasion, my pride did have a nasty habit of getting in the way of common sense.

"Shooting Eli sounds like a splendid idea," I said. "I don't get it. She should've moved onto something else months ago. This is excessive, even for her."

A buzz in the background became a jumble of loud voices. "It's because you're irresistible. On that note, I gotta run. Some briefcase-toting chicks in designer power suits just walked in. See you tonight." Alex disconnected and almost immediately another call lit up my phone screen. Bad sign—my workplace was on the line. I had a hunch my weekend was about to go up in flames.

"Sorry for the call, McKenna," my direct boss, Supervisory Special Agent Allen Weatherspoon said without preamble. Weatherspoon was a decent guy and still remembered what it was like to run hot in the trenches. When his agents had a rare weekend off, he was loath to interrupt. He had a wife and three kids and liked to keep to a regular schedule himself. If the SSA was expressing an apology to me on a Friday evening, something very bad must have happened.

"There's been another school shooting."

"Oh, shit, no." I wasn't sure if I said that out loud or if the words only echoed in my head.

The previous week a shooting occurred at Steven's High School in Minneapolis, and we'd been called in to assist. Minnesota hadn't seen a school shooting since the Rocori High shooting in Cold Spring in 2003 and the Red Lake massacre in 2005.

The Steven's High shooter had killed himself after dropping four students and the vice principal. The investigation into the incident was ongoing. There didn't seem to be any effective federal solutions, thanks in part to a government that couldn't agree on anything and a noisy portion of the public terrified of losing their right to bear arms.

"Where?" I asked.

"Gray Academy Charter. Minneapolis has asked us in, and Nakamura's on her way. Coordinate with the responding agencies and the locals. You know the location?"

"The alternative school? 31st and Nicollet?"

"That's the one."

"Is it secured, or is the shooter still on the loose?"

"Secured. The shooter took out two kids, a security guard, and at least one teacher. Funny thing, he was waiting on the front steps of the school when the cavalry arrived. He stood up, hands in the air, and turned himself in."

"Weird. I'm on my way, sir."

I texted Alex that I'd been called out and that she was on her own for the evening. I had a feeling I wouldn't be home anytime soon.

✲ ✲ ✲

Twenty minutes later I parked near the entrance to Gray Academy. The structure was imposing—the early twentieth-century brick building had housed the Twin Cities Rapid Transit Company, and many of the city's streetcars had been built there in an era long since gone.

The wind had picked up, and I shivered with an inner chill the warmest heater wouldn't chase away. Dusk was eerie, far earlier than usual at this time of year thanks to low-lying, battleship-gray clouds and the nonstop rain. Mother Nature seemed to be weeping for what had taken place.

Squads and ambulances, their red and blue lights flashing, were parked within the cordoned-off parking lot. Across the lot, on the sidewalk next to the street, three dozen gawkers had gathered. Reporters crowded together in a designated area, their bright lights shining and cameras ready to roll.

Yellow crime scene tape wound from tree to signpost to garbage can around the school. A number of crime scene guys hovered over something on the ground to the right of the front doors. Intensely bright police spotlights flooded the area.

I caught the attention of one of the officers valiantly engaged in staving off the morbidly nosy. When I flashed my NPIU credentials, he said, "It's an ugly one, McKenna."

"They all are." I ducked under the crime scene tape. Trampled brown grass ended at a sidewalk leading to a flight of ten stairs and the wide, double doors of the school's entrance.

Five people had gathered halfway up the stairway. I recognized my NPIU counterpart, Agent Rosie Nakamura, by her short, angular profile. Beside her stood the Minneapolis Chief of Police, Howard Helling, along with MPD Officers Manuel Martinez and Bryan Peterson who were a couple of Minneapolis Homicide guys I'd worked with in the past. They moonlighted on the MPD's Special Response Team. I didn't know the fifth man.

Peterson and Martinez reminded me of a mixed up Laurel and Hardy. Martinez was laid back, rotund, and balding. A thick, black moustache hovered over his upper lip. Bryan Peterson's thin, six-foot-tall frame was topped by a mop of straw-colored hair.

Martinez said, "Would be nice to see you, McKenna, if we were at the bar."

All business, Peterson said, "Let's get the intros out of the way. Agent Cailin McKenna, Principal Nyland Nash."

He jerked his head toward a solidly built man with salt-and-pepper hair. I reached for Nash's hand and gave it a quick shake. His paisley tie had been loosened, and the knot sat crookedly at the base of his throat. Sweating and shaky, he looked like he might lose his marbles any moment.

"Miles Johnson," Peterson continued, "is running the scene along with MPD's crime lab. Here he comes now."

Johnson took the steps two at a time. "Hey." A man of few words, he was the head of the Bureau of Criminal Apprehension's Forensic Crime Scene Team. I'd worked with Johnson a couple of times. He was a decent guy and had a great nose for finding shit that was often overlooked.

I gave him a nod and turned to Helling. "Chief."

Every time I saw Chief Helling, he reminded me of Bryan Cranston from *Breaking Bad*—minus the terminal cancer diagnosis. His face vacillated between bluish-gray and reddish-green in the reflection of the flashing lights. The stress of dealing with a cancer of a different kind that encompassed our entire city had to be monumental.

Might as well get on with it and maybe we could get out of the drizzle. I asked, "What have we got?"

Principal Nash found his voice. "A little after three this afternoon, one of our students opened fire."

In report mode, Miles Johnson picked up the narrative. "We have two dead."

Chief Helling crossed his arms, his face anguished. I would not want to be in his shoes.

"Three wounded," Johnson continued, "including the security guard at the front door who was shot in the upper thigh, one teacher who was knocked unconscious by a door the shooter kicked in, and another teacher who was shot in the abdomen. The dead are two seventeen-year-old male students. The injured have been transported to Hennepin County Medical Center, and the deceased are still in place. The shooter has been taken to the Juvenile Detention Center."

Helling said, "Students awaiting pick up are in the library, along with a few kids who came forward wanting to talk to us about the shooter. We need to find out what they know. One fortunate turn of events is one of the kids is the shooter's best friend, and she's willing to talk."

Rosie asked, "Do we have an ID on the shooter?"

Peterson flipped open a notepad. "Michael John Lorenzo, age sixteen."

The air suddenly thickened. I felt like I was choking in a vacuum of disbelief. "Michael Lorenzo?" Cold sweat broke out on the back of my neck. For a second I thought I might go toes up in front of everyone.

"Cailin?" Rosie asked. "What's wrong? You know him?"

It would be easier to think if the roaring in my ears subsided. "I know a kid, a teen, with the same name."

Off-duty, I occasionally picked up off-the-record cases, cases typically outside the scope of my job. Behind closed doors, I admitted to sometimes wielding the power of my badge in ways my bosses might not approve of. Most of those cases involved trying to pull runaways and homeless kids off the streets and get them somewhere safe. Provide them resources they might not know were available. The MPD had a small unit assigned to do just that, but they were often swamped. I was more than happy to lend a hand when I could. The intent was noble enough in my eyes, and that made it easy to rationalize away my legal indiscretions. How many Michael John Lorenzos could there be attending this particular high school?

I snapped my mouth shut. "I pulled a Mike Lorenzo off the streets and helped him get placed in foster care. He attends Gray Academy."

"McKenna." The chief faced me. He pensively tapped his chin with a finger. "Since you might know this boy, maybe you should be the one to talk to this friend of his."

"Who is it?" My voice still sounded thin.

Martinez consulted his notebook again. "Olivia Chapman."

"Goddamn it." The words were out of my mouth before I could censor myself. I tilted my head back to the dark sky. "The shooter is my Mike." A second later I returned my gaze to Helling's. "A year or so ago he told me he'd actually made a friend. Her name was Olivia. Yeah, I'll talk to her."

"Where are the teachers?" Rosie asked. She was one of the NPIU's high tech, detail-oriented computer magicians, and she approached life like she did her work, with a single-minded focus.

Chief Helling said, "Teachers are in the gym. Martinez, head downtown. Make sure the foster parents are notified." He pointed at Rosie and Peterson. "You two go with McKenna. Johnson, get back in there and make damn sure no one is contaminating the crime scene. I'll have enough people crawling all over me without having to deal with that problem."

"Sure thing, Chief." Miles Johnson made for the front door of the school, the big yellow "CST" on his burly back reflecting the sweep of the emergency lights.

Helling rubbed his hands together briskly and attempted a smile that came across as a tired grimace. "Mr. Nash, if you'll come with me, I'd appreciate it. Time for us to face the cameras."

The two men moved down the stairs, Martinez following in their wake.

Martinez stopped after he'd descended a couple of steps. "Jesus, McKenna. I'm sorry."

"Yeah, me, too."

Rosie nudged me. "Come on. Let's get this over with."

Chapter 2

After almost getting lost within the corridors of the school, we found the library. A dozen students milled around inside the entrance. Peterson went off to organize individual interviews with the students under the keen eyes of a few uniformed patrol officers.

Rosie and I passed through the open entrance area and stepped into the warmly lit library lobby. I asked one of the cops where Olivia was, and he pointed to a heavyset girl of about sixteen seated on one of the benches across from the checkout desk. She wore baggy jeans and a black hoodie that partially obscured an acne-riddled face streaked with tears. One of the uniforms sat next to her, murmuring quietly.

The cop, who looked plenty young herself, glanced

up at our approach and rose quickly. The consternation on her face melted into relief.

"Thanks, Officer," Rosie said. "We'll take it from here."

I crouched down in front of the girl, and Rosie sat next to her on the bench.

"Olivia?" I asked softly. She sniffed, dragged a forearm across her face, and slowly raised her eyes to mine. They revealed an anguish that burned into my soul.

"Yeah?" Her voice sounded low and raw.

"I'm Agent McKenna, but you can call me Cailin." I tilted my head in Rosie's direction. "This is Agent Nakamura who you can call Rosie. Cailin and Rosie. Can we talk to you a little bit about what happened?"

Olivia sniffled again and took a jagged breath. "Yeah." She tugged the hoodie off her head, and straight, pitch-black hair touched the nape of her neck.

"Can you tell us what you saw?" Rosie asked.

Later, we'd take a formal statement from her, but for now, we needed to listen.

Olivia gripped the edge of the bench with both hands, hard enough her knuckles turned white. She stared straight ahead. Her lower lip trembled. "I was in math. Last freaking class of the day."

I asked, "Is school over around three?"

"No. Four. Hours at the Academy are different."

I nodded but kept my mouth shut.

"Anyway"—she pulled in a shuddering half-sob— "there were some loud booms out in the hall." She closed her eyes. "Then everyone was screaming. That's when we knew something was majorly wrong." She drooped back against the cold brick wall and played with a frayed piece of cloth on the cuff of her hoodie.

Rosie reached over and gently rubbed Olivia's shoulder. "We're here for you, Olivia. Go on."

"I had this horrible feeling." She sucked snot and wiped her nose on her sleeve again.

I glanced around for some Kleenex, but I didn't see any.

"I—" She coughed thickly, and for a second, I wondered if she was going to puke. She rallied. "I was afraid it had something to do with Mike."

Rosie said, "Why did you think whatever was going on might have something to do with Mike?"

"He was so angry. It was getting worse. His anger. Ever since..." Olivia trailed off and shut her eyes again.

We waited.

"Ever since what?" I finally asked.

"The blimp incident."

My quads were starting to burn. "Tell us about that, will you?"

"Billy Cornwall and Hunter Anderson had been messing with both me and Mike all year. Two weeks ago Billy made copies of the Goodyear Blimp and put my name on them and taped them up in all of the boys' restrooms in the school." Olivia's face burned bright red. "But this time it was kind of like a breaking point. I told Mike it didn't matter, but he was so fucking pissed."

She looked up sharply, probably expecting a reprimand, which wouldn't come from either Rosie or me.

We both had mouths on us that could make the devil's tail curl.

Once she saw we weren't going to chastise her, she continued. "He wanted to confront them. I wouldn't let him because I knew for sure they'd just beat him up again."

Rosie asked, "What else did they do?"

"Lots of stuff. Ever since I started going to school here, they've been on me. One of the things they do, every morning, actually, Hunter stands next to my locker and slams it shut just as I get it open. He keeps doing it until it's too late for me to get to class. That's not so bad, though, compared to what they do to Mike. When Mike came to the school, they started in on him, too, way worse for him than me."

She leaned forward again, elbows on her knees, her eyes on the floor.

"How?" I asked. "How was it worse?"

"One time they caught Mike in the restroom. Held his head in the toilet bowl until he passed out. Those assholes left him there. On the floor."

We waited for Olivia to say more. She finally took a deep breath. "Another time, they cornered Mike in the locker room after gym. Beat the shit out of him." Olivia's voice broke. "He could hardly walk after. Had two black eyes and I think something was wrong with his eardrum. He had a hard time hearing on that side afterward."

Little bastards. I reached out, tucked a loose strand of hair behind Olivia's ear. "Did either of you report what was going on?"

Olivia straightened and breathed deeply in an attempt to regain her composure. "Who do you think they'd believe? A fat girl and a skinny loner, or the captain of the football team and another kid who would be voted most popular if we did that crap?"

"Goddamn," Rosie muttered under her breath.

"A few months ago things went down the shitter when Mike got ahold of some music that a couple of kids were handing out. It was horrible. I mean, the things they sang about were horrible. Actually, the music sucked, too. Speed metal. It was like Mike got addicted. He downloaded it onto his iPod and listened all day long. His whole attitude changed. He got madder and madder and started making up these revenge plans he wanted to do to Hunter and Billy. Never thought he'd actually do it. I thought he was blowing off steam. Honest. I didn't think he'd do something like this." The girl dissolved in heaving sobs.

I wrapped an arm around Olivia.

Rosie mouthed, "Kleenex," and took off.

After a minute, Olivia hiccupped and pulled away from me. She leaned back against the brick, her head tilted toward the ceiling. Tears continued to snake trails down her cheeks.

Rosie returned with a box of tissues and held them out to her.

"Thanks." Olivia plucked a couple and blew noisily. She pulled out another and dabbed at her eyes before dropping her arms into her lap, the damp tissues clenched in a wad.

Rosie settled beside her again. "We know this is hard. Are you okay to keep talking?"

"Yeah. My mom won't be here for a while yet anyway."

"So when you heard the ruckus," I said, "you thought it might be Mike?"

"Well, not really. Maybe. I don't know. He wasn't in school today. We always have lunch together, but he wasn't here. I walked by his biology class. Didn't see him there either. He loves biology."

"What happened next?" I asked.

"First I thought I heard firecrackers—kids do stuff like that sometimes—then I heard screams. That's when I knew it wasn't fireworks. Someone was shooting like last week at Steven's. Mrs. Drake tried to lock the door, but the lock wouldn't work. So she moved us toward the back of the classroom."

Olivia shuddered. "Kids were tripping on desks, and everyone was panicking. I heard a voice next door. I—it sounded like someone was yelling 'Mike.' And then I knew, well, I thought—if it was Mike, I had to see what was going on. I took off. Mrs. Drake yelled at me to come back, but I made it into the hallway. Kids were running out of Mr. Hedberg's class next door. He teaches history.

"I went to the door and looked in. Mr. H. was on the floor. So much blood. I couldn't believe it. Mike had Billy backed up against the window, and he had a gun. All I could hear was that stupid music of Mike's. It was so loud, even through his earphones."

Olivia's eyes glazed over. I met Rosie's gaze and we

waited patiently. After a minute, I said, "So you saw Mike and heard his music. What happened then?"

In a flat voice, Olivia said, "I didn't know what to do. I begged him to stop. Mike told me Billy and Hunter killed Otis. That's Mike's dog." She looked at me and I nodded, encouraging her to continue. "Mike loved Otis so much. I knew if those assholes hurt Otis it was the final straw for Mike." Another tear escaped and rolled down Olivia's blotchy cheek. "I knew from the tone of Mike's voice nothing I said would change his mind, so when he screamed at me to get out, I did. The gunshot was so loud I felt like my eardrums popped." Olivia's eyes searched my face. "Mike's dead, isn't he?"

"No, Olivia," I said, "he's not."

"He's going to jail, isn't he? I'll never see him again. Oh, God." She covered her face with her hands and rocked back and forth, weeping now. "I should have done something. I should've seen this coming. Mike's my best friend. He's my only friend."

☆ ☆ ☆

Rosie and I stood side by side next to my car, leaning against the ice-cold metal. As we exhaled, our breath curled in white wisps.

I said, "I know firsthand what it's like to be bullied. The dread. The anger. The lack of self-worth. But what tips the scale and pushes someone to take that fatal step? And why is it happening so damn often? Where does it fucking end?" I jammed my freezing hands deep into the pockets of my jacket. The misty rain had stopped, but the chill seeped into my bones.

"I don't know. Being Asian, even if I was born here, hasn't exactly been a piece of cake. There's a lot of ugliness in human nature."

Silence settled heavy between us.

Eventually Rosie said, "I wonder if Billy and Hunter did do something to Mike's dog. That's low, man. To hurt someone's pet? Almost pushes me over the edge myself."

"No fucking shit."

Long seconds ticked by. I shivered. "Olivia said something about Mike getting mad after he started listening to that music. I'd sure like to know what he was listening to. We all know music can influence mood and emotions. Every time I hear "Need You Now" by Lady Antebellum it feels like my heart's being ripped out again. When Eli and I were first getting together, the radio played it so often that it became the unofficial soundtrack of our doomed romance."

Rosie gave me a sympathetic glance. "I know what you mean. Olivia said somebody gave the music to Mike. But who?"

"Good question. Last week's shooting had a musical component. The kid had an MP3 player on him."

Rosie zipped up her fleece jacket. "Might be a link, might not. Kids love tunes. Adults hate what kids like. Fucking A. Let's pick this up tomorrow. I've had enough for one day."

I dropped Rosie at her car and headed home.

Chapter 3

The gloomy drive home did nothing to cheer me up. I was still stunned that the Mike I knew could've been involved in a school shooting. I flipped from one radio station to another, but found no solace in any of the songs. I finally bluetoothed into the music on my phone. Even Jim Brickman, an artist I often turned to for stress relief, did nothing to ease the ache in my chest. Too many memories were crowding my mind, memories I wanted nothing to do with.

I parked in the garage and followed the path through the postage stamp-sized yard to my back door. My side of the duplex was dark, while the neighbor's half was lit up like a Christmas tree.

Alex's car wasn't in the garage. Since she'd started

working with Gin at the gallery and displaying some of her own art, business had picked up. She'd come home late three days this week alone.

Alex was a great artist. Her signature pieces were two-and three-panel landscapes. First, she painted in black and white, and then in contrast, she painted the same view in bright, vivid colors. When I'd been in New Jersey and seen a few examples, I was blown away. I knew they'd be a hot commodity. So, with Alex's permission, I sent a few of the pieces home to my foster mom, Gin McKenna, who owned Northstar Gallery in Uptown Minneapolis. They practically flew out of her shop. When Alex moved back to Minnesota with me, Gin was only too happy to get her claws into my girl. I was grateful that she and Alex had taken to each other so quickly. Both had been working hard to score some big names in the Twin City's art world and had succeeded in pulling off some high-classed showings.

At the stoop, I fumbled with the keys and opened the door.

My feet felt like lead. I dragged myself into the kitchen. The Keurig was low on water, so I filled the tank, dropped in a pod, and hit start. A perfect cup of coffee in less than a minute did little to boost my wrung-out mood.

I sunk into a chair at the table, one hand holding my head up and the other wrapped around the coffee cup, the heat against my palm comforting.

My gaze fell on the neat pile of Eli's notes. Now that I thought about it, Eli was a bully herself. I had to handle her somehow, but I didn't have the energy to think about it.

My phone rang, snapping me out of my malaise. I let out a pent-up breath of relief when I saw it wasn't anyone from work calling. Sooner or later I should probably figure out how to customize rings for different people. I wasn't afraid of technology, but I never could find the time to mess around with it, and when I did have time, I was more likely to play Angry Birds or Sniper Shooter.

My best friend's name, "Pick," popped up on the screen. For a moment I debated ignoring the call. It wouldn't do any good, anyway. Pick was persistent.

"What?" I answered more sharply than I intended.

"My, we're in a mood, aren't we? Where are you?" Music and voices echoed in the background.

"Just got home."

"Well, get your booty over here, girlfriend. We're having a little par-tay."

That was the last thing I needed. "No thanks. You been drinking?"

"Maybe. Come on, Cailin. It'll help you forget whatever you need to forget." Pick's voice softened. "Alex told us you got called in. We heard about the shooting. Is that where you were?"

"Yeah."

For a long moment, I heard nothing save the noise in the background. Finally Pick said, "Alex is here. We have something to talk to you about. Just come on over for a while. Chill."

I knew if I didn't go, they'd appear here in a heartbeat and drag me right through the door. Puffing out a cranky breath, I gave in. "Okay. But only for a few minutes. I want to go to bed early and pretend this day was a bad dream."

"Okay, see you." Pick hung up on me.

Pick Pickford, first name Eleanor—but don't call her that unless you have a death wish—resided in the other half of the duplex I lived in. Sometimes it was a handy thing, sometimes a royal pain in my ass.

Pick was a reporter for the *Star Tribune* and lived up to the reputation that blondes do have more fun. Her light locks were usually standing artfully on end, and she was the definition of high energy. Pick's latest endeavor—and she was always endeavoring at one thing or another—was the Life Time Fitness Triathlon. She'd been in training all winter. Tonight she'd apparently decided she needed a break.

After wallowing another five minutes, I locked my door and trudged down my steps and up Pick's, not bothering with a jacket. The door was unlocked, and I let myself in.

Pick's half of the duplex was a mirror of mine. I heard laughter and music spill into the hall, and headed toward the living room.

Before I made the doorway, Grady, Pick's German shepherd, trotted up and greeted me with a cold, wet nose and warm tongue. Some watchdog. I knelt down and wrapped my arms around her thick neck, trying but failing to avoid a tongue facial.

Pick had adopted Grady from the Humane Society the previous fall after she did a story on the organization. I'd call her a sucker, but her heart is too soft for that kind of observation. Now the mutt was the queen of the castle, along with Hightail, Pick's huge, twenty-five-pound tabby.

I gave Grady's head a final stroke and entered entertainment central.

Sirius Hits 1 came from a high-end Pioneer Micro System that was hooked up to surround sound.

To my surprise, Pick, Alex, and our good friend, Jada French, sat on the floor, huddled around a game board on the coffee table.

Jada was the chef at the Blue Fin, a bar and grill in Uptown. She had one of the most eclectic backgrounds of anyone I'd ever met. Her personal religion dictated free expression of her happiness as well as her outrage, her contentment as well as her sorrow. She was thoroughly outspoken. Jada was great to have in your corner, and it didn't hurt that she was a true African-American Amazon, over six feet of luscious curves.

As soon I came in, all chatter stopped. I slung myself onto the couch behind Alex, kissed the top of her head, and settled on my side, chin propped on my fist.

Alex shifted around to face me. Long, black hair fell down to the middle of her back, the silky strands brushing against my arm. Alex wasn't beautiful in the classic sense, but she was the epitome of all I desired. Jada said she was just plain hot.

Midnight eyes caught mine, and Alex leaned in for a kiss. "You okay?"

I smelled tequila on her warm breath, and when our lips met, I tasted its tang on my tongue.

"Yeah. Fine enough." My eyes felt gravelly, and I rubbed them, exhaustion weighing on me like a physical thing. I could wallow enough for everyone, but why bring my obviously feeling-no-pain friends down with me if I didn't have to? "Who's winning?" I asked, trying to redirect the conversation. "And where is everyone?"

Pick stood, swaying slightly. "Jada's the queen of the game, as usual. The rest of the revelers took off about a half hour ago. You want something to drink?"

Oh, did I. "I'll take a Surly." Couldn't beat local craft beer, and—bonus plan—the name matched my mood. I sat up and slouched against the back of the couch.

"Coming right up." Pick wandered out to the kitchen with Grady trailing a step behind, hoping for a snack.

Jada's sharp gaze assessed me. "You need yourself a massage and some hot sex."

I rolled my eyes. For once, sex was the last thing on my mind, although a massage sounded good. "I don't think I'd recognize you if your mind wasn't on getting some. What's the occasion for game night?"

Jada laughed, and the sound boomed around the room. "Pick decided she needed a little, what did she call it?"

"A triathlon training time-out," Alex said. A teasing grin played at the corners of her mouth.

I managed a smile and felt the knots loosening in my shoulders. Alex leaned back between my knees, and I absently ran my fingers through her hair. I loved her. I still got a jolt whenever I thought about how incredibly lucky I was that we'd met. Somehow, simply being near her grounded me in ways I still couldn't identify.

Pick returned from the kitchen with a can of Surly Furious and handed it to me. I idly wondered for the millionth time why they didn't put this particular beer in bottles. Then she resettled her lanky frame on the floor, leaned back on her hands, and crossed her ankles. "Okay, superhero cop. What's going on?"

I took a healthy swallow. My friends were good about helping me unload when I needed to instead of keeping things stuffed inside. But sometimes, I couldn't do it. Amazingly, they understood that, too.

Now was one of those times. Instead of getting mad that I didn't answer her question, Pick sighed and looked at me sympathetically. Jada heaved herself off the floor and settled into a recliner, drumming her fingers impatiently on the arm of the chair. I glanced at Pick, who could play poker with the big dogs, and then at Jada. She gazed expectantly at me. I dropped my eyes to the back of Alex's head, which did me no good at all. Did I forget something? It wasn't anyone's birthday, or anniversary. Was it?

"For Christ sake," Jada said.

"What?" I asked.

"Alex." Jada shot her a look. "If you won't tell her, make no mistake. I will."

"All right. Okay." Alex hoisted herself onto the couch beside me, rested a hand on my thigh, and gave it a gentle squeeze.

I frowned and shifted restlessly, sure I was being set up, but unsure why.

Alex said, "Cailin, I want you to stay calm, okay?"

Conversations starting that way were never good. "What, did I grow two heads while I was gone?"

The look of affection on Alex's face told me I had nothing to fear between the two of us. "Did you notice my car wasn't in the garage when you came home?"

"Yeah, I assumed you were still at the gallery." Then it dawned on me. A bolt of fear fizzed down my spine. "Did you have an accident?"

Alex's eyes widened, "No, no. Oh, Cailin, I didn't mean to scare you like that."

"For Pete's sake," Jada boomed. "Alex's tires were slashed when she came out of the gallery tonight. I had to go and pick her up."

I tensed. "What the hell happened?"

"There was a note," Pick said.

My head snapped from Jada to Pick. "From who?" I had a sneaking suspicion I wouldn't like the answer.

Alex said, "It appears our friend is changing tactics, from cards and flowers to some controlled violence."

"Eli slashed your tires?"

"Looks like it." Alex extracting a folded piece of paper from her pocket and handed it over. "This was under the wiper."

I unfolded the sheet.

Alex, give it up. She's mine. Go back to New Jersey and everything will be fine.

I wanted to get up and do a little controlled violence myself. "She went to Northstar and slashed your tires in broad daylight. Broad fucking daylight."

"Cailin. Baby. She can try, but I can kick her ass six ways to Sunday."

I didn't doubt that for one second. Alex grew up in a tough neighborhood. She definitely knew how to take care of herself.

"How many tires?" My restraint was wearing thin.

"Three," Pick said.

"Three?" My voice rose. "Three tires?"

"Cailin, calm down." Jada said. "Grady will have a heart attack if you don't." The poor dog was huddled in the corner, eyes wide. She didn't do well when things got loud, and I knew better.

"Shit." I blew out a breath. Way to go, Cailin. Scare the shit out of an abused dog. "Grady, come here."

That earned a flag of her tail.

"It's okay. Auntie Cailin is a bit worked up. I'm sorry." The dog padded warily toward me. "That's right. Come here, Grade." I patted my knee in invitation.

Grady hopped up on the couch. She circled and settled with a heavy sigh next to Alex, peering up at me with big, brown eyes. My body relaxed against the couch cushion. I felt my remaining irritation melt into something more manageable.

Alex gave my forearm an affectionate squeeze, and I

met her eyes with gratitude. That she was willing to put up with the sometimes mercurial me was both thrilling and terrifying. Trust had never come easily. I still had to work at it. I said, "Did you report what happened to the police?"

Alex leaned against my side, her physical presence further settling me. "I did. Since I couldn't prove it was Eli who filleted the tires, letter or not, they put it on record."

I tipped the can to my lips and took another deep swallow, the beer rolling coolly down my throat. "Where's the car?"

Pick said, "We had it towed to Bobby and Steve's. They said they could have it fixed up by tomorrow afternoon."

Jada popped the footrest on the recliner and tucked her hands behind her head. "So, Cailin, what are you gonna do about Little Miss Thang?"

Yes, indeed, what was I going to do? I was calm again, but I felt outrage bubbling just beneath the surface.

Alex tugged on my hand and shifted to pull my back against her chest, careful not to disturb Grady or my beer. I melted into her like an overheated candy bar. She sifted my hair between her fingers, and I felt her lips against the back of my head.

I took another pull off the can, feeling my body relax for the first time since the call about the shooting came. "In answer to your question, Jada, I don't know. My threats obviously aren't working. I'll talk to her again. This time I'll make sure things are absolutely, one hundred percent, crystal clear."

Pick looked at me thoughtfully. "You could go slash her tires." She raised her refilled glass. "Or I could."

Jada wriggled into a more comfortable position. "Damn, I love me this chair. If it's gone one day, don't come looking for it." She crossed her arms and nailed me with now-serious eyes. "Maybe we should confront her together."

Neither of those things was about to happen. There was no doubt Eli would hear from me, but not with this crew tagging along. That would be an invitation for trouble I didn't need.

"If only she'd show her sweet innocent face," Alex said. "I could give her an attitude adjustment."

Up to now, Eli had been careful not to put in any appearances when Alex was around. I figured Alex had thoroughly intimidated her when they met last fall in the New Jersey hospital where I'd been temporarily laid up. Alex let Eli know in no uncertain terms to back the fuck off.

After an awkward silence, Pick said, "So what happened at the school?"

I knew the question was coming sooner or later. "I can't believe it. This time, two boys dead, two teachers and a security guard injured." I paused. "I know the kid who did it."

"What?" Pick's eyes snapped to mine.

"You do?" Alex's chest vibrated beneath me.

"I ran into him a couple years back. He was a runaway. Hadn't been on the lam very long. I hooked him up with a gal I know who found him a great foster family."

I downed the last dregs swirling in the bottom of the can and let my head fall back again to Alex's shoulder. "Jesus. What they must be going through."

Alex's arms tightened around me.

"His name's Michael Lorenzo, goes by Mike. Had a very abusive situation at home and finally bailed. He'd been on his own for a few weeks when I ran into a group of homeless kids he was hanging with."

"You're always helping out those kids." Jada raised her glass in a mock salute to me. "They're lucky to have you."

"Some help I was this time. I thought he'd been doing so much better." My brain felt like a giant hand was squeezing the hell out of it. "I can't believe he'd do this. Kid's really sensitive. Somehow the time he spent on the dodge didn't burn that sensitivity out of him. I don't get why this happened."

Pick asked, "What's his background?"

"Mike was a quiet kid," I said. "Before he was placed, we periodically met up. I'd take him somewhere to eat, buy him some new clothes. Once he realized I wasn't hauling him off to juvie, he loosened up. Told me his story." I held my empty toward Pick.

"Lazy ass." She got up and snatched the can. "Same thing?"

As much as I wanted to feel the burn of Tanqueray hitting the back of my throat, beer was probably a better idea. "Yeah."

Alex rested her cheek against mine. "You don't need to tell us now if you're not ready."

I turned my head and caught the corner of her mouth with my lips. "I'm okay." I held her gaze a second longer in reassurance before settling back against her again. Pick returned and handed me another beer. Then she stretched out on the floor and waited expectantly.

The cold can in my hand helped my focus. "Generally, Mike had a terrible time in school. Shy, introverted. Total nerd. I can see now that he must have been a natural target for bullies. You know how that goes."

"Sure as hell do." Jada had her share of problems throughout the years and came out stronger because of it, instead of allowing it to ruin her.

I wondered what made one person persevere and another buckle. "His mom died when he was a toddler. His father was usually too busy or too drunk to pay much attention to the fact he had two kids to raise."

Alex asked, "He's got a sibling?"

"Did. One night Mike's five-year-old brother got into the Liquid-Plumr. He chugged most of the bottle. Mike was seven, knew his brother was in big trouble. Tried to wake his dad for help."

I shuddered. Alex's arms pulled me even closer. "The bastard slapped Mike across the face for waking him up. Split the kid's lip. Then Daddy-O rolled over and went back to sleep. Mike called 911 himself. When the paramedics showed, Mike's dad had come around and he acted like he'd known what happened all along. He even told the paramedics he'd had Mike call an ambulance because he was too busy trying to help his youngest."

The cork had been popped and the story poured out.

"Mike's brother didn't make it. The dad blamed Mike for not watching his brother carefully enough. He started really laying on the physical abuse with Mike. It kept getting worse. Mike withdrew even more.

"Not long after Mike turned thirteen, his dad dished out a particularly vicious beating that"—I took a deep breath—"fractured a rib, blackened both eyes, among other injuries. Later that night, when his dad passed out on the couch, Mike stuffed some clothes in a backpack, swiped some money out of the bastard's pocket, and took off.

"He left in late spring and made do sleeping on benches or out of sight in the parks. Managed to avoid getting picked up by the Park Police. Had to give him credit for that. Then he fell in with some other homeless kids. They'd break into abandoned buildings to hide out, hunker down in one of the entries of Calhoun Square when the weather was bad.

"I met Mike when he was running with that crew. Convinced him to talk to a social worker I knew who was great at finding suitable foster homes. She worked her voodoo, found a great place for him. He was willing to give it a whirl and wound up remaining with that foster family."

Pick asked, "What happened to his dad?"

"He basically turned his back on Mike, relinquished all rights."

I lapsed into silence for a moment and lost myself in memory. "Last I heard, the kid was doing okay. The foster family enrolled him in an alternative school that I thought suited him better. They even bought him a puppy he named Otis. That damn dog is, or was"—my words turned bitter—"his world. Hard to believe it was almost three years ago."

"Have you talked to the foster family yet?" Jada asked.

"No, but we did talk to his best friend tonight." I closed my eyes and the tormented anguish that rolled off Olivia flooded me again. Grady must have absorbed my tension because she raised her head off Alex's leg and whined softly.

I said, "The girl, Olivia, tried to talk him down, but apparently Mike blamed the two boys for killing his dog, so he exacted revenge. She told us the two dead students had been bullying her and Mike for some time."

"Kids can be shits," Alex said. "When I dropped out of school the beginning of my junior year, it had a lot to do with kids on the bus. They picked on me, called me names, pushed me around. I had a pretty heavy accent back then. Bunch of ass-hats." Alex was born in Puerto Rico. Her parents were killed in an accident when she was eleven, and she and her brothers moved to New Jersey to live with extended family.

"Bullying's the link in most school shootings," Pick said. "Two shootings in a week in Minnesota? I can't believe it. It's sick. Fuck the Second Amendment. Something has to be done with gun control."

I understood how she felt, but I was torn. On one hand, if no one but the good guys had weapons, my job would be a lot easier. But I also understood the intrinsic need some people felt to protect themselves and their property.

"One thing Olivia mentioned," I said, "was that Mike had gotten hold of some music, and after he started listening to it, his personality changed. In fact, he was listening to it when the shooting went down. Music apparently played some role in the Steven's High shooting, too. I'm thinking there could be some kind of connection."

Jada said, "Music can have a tremendous effect. I'd hazard a guess it wasn't Barry Manilow."

I allowed a smile. "No. It wasn't. It bothers me, this whole thing. It doesn't add up. Mike's a decent kid. He had his problems, but he was making it. What was I missing? I should've goddamn well picked up on it."

Pick carefully set her empty glass on the coffee table and leaned back. "Cailin, you can't take this personally. You're a hero to those lost kids. You were one of them, and they sense that. Just because one of them self-destructed doesn't mean you failed."

I tensed.

Alex's fingers stilled their movement on my arm, and Pick's eyes widened.

Up to now, I hadn't told Alex anything about my life before the McKennas. My past was something I wanted only to forget. The horror of it was crammed away somewhere in my skull, and that's where I wanted it to stay.

Alex spoke gently, as she would to Grady when the dog was freaked out. "You were a street kid?"

Oh, God. I always intended to tell Alex when the time was right. But every time I thought the time was right, it wasn't. I opened my mouth and shut it again.

Jada shook her head. "Girl, I can't believe you haven't told Alex."

I scrambled out of Alex's arms to sit upright. Grady chuffed at me in irritation.

Alex leaned against the arm of the couch and leveled an even gaze at me. She had an uncanny way of remaining calm when the shit started flying. The first time I confided something potentially deal-breaking to her, namely, that I was a federal agent and not a writer out to do a story about her livelihood, there'd been a few tense moments. But in the end she'd come around, in more ways than one.

Finally I worked up enough spit to speak. I met Alex's eyes. "I wasn't trying to hide anything."

"Cailin," Pick said, "I'm really sorry. I didn't know Alex..." She trailed off and snapped her mouth shut.

Sighing, I leaned forward, planted my elbows on my knees, and interlocked my fingers. "Alex, I ran away from foster care when I was fourteen. I survived on the street pretty much like the kids we've been talking about. For almost two years. Pick helped me, and I tried to keep up in school."

The living room was so quiet I heard the whoosh of Grady's exhalations.

Alex put her hand on my back. "Cailin, it's o—"

"No. Let me say this." I suddenly felt ten thousand years old. "I did some pretty harsh things back then. It's...hard to explain. I don't like to talk about it." I folded a leg onto the couch and pivoted to face Alex. "I didn't mean to keep this from you. I wanted to tell you but never could find the right time."

Her face was impassive, black eyes steady on mine until I couldn't take it and dropped my gaze.

With gentle fingers, Alex caught my chin and brought my head back up, forcing my eyes to hers. "Cailin. I don't know exactly what to say, but, God, I'm so sorry." She reached over with her other hand and pulled my rigid body to her.

I yielded. "Let's go home, and I'll explain."

"Okay, but you don't need to. It's the past."

Jada and Pick followed us to the door—neither saying a word—which must have taken some effort on Jada's part.

"Thanks for the evening, ladies," I said with a wry smile. "It was enlightening."

Pick hugged me and whispered, "I didn't know."

"It's okay."

"Now you two trot on home." Jada pushed us both out the door. "Talk 'til four in the morning if you like."

"Thanks again for the lift, Jada," Alex said. "I had a great time tonight. Everything's fine." She gave Pick a raised brow to drive her words home and grabbed my hand.

I hoped she was right.

Thirty seconds later I closed my own door and leaned

against it, feeling like every bone in my body had departed. Alex turned toward me, and I almost cringed, expecting some kind of rebuke. Instead, she shrugged out of her jacket and hung it up.

If I wasn't careful, my brain would shift itself into reverse, and the memories I tried so hard to hold back would surely drown me with their power. My feet felt like they were glued to the floor.

Alex held out a hand, and I obediently took it. She tugged me toward the staircase and led me up to the bedroom. As we undressed, we exchanged inane comments about the state of our dirty laundry and what was on the agenda for the next day. Then we shared the bathroom sink and brushed our teeth. The simple ritual gave me a certain amount of comfort.

In a tank top and boxers, I slid between sheets that had never felt colder. The bed dipped. Alex crawled in and turned off the light. She slid over and molded herself against my stiff form.

I clenched my teeth, furious that I'd allowed myself to be reduced once again to a trembling heap. I functioned well on common sense and hard facts. Not so well when it came to dealing with my past or the emotions surrounding it. Memories long repressed were suddenly on the razor's edge of swallowing my soul. The feeling terrified me. I opened my mouth to speak and closed it in an angry breath. I had no idea what to say, no idea how to manage the vicious roiling in my guts.

I felt a warm exhale against my neck. Alex whispered, "Sleep. We can talk tomorrow." I rolled onto my side. She wrapped an arm around me and tucked her thighs tight against the backs of my legs. After a second I felt her lips press against my neck. I rested my arm atop hers and allowed exhaustion and the horrible feeling of anguish I thought I'd banished pull me under.

"Come on, slut. I'm a paying customer."

"Fuck you," I snarled and struck out at the hand holding the five-dollar bill. That bill would allow me to fill my stomach, would stop its ache, but I couldn't, I wouldn't accept it.

The stench of sour sweat and rotting garbage filled my nostrils. The man laughed obscenely. Roughly he pushed me to my knees on the dirty asphalt of the dark alley. "I like 'em fighting," he said to another guy who stood behind him. He grabbed my hair so I couldn't retreat and fumbled with his zipper.

"No!" I yelled. "I'm not—let me—"

I jerked awake and sat up with a ragged gasp, my own name ringing in my ears. Someone was shaking me none too gently.

"Cailin!"

I pulled in another shuddering breath and realized Alex was kneeling beside me, her hands on my shoulders. The panic on her face was obvious even in the dark.

She leaned over me and turned on my bedside lamp. A warm glow filled the room but did nothing to banish the darkness that had settled in my chest like a blanket of demon snow.

I tried to swallow but my throat was too dry. The air felt like soup.

Alex pulled me into her arms and hung on. "You're okay. You're right here. It's just a nightmare."

I struggled mightily against the overwhelming need to run. Anywhere.

"Do you want to talk about it?"

I squeezed my eyes shut. The terrible scene replayed against the inside of my eyelids. The worst part was that it wasn't a nightmare.

"Alex." My voice was so hoarse I hardly recognized it. "I did a lot of shit I'm not proud of." I laughed bitterly. "Took years of therapy to understand I wasn't weak. It was survival."

To her credit, Alex didn't say a word and she didn't let go.

My cheeks felt hot under my palms. "I was so hungry. There was never enough. Too often not enough." More unbidden images flashed through my mind. "These fucking monsters came and preyed on the homeless, especially the kids. Used them." The words were so hard to verbalize. "Us. They preyed on us, not them. Us. Me. They'd be good for—Jesus fucking Christ. For a few bucks. The beatings, the drugs." The words stuck in my throat. I was so close to the brink, terrified I'd slip over the edge and wouldn't be able to stop what was perilously close to spilling out. Wouldn't be able to shove the memories away. I was still disgusted with myself. How could Alex not be?

She squeezed my leg. "Cailin, whatever happened,

whatever you did, it's what you had to do to survive."

"There was a lot of...horror. It was horrible. Horrifying." I swallowed thickly and risked a glance at Alex's face. Compassion was in place of the revulsion I was so sure I'd see.

"I prostituted myself, Alex. Blackmail—physical, emotional. I ran dope. And...that's the least of it. They used us. For about anything you can imagine." I shook my head, trying to clear it. "So many of us were pimped, sold for sex, taken out of state. In some cases out of the country. I guess I was fucking lucky." My heart thundered like a sledgehammer, and oh-so-familiar shame burned through my veins.

The fury in Alex's voice was unmistakable. "Call it what it was Cailin. Rape. Torture. I am so, so sorry. Believe me when I say it doesn't change the way I feel about you one bit."

Alex tugged my rigid body into her. With her cheek pressed against the top of my head, she murmured reassuring words. Eventually the black curtain of dreamless slumber knocked me out.

Chapter 4

The smell of freshly brewed coffee woke me. I blinked a couple of times and squinted at the clock. 8:03. My head felt hollow, and I dropped it back onto the pillow.

Recall fluttered on the edge of my consciousness and suddenly returned with far too much clarity, pinning my body down with its weight.

Mike and the massacre at school.

The incredulous look on Alex's face when I told her about my runaway past.

Pick's heartfelt apology.

The nightmare in the alley.

Oh, my fucking God.

Then my bladder took over and I staggered toward

the bathroom. Once I was done, I found the aspirin, brushed my teeth, and crawled back into the warmth and security of bed. I rolled on my stomach and dragged the pillow over my head. It wasn't long before I felt the side of the bed dip, and a hand settled on the small of my back.

"Are you still talking to me?" My voice was muffled by down.

"Oh, Cailin. Of course I'm still talking to you."

I peered out from under the pillow's edge. Alex perched on the edge, a leg bent at the knee pressing against my side. She was dressed in faded black jeans and a paint-stained sweatshirt, ready to create something out of nothing. Her still-damp obsidian hair hung loose. She slapped me on the butt. "Out of bed, sleepyhead."

I didn't move.

"We can talk about last night if you want. Or not. I'm here, no matter what."

I snaked a hand out from under the covers and grabbed her wrist. She was my anchor to the here and now. I curled around her leg and rested my head on her thigh. My fingers slid down to her hand, and I brought her palm to my lips. Alex was real, and she was mine. I needed her touch, needed the connection, needed to remind myself I was alive.

Alex read my emotions, and the banked fire that was a constant in her eyes flared to life.

"I need you," I whispered and propped myself on my elbow. My thumb caressed her cheekbone, then I slid my hand to the back of her neck. Our lips touched gently, and Alex's tongue slithered wetly into my mouth.

In the space of a heartbeat I fought my way out of the covers and had Alex on her back, my mouth plundering hers. Hands tangled in my hair, Alex shifted, allowing me better access. Alex. My safe harbor, my rock. She grounded me in ways I didn't understand but needed as desperately as the air I breathed.

The tenuous control I had snapped.

Clothing flew.

Finally, finally we were skin-on-oh-so-achingly-hot-skin, and I lost myself in salvation.

★ ★ ★

I was chewing on the last bite of my breakfast when the phone rang. Alex waved me off and answered it.

She listened for a few seconds. "Hang on." She held the receiver out to me. "Martinez."

Manny Martinez and his partner Bryan Peterson had worked with me periodically, most often on the Fugitive Apprehension Team, also called the FAT team. They were great at keeping everyone apprised of what was happening, and I was glad they were the investigators who'd caught the school shooting case.

I polished off the last of my orange juice and took the handset. "Yo."

"You sound like a female Rocky Balboa. Doesn't the NPIU teach their agents manners?"

"Better manners than the MPD imparts on you, lush."

"I hold my booze just fine. Frankly, I don't know

how that hot thing you call a girlfriend can put up with your pain-in-the-ass self."

"What's up? I don't suppose you called to trade jabs."

"Talked to the kid last night. He asked to see you, by the way. Maybe you can get more out of him than I could, which was pretty much zilch."

Not surprising. "I can do that."

"Tried to ask him about the music Olivia mentioned. Pretty much stonewalled me. I did discover that the album's a dupe of what the kid who did the Steven's High shooting had on his player. Not that music is a reason for a kid to kill, but it can certainly play a part. We're trying to ID who was doling it out, see where that trail leads. With the second school shooting, it's balls-to-the-wall to find a reason. Any reason. The music's as good as anything to focus on right now. Governor's upping the pressure, Helling's sweating. They're talking task force now because the music's been traced to a hate-based label. It's a stretch, but the Gov wants action."

"White Power music?" I chewed on that for a moment. "Panzerfaust Records?"

"No, maybe an offshoot."

"Panzerfaust fell apart after it came out the owner was a Mexican. But I can see one of the jokers involved continuing on."

Panzerfaust had been based out of Minnesota and was once the main competitor to Resistance Records, the biggest of the White Power labels. Resistance had fallen into hard times in the mid-two thousands, and Panzerfaust had imploded entirely. Since then, distributors who marketed and sold individual bands' albums generated the majority of white-power metal music.

A lot of residents would be stunned to learn hate groups existed within the state. The Southern Poverty Law Center kept a map of these groups throughout the country, and Minnesota had at least eight that the SPLC and the NPIU monitored. The Ku Klux Klan even had a foothold, as well as a variety of Neo-Nazi and Racist Skinhead groups. There were two suburban anti-LGBT groups, a Black Separatist organization, and a Radical Catholicism group. Not all of these associations were racist or used violence to intimidate the larger population, but some were and did. When violence or a viable threat of violence occurred, that group slid into terrorism territory, and thus fell squarely under the NPIU's jurisdiction.

Martinez said, "I know a few other labels have popped up in the state, but this particular one is based in Minnetonka."

"Minnetonka? Again?" The city was an affluent suburb west of Minneapolis. At the tone of my voice, Alex looked curiously over her shoulder at me from the sink where she was finishing up the dishes.

"Yeah. Again. Listen to some of the shit Mike was listening to. *Skinhead Way to Live, Retribution Youth, The Time is Now, Glory is in Hand, Hate Train of Defiance.*"

"Jesus."

"The lyrics are enough to curl your short hairs. Okay, hold on," he said. I heard rustling in the background and the sound of paper being unfolded.

Grim reaper waits grinning
Will to survive, death marks our path
There is nothing to think besides winning
Entirely against the system, mark your staff

Feel the pain and give it back
Only the strong prevail
Stir the chaos, feel the hate
Kill them all, we cannot fail

I sat motionless, repulsed. "Holy crap."

"Group's called Brutal Hate. The rest of their stuff's not any better. It's head-pounding, ear-searing hell. I can see it how it could influence someone, especially a teenager who's already knee-deep in angst and bullshit."

"Has anyone interviewed Mike's foster parents yet, the Nordquists?"

"Bryan notified Larry and Ellen last night and did a preliminary interview, but as you can imagine, they weren't exactly in the frame of mind to do much more than nod their heads and hold back tears." Martinez cleared his throat. "SSA Weatherspoon and Chief Helling want us to stop by the Nordquists' and see what they have to say now that the shock is over. Peterson's still tied up with the BCA at the scene."

"No problem. I met them a couple of times, nice people. Goddamn, I just can't wrap my mind around this whole thing."

"You and me both."

"Meet me in forty-five at the Fifth."

"See ya."

I disconnected.

Alex settled across the table from me with a cup of coffee. A ray of sunlight filtered in from the window above the sink and fell across her and part of the table, making her hair shine a deep blue-black. She absently stirred the contents of a travel mug with a spoon. "What was that all about?"

I told her what Martinez had said and ended by explaining that I was meeting him to reinterview Mike's foster parents."

"I take it you've met them?"

"Yeah. Twice. Once when we first placed Mike and then again about a year ago. Nice folks. They'd been doing the foster thing for a long time, had some ideas how to handle a sensitive kid in a world of pain."

Alex put a hand on mine and entwined our fingers. "I'm sorry to leave you like this, but I have to get to work. Your mom has an appointment at ten-thirty, and I have to cover, and then I need to paint." Since Alex had moved to Minneapolis with me, her work had evolved. She spent hours at a time in the spare room we'd turned into a studio, lost in her art.

I leaned over the table and kissed her. "Okay. I imagine I'll be tied up most of the day. Hopefully I'll see you later, maybe for dinner, since yesterday's kind of went down the toilet."

Alex twisted her hand in the collar of my T-shirt and pulled me in, her tongue lightly skimming mine. For just a moment I deepened the kiss, tasting the coffee with vanilla coconut milk creamer she was drinking. If she wasn't careful, I was going to drag her ass upstairs to bed again.

She pulled away, a regretful smile on her lips. "Do what you can. I know now's the time you have to get a jump on things." Alex got up and headed for the back door.

I followed her down the hall. She grabbed her jacket off the hook. As she pulled it on, I walked her backward, not stopping until her back hit the door.

I was still in awe that I felt so much for this person, when less than a year ago I decided I'd never get involved again. The break with Eli had cured me of harboring any of those silly happily-ever-after notions—or so I had thought. Once I emerged from the fallout less than whole, I swore I was done. But Alex found a chink in my armor and blew out every wall I'd so carefully constructed.

Now, I was happier than I could ever remember and periodically had to stop and remind myself it was real. I braced my hands on either side of her head and nipped at her bottom lip. She deepened the kiss, allowing me full access. My hands settled on her hips, and I pulled her hard against me. She felt so solid, so *there*. With a regretful sigh, I trailed my mouth over the soft skin of her neck and reluctantly stepped away.

From the rapid rise and fall of Alex's chest, she was wound as tightly as I was. "I love you, Cailin." She pressed her hand over her heart and then placed it on the left side of my chest. I knew she felt the rapid pounding beneath her palm. Her heart to mine.

✷ ✷ ✷

In the back lot of Minneapolis's Fifth Precinct I saw Martinez leaning against a crap-brown unmarked Crown Vic, chatting with a couple of patrol cops. They took off when I approached.

"You ready for this, McKenna?"

"No. I am not. This heap our ride?"

Martinez scowled. "Don't call this thing of everlasting beauty a heap." He stroked the dented hood affectionately.

I eyed the car and climbed in the passenger seat, after I kicked an empty McDonald's paper bag and two stained coffee cups out of the way.

Martinez hopped in beside me and cranked the motor. Grinding sounds emanated from under the hood. Just before I thought he'd run the battery down to nothing, the engine caught. At this rate, we'd be lucky to make it out of the parking lot.

I pulled at the seatbelt. It didn't budge. Batting a thousand today.

Martinez clicked his own in place. "Gotta put some oomph behind it."

I gave the belt a good yank. It popped free and my hand nearly hit the dashboard. "I agreed to talk to Mike's foster folks, not take my life in my hands."

Martinez pulled out of the cop shop lot and headed south on Nicollet. "You'll be fine. You're with a trained professional."

"That's what I'm afraid of."

Less than five minutes later, we pulled up to a light blue, ranch-style house. A white fence encircled the yard.

The gravity of the visit blossomed in the air like a specter. This kind of thing had to be one of the worst parts of the job. Solemnly, we trudged resolutely through the gate.

Martinez knocked on the door.

I glanced at him. "Did you call ahead?"

"Naw."

We waited as seconds ticked by like minutes. I was so not looking forward to the upcoming conversation. Eventually we were rewarded for our patience with the sound of a deadbolt being thrown, and the door opened.

Larry Nordquist blinked against the light of day. The man had aged since I'd last seen him. The shock of red hair on his head had gone completely white, and while I guessed his age to be mid-fifties, he looked like he'd roared past seventy overnight. The man resembled a giraffe—rangy and thin with oversized ears, long neck, and mottled skin. An unbuttoned gray sweater hung loosely from his bony shoulders, covering a white, untucked polo with what looked like a coffee spill down the front. Every other time I'd seen him, he'd been impeccably dressed, and I'd be willing to bet he wouldn't be caught dead in stained clothing.

I held out my hand. "Mr. Nordquist, I'm so sorry."

Haunted eyes met mine and Nordquist grasped my hand, his grip firm but not bone-crushing. "Yes, Cailin. Thank you."

I waved a hand at Martinez. "This is Officer Manuel Martinez from the Minneapolis Police Department."

Nordquist exchanged my hand for Martinez's and took a step back. "Come on in. Have a seat in the living room while I go get Ellen. She's lying down."

We wandered into the living room and settled on a burgundy leather sofa.

A random scattering of magazines and books occupied the coffee table. In one corner were a half-chewed rawhide bone and a couple dog toys. A drafting table was set up against another wall, blueprints spread across its surface.

Martinez sat back and crossed his arms. "What's the old man do?"

"He's an architect. His wife's E. A. McGregor, the romance writer."

"No shit. The ex loved her books. Loved them more than she loved me, if you can imagine that."

Mr. Nordquist returned to the living room with his wife in tow. Ellen Nordquist was a tall, lean woman with white-silver hair teased into a flowing mane. Her makeup-free face was pale, and black circles smudged the skin below her eyes. Dressed more casually than her husband in jeans and a T-shirt, she had the brittle appearance of someone very close to the edge.

The Nordquists sat across from us on two overstuffed chairs. Larry looked like he hoped the chair would open up and swallow him.

Ellen perched on the edge of hers, ready to take flight. She put a hand to her throat. "I'm forgetting my manners. Would either of you like something to drink?"

We both declined, and Martinez said, "I know this is a hard thing for you to do. We have some questions, and I'd like to tape it if you don't mind."

The Nordquists consented. Martinez clicked on a digital recorder and set it on the coffee table.

"How are you two holding up?" I asked, even though it was obvious they weren't.

Larry made an effort to sit up straighter in his chair. "This has been a terrible shock. Two terrible shocks, first with Mike's dog and...and—" His voice broke but he maintained his composure. Ellen reached over and put a hand on his knee.

Martinez gave him a second then asked, "What exactly happened regarding the dog?"

Ellen said, "We let Otis—that's the dog's name—out into the yard the evening before last." Her features became slightly more animated. Apparently it helped that she had something specific to think about. "That dog was the absolute light of Michael's life. Never a problem. He never ran away, never seriously misbehaved. Thursday night Michael went out to bring Otis in about, oh, nine-thirty. The gate was wide open, and he was nowhere to be found."

I asked, "Otis wasn't one to take a spin around the neighborhood?"

"Oh, no." Ellen swiped at a stray tear that rolled down her cheek. "He adored Michael. I think that dog would go to school and sit next to Michael's desk if he'd been allowed."

"What," I asked, "did you do when you couldn't find him?"

Larry said, "We walked the neighborhood, but no sign of Otis. Finally Ellen and Mike took one car, I took the other, and we drove around half the night looking for that damn dog."

Silence settled over the room. Then Martinez said, "You didn't find him."

"No." Ellen straightened. "Poor Michael. He was beside himself. Took a sleeping bag and sat on the front step hoping Otis would show up. Next thing we knew, Michael burst into our room in tears—he'd never cried in front of us before. We could hardly make out what he was trying to say."

Ellen took a shuddering breath, her eyes locked on hands fisted in her lap. "We got dressed and went downstairs to find the dog lying in the grass next to the stoop. He couldn't get up. He was so sick, throwing up, so very weak. We got him into the van and took him to the all-night emergency vet." She looked at me. The pain reflecting from her made it difficult to meet her gaze.

Larry reached over and Ellen grabbed his hand and held on. "They checked Otis out. Pretty quick they figured out he'd ingested antifreeze. We had him put down."

Martinez asked, "How did Mike handle that?"

Ellen glanced at Larry. I wondered if she tended to defer to him or if she was simply checking to see if he would answer. She said, "He went silent and withdrew completely."

Larry nodded. "Yes. He regressed to the point he was

at when he first came to us. Sullen, silent. He didn't say anything on the drive home, and we decided we'd call him in sick yesterday so he'd have a chance to pull himself together over the weekend. I don't think we got him to bed until close to six a.m."

I asked, "Did either or both of you stay home with him?"

Ellen tensed. "No. I had meetings and Larry went to work." Her voice went up a couple of octaves. "If only I'd come home sooner—"

"No, Ellen." Larry faced his wife. "You can't think that way."

The brightness in her eyes turned into tears that trickled down her cheeks. "Michael came to us painfully shy. Withdrawn. He'd come so far. And now—all those he hurt." Ellen's composure crumbled. She ducked her head and wept quietly.

Martinez glanced uncomfortably around the room.

Ellen pulled a tissue from a box on the floor next to her chair and dabbed at her eyes. "I'm sorry," she said, her voice now low and thick, but she was back in control, however tenuous.

Martinez asked, "When was the last time either of you saw Mike?"

"I stuck my head in his room just before I left." Larry swallowed with difficulty and gazed out the window. "About seven-ten or so. I thought he'd fallen asleep. I remember hoping we would be able to ease him over this hump. I was so wrong."

These people were givers. They gave time, money,

and love freely, only wanting the best for the kids who came though their doors. The circumstances and their pain were devastating to witness.

Ellen blew her nose and pulled out another tissue.

I hated to turn the conversation, but I needed to. "Do either of you have any idea where Mike got the gun?"

"My husband hates guns." Ellen's voice was steadier. "I'm terrified of the things. We have never had weapons in the house. I have no idea where Michael could have gotten it."

Larry stared blankly at the coffee table and didn't say anything.

I leaned forward, elbows on my knees, hands clasped. "How had Mike's attitude been before this?"

Ellen twisted the tissue in her hand. "Michael's been quiet. He's always been kind of moody. He swings from boisterous and manic to retreating into his bedroom for days listening to that infernal music."

"Were you aware he was being bullied in school?" Martinez asked.

Larry snapped out of whatever haze he'd fallen into. "He told us about a few incidents. We did talk to the school administration. They made note of it. Mike stopped mentioning trouble at school, so I guess we figured it had stopped." His lips were pressed tightly together. "God damn it. I should have followed up."

I asked, "Did Mike ever mention who was bullying him?"

Ellen said, "It started with an H."

"Hunter," Larry clarified. "The other name he

mentioned was Bill, or Billy something."

I opened my mouth, but Martinez beat me to the punch. "Did Mike ever tell you what they did to him?"

Ellen's brow furrowed. "He mentioned trouble in the cafeteria. Something about his friend Olivia. I'm sorry, I don't remember specifically what."

"I don't think he told us any specifics, Ellen." Larry met my eyes. "I pushed him, but he wouldn't say."

Remembering Olivia's comment regarding Mike's changing demeanor and Ellen's referral to Mike's "infernal music," I said, "There was a particular band Mike was listening to yesterday when this happened. Do you know about it?"

Larry said, "We don't usually keep track of particular bands the boy likes. It's been our policy to stay hands-off of stuff like that, but if it's the same thing he's been listening to lately, it's ghastly."

"He'd walk around with the music turned up so loudly in his ears I was afraid he'd go deaf," Ellen said. "I tried one day a couple weeks ago to ask Michael what he was listening so intently to. He wouldn't say, but he did turn it down, at least around here. I know music sounds different when it bleeds through headphones, but this was really hard-core." She laughed once, the sound a harsh bark that held zero humor. "He once called it death metal. Like I even know what exactly that is. Kids always listen to music adults are horrified by."

Martinez said, "We're in the preliminary stages of the investigation, but we've learned the music was made by a Neo-Nazi-founded production company."

Larry's eyes narrowed and Ellen uttered, "Oh, God."

"It looks like this company recruits young adults," I said, "probably kids under eighteen, to give the music away at schools."

Ellen whispered, "Why? Why would they do that?"

"We're working on it," Martinez said.

Neither one of us was geared up for a lesson in hate group recruitment techniques, so I asked, "Have you noticed anything different in Mike's personality, in his demeanor lately?"

Ellen's hand quivered as she raised it to rub the back of her neck. "He has been losing his temper more easily. Just the other day he was doing some homework and had come out to the kitchen for a snack." She glanced at her husband. "You weren't home from work yet. The lid on the jam jar was stuck, and he got frustrated. Finally I took it away because I was afraid he'd slam it on the floor."

Martinez asked, "Does he tend to have a short fuse?"

"No," Larry said, "I'd say he's usually very self-controlled. Rarely lets much emotion show. The exception was that damn dog. He lit up when he was near Otis."

"Does Mike have a cell phone?" I asked.

"No," Ellen said. "We told him for his last two birthdays we'd get him one if he wanted, but he's never shown interest. He'd rather have a video game. Now he'll never—"

Larry put a hand on her leg.

They'd had enough, I could tell, and it was time to go. I said, "That's about all we have for now. Before we go, would you mind if we took a peek in Mike's room?"

Ellen stood and leaned into Larry. "Certainly. Follow me."

Martinez and I trailed Ellen upstairs. She stopped in front of a closed door and rested her hand on the knob. She took a deep breath before she opened it.

"Thank you, Ellen." I gave her shoulder a gentle squeeze. "We can take it from here if you want to go back downstairs."

"Thank you. It's so hard to see Mike's room without him in it."

How did a parent, adoptive, foster, or otherwise, deal with pain like this? It had to be unspeakable.

Once Ellen left, Martinez and I surveyed the room before crossing the threshold.

The room was typical teenager; in other words, a mess. A twin bed was unmade, and clothes were lumped across the floor. A twenty-two-inch flat-screen TV sat on a pressboard stand, hooked up to an Xbox. Video games were stacked next to the TV, and a number of them lay in a pile on the floor nearby.

The only place that was neat—almost obsessively so—was a student-sized desk beside the bed. In stark contrast to the condition of the rest of the room, schoolbooks and notebooks were neatly arranged on one side, and pens and pencils nestled in a tray.

I moved closer to take a better look. A small notepad sat on the corner of the desk. A reminder that Olivia's birthday was coming up was written in cramped, precise printing. A half-eaten Snickers bar lay nearby, along with a stapler, a solar calculator, a bottle of White Out, paper clips, and a 4x6 picture of Mike and Olivia on a roller coaster, their mouths open wide in silent screams, round eyes reflecting terrified delight. Probably on one of the coasters at Valley Fair.

While I rifled through Mike's desk drawers, Martinez stood before a bookcase, head tilted. "Kid was into sci-fi. Lots of Robert Jordan. Some books on biology. Goddamn, what a waste."

Waste it was. The last drawer stuck and I had to give a good yank to open it. A well-loved, one-eyed, stuffed teddy bear sat atop some old notebooks and comic books. Underneath it all was a dog-eared Playboy. Such is the transition between innocent child and young man.

I slid the bottom drawer shut and shifted my attention to the bed. The headboard was essentially a long shelf, and it was full of CDs. My heart sped up for a minute, but I quickly saw that, with the exception of a couple discs by Marilyn Manson, most of the stuff was standard teen music. Nickelback, Eminem, Train, Ne-Yo, and a host of other pop and rap artists rounded out the stash. "All his tunes are pretty mainstream. No questionable music here, unless..." I trailed off and opened a few of the cases. They held what was advertised on the outside. "Never mind." I straightened and sighed heavily. "Wonder if he has a laptop."

Martinez moved on to the kid's closet. His voice was muffled. "Don't know. We'll ask on the way out."

I halfheartedly shoved through the mess of clothing on the floor with my foot while I waited for Martinez to finish. The video games piled around the TV caught my attention. "Splinter Cell: Conviction." "Assassin's Creed." "Castlevania." "Pac-Man Championship Edition."

Five minutes later, we descended the steps to the main floor. Ellen and Larry had returned to their places in the living room.

"We didn't find anything," I said. "Does Mike have a laptop?"

Larry's gaze went to the corner of the room, to a desktop computer. "No. If he needs to do something for school, he does it on the family computer. He hasn't been interested in electronics unless it's attached to his Xbox."

"Or his iPod," Ellen added.

"I imagine we'll be back," Martinez said. "Forensics might want to take a look at the hard drive. In the meantime, here's my card."

I pulled my own business card from my pocket and handed it over as well. "Call either of us, anytime."

We thanked the Nordquists and left.

The car started on the first crank this time, and Martinez pulled away from the curb. I glanced at him. "What do you think?"

"I think this is a fucking mess. Kid doesn't look like he was ready to jump off a building or anything. Had his share of trouble, but who doesn't?"

"You think he preplanned?"

Martinez jerked the steering wheel to swerve around a car. "Only far enough in advance to get a gun. You got a good kid, for the most part, anyway, and he was trying to do his thing. Gets harassed at school. Pushed too far. It happens. If this wasn't the second school shooting incident, that's pretty much that."

"I can't help but think that the death metal music must have stirred the pot. The other thing we need to find out is if the two victims had anything to do with Otis or not. I hate to think of anyone intentionally poisoning an animal."

"But someone did."

We rode in silence for a few blocks. "Do you believe music has the power to affect someone to the point they act out?" I did, in certain instances, but I wanted to hear his thoughts.

"I think it can if the kid is in the right headspace. Vulnerable. Haven't you ever gotten depressed when you heard a song on the radio that reminded you of some shitty event?"

"Oh, yeah. Mix in those God-awful teenage hormones, and you have a boatload of potential trouble."

Martinez pulled into the parking lot of the Fifth, and the car lurched to a stop. "See, back in one piece. Told you I'm a pro."

"Yeah, you're a pro all right. I'm going to see what's up back at the ranch. Keep me in the loop, okay?"

"You know it." Martinez thumped my shoulder. "Thanks for tagging along."

"Right on, Skipper." I saluted him with my middle finger.

"Same to you, sweetheart." Martinez gave me a lecherous grin, then his serious face reappeared. "Mike was asking to see you last night, remember? You wanna give him a go?"

I looked at my watch. It was half past three. "I'll call in the morning and make sure I can get in, then I'll sit down with him." As pathetic as it sounded, I wasn't sure I was ready to face him.

Chapter 5

The offices of the Midwest headquarters of the Bureau of National Intelligence were located in Minneapolis's Warehouse District, northwest of downtown, not far from the Mississippi River. The entire fourth floor of the Amethyst building—a historic, six-floor, late-19th-century behemoth—was taken up by the NPIU. Various other federal agencies occupied the rest of the building.

Before 9/11, security was lax at many federal sites, but not anymore. The lobby had been divided in half by clear ballistic glass and remodeled to funnel all comers toward two sets of metal detectors. A bulletproof security desk situated next to the detectors housed closed circuit TVs and other surveillance equipment.

"Hey, Herc." I scanned my badge and gave a friendly

wave to a thickly muscled man sitting behind the desk. His name was Tim Benson, but somewhere along the line someone called him Herc, and the nickname stuck.

"McKenna." He buzzed me in. "Crazy weekend. Full moon's bringing out the nut jobs."

"Yeah." I crossed to the elevator and pushed the button. As the double doors shut, I waved and said, "Keep 'em outta here, okay?"

One corner of his mouth quirked up and a deep dimple appeared. Ten to one he'd received more than his share of old lady cheek pinching when he was a kid. "I'll do my best."

Inside the elevator the smile melted off my face.

The weekend usually found the 4th floor essentially abandoned, but today, light leaked around the closed blinds of Weatherspoon's glass-fronted office. I heard the low murmur of two or three one-sided conversations as I made my way through a honeycomb of drab beige cubicles toward my little piece of government property.

As I neared my cube, a familiar, but out-of-context voice floated through the air. Agent Rosie Nakamura's distinctive, sharp laugh followed.

I stuck my head into my office space. Sitting in my chair, his feet flung carelessly across my desk, was an agent I hadn't seen in some time. What the hell was Dirty Harry doing in Minneapolis?

Across from Harry, Rosie was in the process of wiping her eyes with her fingers.

Harry Robinson was an NPIU legend. Rosie and I met him in New Jersey. Harry had been an undercover wino working the traffic ramps leading into the Holland tunnel. He portrayed a very realistic bum, complete with filthy clothes, a ratty trench coat, and more than one layer of grime coating his skin. When I first saw him, I thought he was the real McCoy. I'd dropped some change into his dirt-crusted fist more than once.

We'd gotten to know Harry pretty well. Despite the nasty habit he had of sucking discarded cigarette butts for the nicotine rush, I thought he was all right. In fact, he'd saved my ass by bringing down a gun-wielding ex-con bent on revenge. The con managed to skin my skull with a potshot before Harry walloped him. My hair was finally growing back after the ER doc creatively shaved the area around the wound in a surprisingly realistic reproduction of the state of Florida.

I propped both hands on the cube walls on either side of the entry. "Harry. What the hell are you doing here?" I was shocked at the change in his appearance. The same bright blue eyes peered through dark lashes, but that was where the familiarity ended. His shaggy blond mane had fallen victim to a pair of scissors, and he had a stylishly tousled Bradley Cooper look going. Gone was the scruff that had adorned his concave cheeks, and I saw he actually had a divot in his chin. Instead of baggy, horrifyingly aromatic rags for clothes, Harry's new attire was *GQ* worthy.

A ribbed red sweater over a gray oxford shirt clung to his sinewy frame, the sleeves pulled halfway up his forearms. Faded blue jeans and a newish-looking pair of Danner boots finished the transformation. An M-65 military throwback jacket hung from the back of my chair.

Momentarily robbed of speech, I couldn't do more than gape.

"What's wrong, McKenna, tongue fall out again?"

There. That was the Harry I knew. Mr. Sarcastic.

He tilted his head. "Your hair's finally growing back. I think I like the short look. Makes your ears stick out."

"So smooth. Bet you're popular with the ladies."

Rosie said, "Time for me to get back to it. Cailin, come see me after you two catch up. Agent Robinson, you'll have to finish your story later. We'll grab a cup of coffee or something. Didn't think we'd ever see your ugly mug again."

Harry flashed a smile. "I still like you, Nakamura."

Rosie ducked under one of the arms I still had braced on the cube entrance, her short black hair swaying with her movement. She waved and disappeared around the corner.

I dropped my arms, stepped into my dinky workspace, and settled in the chair Rosie had vacated. "What brings you to the cold streets of Minneapolis?"

"And a nice hello to you, too. Forget your manners?"

I smiled. "God, Harry, it's good to see you. Although I'm glad I heard your voice first. I'd never recognize you. For a bum you clean up well."

He grinned. I could now see he had more than just the dimple on his chin. He'd be a definite danger to the hetero female, and to the gay male population if he rolled that way.

"Finally got off dirt duty and was about to take a nice,

long, relaxing vacation. Thought I'd come visit the northland."

Harry threaded his fingers behind his head and crossed his feet, which were still propped up on my desktop. "Unofficially, thought maybe I could lend a hand."

"Not that I'd ever mind a hand from you, but why?"

Harry flung his feet off my desk, sending a file to the floor, the contents skidding across the industrial carpet. "Come on, you can tell me all about your case while I have a smoke."

I bent to retrieve the file, straightened the scattered pages, and tossed it back on my desk. "Thought you gave that shit up."

"Hell, no."

I led him to the parking ramp and propped a pocket-sized notebook between the exit-only door and the jamb and waved at the close circuit camera that covered the area. We meandered through the mostly empty fourth-level ramp with its grease-stained cement and faded parking lines until we got to the edge of the lot that faced west. Target Field's huge stadium lights were ablaze, and I wondered what was going on over there.

Harry eyed the view, lit up, and inhaled deeply. When he exhaled through his nose, I was reminded of a pissed bull in January.

"So." I propped my elbows on a metal rail that rose about six inches above the half wall.

"So," Harry echoed and took another long pull, the cherry of the cigarette glowing bright red.

"God, you're a pain."

That roguish smile appeared again.

"Didn't know you had so many dimples."

"Mom's the culprit. Became an overnight chick magnet at puberty."

"No ego there. Seriously, why are you here?"

Harry lifted a shoulder. "Like I said, I'm here to help."

"I didn't know you had any interest in Minnesota hate groups." I shifted to stand upwind of the smoke and tucked my hands in my pockets.

"There's a lot you don't know about me, McKenna." Harry squinted through his fumes. "I've been fascinated with the concept of hate groups of all kinds since college. Motivations, practices. I've worked with some of the guys at the Southern Poverty Law Center. The breadth and scope of these radical nutcases scares the shit out of me. Thought I might be an asset. Since I'm on leave, I thought why not swing by and see what's happening."

While it might be irregular to have an agent fly halfway across the country on his own dime to offer help on a case, it wasn't unheard of. All part of that sharing and caring NPIU mandate.

"Why are you on leave?"

"The brass decided I'd been undercover long enough. Told me to use up some of the vacation hours I've got piled up. Been five years since I've taken any substantial time off. I hate to admit I forgot how good it feels to be squeaky clean for any length of time."

"I'll bet. If you want to use your break helping us

figure this out, I'm not going to argue." I took a moment to order my thoughts. "I don't know exactly where we are on things yet, but let me fill you in on what I do know." I told Harry about Olivia and about what little I knew about the hate music and where it had come from.

Harry listened quietly. When I finished, he stubbed out a second smoke against the sole of his boot and flicked the butt over the wall.

I watched it spiral downward. The back of my brain itched to say something about littering, but my frontal lobe countered with the reasoning that I'd serve myself better to shut the hell up and not tick off a potential ace in the hole.

After another moment, I gave Harry a sideways glance. "Thoughts?"

"Dunno. I've heard of one hate label casing schoolyards around the country, but I haven't been keeping up on that shit since I started the Jersey City detail. Wasn't aware music was being produced right here in your own backyard."

"Come on inside. I'm freezing."

I retrieved my notebook with another salute to the video camera. "I suppose we better let the big boys know you're here and willing to help. Then I'd like you to talk to the lead Minneapolis PD guys on the case, Martinez and Peterson. They're good."

"Okay. Before I'm cleared with your people, I have some calls to make, and I need a computer. I'd like to do a little research before I talk to your boss."

Back at the cubicle, I gestured toward my desk. "Use

mine if you want. I need to help Rosie finish up some reports. Speaking of Rosie—" I shot him a warning look. "Don't be playing that good guy act on her. She's a straight shooter, man, and you're nothing but trouble."

Harry's expression was wary, and was that guilt I saw? Suddenly I understood. "You really are here to see Rosie." I poked him. "Aren't you?" There had been a whiff of interest between the two of them in Jersey, but I thought that fire had died. Apparently not.

"Maybe she's added incentive." Harry held his hand over his heart and settled down behind my desk. "I'm nothing but a gentleman, but even a gentleman would notice Nakamura does have a mighty fine ass."

I rolled my eyes, told him where to find Weatherspoon, and walked out.

Rosie's often unused, tiny piece of tarnished heaven was around the corner and halfway down the row. She was furiously pounding away on her keyboard. I filled her in on the discussion I'd had with Harry except for the part about her nice ass and Harry's possible intentions.

When I finished, she said, "Weatherspoon stopped by while you were out with Harry. They're calling a meeting for nine o'clock tomorrow morning. I told him I'd let you know. With the second shooting, and the commonality of the hate group tunes, it's task force time. We need to examine the recruitment angle, see what else might be in play. They want the group identified and investigated to see what exactly might be behind the music distribution. If these White Power groups are recruiting, they're trying to ramp up. The question is why." She stuck the non-business end of a pen in her mouth.

"One of these days that ink's going to wind up all over your face. Who'll make up the task force?"

"You, me, Harry, if all goes well—"

"About Harry. You know he's a smooth operator, Rose."

Rosie's almond-shaped black eyes bore into mine. "I can handle myself, Cailin."

"I know that. I'm just saying."

"Duly noted."

If anyone was up to the task of tangling with Harry Robinson, it was Rosie, but I didn't want to see her get hurt. Harry was a great guy, but I got the vibe he was something of a playboy. Still, Rosie was a big girl, and I knew when it was time to back off. I leaned against the edge of the cube door. "All right. Just don't say I didn't warn you. Back to the task force. Who else?"

"Cirilli and Smith, on our end. Martinez, Peterson, whoever else MPD wants."

I nodded at her monitor. "Where are you at?"

"I'm just about done. You're off the hook this time, McKenna." Rosie's smile faded. "They're trying to keep the Neo-Nazi White Power music thing out of the media, and things are going to get"— she floated quote signs in the air—"intense. Weatherspoon said we better catch up on our sleep, because tomorrow the shit-storm hits."

I left Rosie finishing her computer work and headed back to my desk. Harry was absorbed in whatever he was doing. I told him about the nine o'clock meeting and offered him our spare bedroom. He grunted, which I interpreted to be thanks, but no thanks, and mumbled that he'd already talked to Weatherspoon and was checked in at the Sheridan.

That was much more the Harry I was used to, and it gave me a strange sense of comfort.

✯ ✯ ✯

Darkness had fallen, and streetlights glowed softly at either end of the alley. I pulled into the garage and parked.

In the hallway I caught the scent of home-cooked food. My mouth watered. I hadn't realized how hungry I was, and my stomach chose that moment to noisily agree with my salivary glands.

Alex was at the stove, her hair up in a loose ponytail. The sleeves of her sweatshirt were pulled past her elbows.

"Hey, baby." I wrapped my arms around her, buried my face in her neck. I could still smell her shampoo faintly, and inhaled deeply, cherishing the feel of her relaxing against me.

"You made it home for dinner."

"I did." I nuzzled the smooth skin behind her ear.

Alex sighed and tilted her head to give me better access. "How did things go?"

"Talked to Mike's foster parents. They're pretty broken up."

Alex squirmed. "Stop. You know I can't think when you do that."

With a satisfied smile, I released her and dropped into a chair at the table. "You won't believe who's in town."

"Who?"

"Dirty Harry."

"Harry Robinson?" Alex turned to me, loose strands of hair stuck to her heat-flushed cheeks. "What's he doing here?"

"Has some time off, decided to come visit. I almost didn't recognize him."

"He cleaned up?"

"Yeah. It's an amazing transformation. He's rather handsome, actually. Has dimples."

"No way. Can you grab some plates?"

I dropped the front legs of the chair onto the floor and went over to the cupboard.

"You rope him into helping out?" Alex said.

"He already volunteered. It'll be good to have an extra hand. How was your day?"

"Got some good work done on my latest project."

"That's a plus."

"However, you might want to listen to the answering machine."

"What now?"

"Go on and listen. I don't think I can do it justice."

I set two plates and two cups on the table and grabbed the phone mounted on the kitchen wall.

Eli's voice filtered through the receiver. "Cailin, it's me. I wanted you to know I'm thinking about you. Wondering if you're thinking about me. Wondering how your bitchy girlfriend is getting around. I heard something happened to her car. What a shame. Call me."

"Jesus," I muttered under my breath and hit the button to save the message.

"Good to know I moved from bimbo to bitch." Alex turned around and crossed her arms. "I should show her what kind of a bitch I can be. I'm getting close, Cailin. Very, very close to doing just that."

The last thing I needed was a catfight between a streetwise, motorcycle-racing, ex-flower hustler from New Jersey and a pseudo-professional used to high heels and highballs. Although that would be a hell of a fight to watch.

"No. Rein it in, Rocky. I'll talk to her tomorrow." I pulled the silverware drawer open. "I don't understand. She was never this bad."

Alex set a couple of steaming bowls on the table. "Seriously. You've got to do something, Cailin. She's escalating, and we don't need a crazy stalker freaking out on either one of us."

"I know. I do know, baby. Don't worry. I'll take care of it."

We sat down to red beans in a sauce with ham and diced potatoes on yellow rice, fried sweet plantains, and yucca boiled in garlic. I was reminded of one of the first meals I'd ever eaten with Alex. "*El Requenion.*" I pointed my fork at her, remembering the Puerto Rican restaurant where we shared that meal.

"Yeah." She smiled. "Afterward, I couldn't believe how you literally slept through our first night together."

"I can make up for it tonight. Again."

Alex gave me a wolfish grin. "Dig in. Time's a-wasting."

Chapter 6

The alarm went off and I hit snooze. Impossibly soon, the horrible noise went off again.

I cracked open a bleary eye and shut it off.

Alex barely stirred, but her hand shifted to rest on my thigh. I rolled over and pulled her against me, her skin oh-so-sleep-warm. She was softness and muscle, danger and home. So many contradictions. I felt desire coiling lazily, even after we'd been up half the night making love.

After soaking in another couple of moments of peace, I kissed her neck and gently detangled from her.

"Wait," Alex mumbled. "Don't go."

I brushed my cheek against hers and caught the shell of her ear with my lips. "I'm sorry. Go back to sleep. Love you."

"I know." She yawned, and then her breathing evened out as the sandman reclaimed her.

✹ ✹ ✹

An hour later I was at the office, seated at a fifteen-person conference room table, polishing off a Sausage McMuffin. Rosie sat next to me, eyeing each bite I took.

"For Pete's sake, take the rest." I thrust the last bite at her. "Did you forget breakfast again?"

Rosie popped the McMuffin in her mouth. "Yup."

I wiped my fingers on a napkin and stuffed it into the bag, which I wadded up and tossed toward a garbage can next to the door. The bag flew through the air as Chris Cirilli strolled into the room. The bag smacked him dead center and fell to the floor. He toed it with his Bruno Magli's and foot-bagged it into the garbage can. Smooth move.

Cirilli was the only former FBI agent in the NPIU. He was sickeningly handsome, resembling a younger, tidier Brad Pitt—tall, blond, muscular—and he possessed one hell of a come-on-and-try-to-fuck-with-me smile. Cirilli favored Armani, cashmere, and probably silk boxers, although I was in no way inclined to confirm that. He was dependable, usually cheerful, kept his head down, and worked hard.

"Where is everyone?" Cirilli asked.

Rosie said, "Weatherspoon's on the phone with Helling. Sounded like the MPD contingent's running late."

Agent Anthony Smith scurried in next and slammed himself into a chair next to Cirilli. Tony was maybe five-six and whipcord-thin. An unbuttoned flannel shirt partially covered a T-shirt smeared with the remains of whatever he'd eaten for breakfast. Between his clothing choices, his worn, off-brand tennis shoes, and male pattern baldness, Tony appeared way older than the late twenty-something he actually was. Although his wardrobe came straight out of the grunge era, his computer abilities were one hundred percent twenty-first century.

He was the sole lead for the Midwest Records and Research Technical Analysis team, which consisted of one member until something went down and more hands were necessary.

Rosie bounced between partnering with me in investigations and helping Tony out in R&R. She'd been an industrial and corporate hacker prior to becoming an agent. Few people knew she'd been given the choice of joining the NPIU or cooling her jets in federal prison. She'd taken the road better traveled and opted out of a lengthy stay in a computer-deprived penal institution.

Tony's leg bounced rapidly beneath the table. The force of it shook his entire body. "I wish they'd get this on the road. I'm running a search string on homegrown hate groups, and I don't have time for this shit." I liked to think of Tony as Agent Brainbucket. Whenever he had to slow down to the pace of us normal humans, he could hardly contain himself.

Cirilli glanced at the silver Rolex on his left wrist. "Ten minutes late now. Who's all coming?"

Rosie stretched her arms over her head and spoke through a yawn. "Everyone including God himself."

"Speak of the devil," I mumbled under my breath. Chief Helling blew in, followed by Manny Martinez and Bryan Peterson. Helling settled wearily at one end of the conference table, his complexion sallow, his suit wrinkled. I wondered if he'd been home at all in the last twenty-four hours.

"Peterson," I said, "you take your life in your hands and ride over here with Martinez?"

"Hell, no. You think I'm crazy?"

"Just because you two are a couple of pansy-assed—"

Martinez's retort was cut off with the arrival of SSA Weatherspoon, Harry, and Arthur Singleton, the Regional Director of the Midwest Bureau of the NPIU.

Singleton was an ex-Marine who still reflected the pride of the corps. He was dressed in a gray pinstripe suit with a teal tie. His graying hair was buzzed, and when the director's gravelly voice boomed out, everyone listened. He was probably James Earl Jones's long lost brother. Rumor had it he was in his mid-fifties, though his dark face was minimally lined and his body held no trace of fat. Not much escaped Singleton's attention. He was hard-nosed, but generally fair. His biggest asset was his ability to actually hear what was being said and then study all sides of a situation before taking action.

Once everyone settled, Singleton passed out file folders like he was dealing from a deck of cards. "First of all, thank you all for coming. Most of you know each other, but we do have one addition." Singleton nodded at

Harry. "Agent Harry Robinson is on loan from the NPIU's East Coast Bureau."

Harry raised a brow and leaned back in his chair.

Singleton said, "Chief Helling is going to run down the status of this case."

Helling slipped on a pair of thin, metal-framed reading glasses and shuffled through a pile of papers. When he finally spoke, a very slight southern accent indicated he wasn't a native Minnesotan. "Here's what we have to date. A sixteen-year-old male, Michael John Lorenzo, shot a security guard, a teacher, and two male students with an unregistered handgun, injuring the guard and the teacher, and killing both students. Another teacher was knocked unconscious when Lorenzo kicked a classroom door open and the door struck her.

"When police arrived, Lorenzo gave himself up without incident. He was placed under arrest and transported to Hennepin County Juvenile Detention Center. Included in the inventory of his personal effects was an iPod. The music he was listening to at the time of the shootings was produced by a supposedly Christian Neo-Nazi group based here in the Twin Cities."

Helling pulled off his glasses and threw them on the table. "It's bad enough I have gangs going after each other, shooting innocent bystanders. Doing drive-bys and killing babies. It's bad enough I have drug lords taking each other out over territory disputes. It's bad enough I have people torching homeless drunks passed out in the parks." Helling pulled a deep breath through his nose and clenched his teeth, the muscles in his jaw standing out in stark relief. "I do not, and I repeat, I do *not*"—he jabbed his finger in the air—"want to see innocent children exposed to the kind of hatemongering expressed in the music that was in the possession of both shooters. It appears the music was handed out on school property for purposes of youth recruitment. The same album was on the phone of the Steven's High shooter although it's unclear if he was listening to it as he acted, as Lorenzo was.

"Violent reaction to bullying and other mitigating factors isn't something new. Adding racist hate to that already volatile mix is untenable. I want to know who's behind this, and I want it stopped. To top things off, the media is already screaming for more information. I've scheduled a press conference for three o'clock today. This is likely going to be a journalistic circus from hell." He sat back, looking spent, and folded his arms over his chest.

After a long moment, Singleton picked up his folder and opened it. "Please take a minute and page through the file I handed out. This is some of the work Agents Smith and Nakamura have put together on local hate groups, their goals, and how White Power music is used to help them achieve what they want."

The sound of shuffling papers filled the room. I rapidly scanned the sheets. Much of the information had been assembled by the Southern Poverty Law Center regarding hate groups in Minnesota I was already familiar with. What I wasn't familiar with was the hate-based record label called Third Reich Records located in Minnetonka. I'd bet my last buck this was the birthplace of the music that Mike Lorenzo and the Steven's High gunman had. The label was related to a group called the Soldiers of Christ, and if I didn't miss my guess, they would be our initial focus.

"The NPIU," Singleton said, "is prepared to assist Chief Helling in any way. I'm putting each of you at the disposal of the MPD. Please consider Chief Helling your lead. As we know, one of the NPIU's mandates is to share resources, information, and manpower with local agencies. This will be a fine example of how well agencies can work together to achieve a common goal. We need to find out exactly what motivated the shooters, the role the music played, and how this hate music was distributed to schoolchildren so we can put a stop to it." Singleton paused. "We will find out exactly who is behind the creation of this vehicle of hate, and take them down. Are there any questions?"

No one said a word.

Chief Helling folded his hands on the table. "Agents Smith and Nakamura, keep working to find out what you can about the group behind the music. Agent Cirilli, you and Officer Peterson continue to question students, staff, neighbors, whoever might have witnessed anything.

"Agents Robinson and McKenna, you'll team with Officer Martinez and follow the music trail. Get to the bottom of what the group is planning, if anything." The chair creaked as Helling shifted. "Maintain clear channels of communication at all times. In your folders are contact numbers you may or may not already have. You can meet here or at the Fifth, whichever works best for you."

Helling glanced at Singleton. "Is there anything I've missed?"

Singleton stood, planted his hands on the table, and leaned forward. "That's about it for now. I'd like to see reports of your initial findings as soon as you can prepare them. We'll schedule another briefing in a day or two."

The rumble of voices in the room rose. Martinez called Harry aside to have a private conversation that lasted about three minutes, tension-filled if I read their body language correctly. I kept an eye on them, but generally stayed out of the way of jacked-up testosterone and hoped I wouldn't have to step in. I was relieved when they parted in a huff and returned to the table.

After some discussion, Rosie and Tony headed for their computers, Cirilli and Peterson left to talk to the kids, and Martinez pushed Harry and me to have a chat with Mike. Maybe with Harry at my side, I could face this. Actually, there was no "could" about it. I had to.

Chapter 7

Harry and I descended some seriously foul-smelling concrete stairs to the ground floor of the parking ramp near the Juvenile Detention Center. As we neared the JDC's front entrance, I asked, "So what was that all about with you and Martinez back there?"

Harry ground out the smoke he'd finished under his boot. "Just one hard-ass making sure another hard-ass knows where he stands."

"You come to some kind of understanding?"

Harry pulled open the door of the JDC. "I believe so."

That didn't tell me much, but since they hadn't come to fisticuffs I couldn't press the matter.

We signed in and were escorted by a detention officer

to a conference room barely large enough to hold a metal table and four dented, metal chairs. A ring was imbedded in the floor for shackles, and a one-foot-square barred window six feet up the white-washed wall let in a minimal amount of light. I slowly sank into work headspace, and my initial distress over this meeting melted away.

Harry rolled a pen back and forth between his fingers. "You wanna play good cop/bad cop?"

"No. Let me take this. I know the kid, and he trusts me. Or at least he used to. If things aren't going well, then we can take another tack."

"Whatever you say."

The door opened, and Mike Lorenzo crept in, followed by a female guard with a truly ripped physique. The county must have thought a show of muscular power would keep the kids in line. She laid a hand on Mike's shoulder and pushed him toward the table. To me she said, "I'll be right outside if you need anything."

When I laid eyes on Mike, my carefully constructed composure almost crumbled. I reminded myself this kid had killed two people, and there was a lot going on in his brain I might never know or understand. He was even thinner than he'd been during his days on the street. His golden curls were limp, and exhaustion shadowed his eyes. The pale skin on his face accentuated the hollows in his cheeks. Dressed in JDC's best, he looked like a lanky, forest-green tree.

I motioned to a chair on the opposite side of the table. "Mike, please sit down."

Mike shuffled over and sank into the chair. His

shoulders slumped, and he kept his hands in his lap.

I leaned forward. "Mike, look at me."

Brown eyes slowly rose and met mine. The hopeless, haunted expression that had been a constant on Mike's face when I first met him was back, along with a new, underlying sense of bleak resignation.

I nodded at Harry. "This is Agent Robinson. He's an investigator from New Jersey."

Mike's eyes flicked from me to Harry and back again and resumed studying his lap.

"Mike." My voice was just this side of cajoling. "Officer Martinez told me you wanted to talk to me." I so wasn't cut out for this. Give me a two-hundred-pound badass, and I was good to go. Put a kid opposite me in a situation like this, and it was like I'd forgotten how to do my job. "Mike?"

His lower lip trembled.

"Would it be better if Agent Robinson stepped outside?"

A shoulder raised.

I glanced at Harry. "Would you give us some time?"

"Sure."

Once Harry exited, Mike slumped bonelessly against the back of his chair as if he were a marionette and someone had cut the strings attached to his limbs.

"Come on, kid. It's me."

Mike's chest expanded, and I thought he was going to say something. Instead, he turned his attention toward the bleak light streaming through the window. A tear ran down his cheek and dripped off his jaw.

I walked around the table and crouched beside him. "Mike."

He cut a glance at me, again, and looked away. "I did it. I know I did it. I know what I did. I—know I let you down. I let everyone down." Mike balled his hands and slammed them onto the tabletop. A wail ripped out of him. He dropped his head, and his entire body trembled as he tried to hold himself together. He moved his hands up to cover his face and started to rock back and forth. "I didn't mean for this."

I hesitantly put an arm around him. Awkward, but it was the best I could do.

After a few long moments he straightened and fixated again on a beam of weak sunlight that hit the opposite wall.

I waited.

Mike eventually looked at me again, his eyes red, his face pinched and pale.

"You ready to tell me what happened?"

"I don't know."

"This was not the Mike I've known these last few years."

Silence settled. I knew I needed to wait him out.

Finally Mike said, "I just...I was so mad. The thoughts in my head. I'm so confused. When Otis came home, so sick, I knew."

"Knew?"

Mike sniffed hard. "Knew they hurt him."

"Hunter and Billy?"

Mike nodded.

"Why?"

"They're assholes. Those two fucking jerks are—" He clamped his lips shut. When he spoke again, his voice had deepened to the point I could hardly hear him. "After we put Otis to sleep, it was like, I don't know. Like I was watching myself in a movie. What I was doing was happening to someone else." He scrubbed his hands on his legs. "I—I went to see someone. Got a gun. It was like a dream. You know what I mean?" For the first time Mike really looked at me.

"Yeah. I get that." Before the McKennas came along, I often used to compartmentalize, mentally remove myself from certain situations. Shrinks had a fancy word for it, but it boiled down to one simple thing—survival.

"It was so weird. I was so angry. I couldn't think. I just did."

"Where did you get the music you were listening to that day?"

"A couple of kids were handing out promos after school."

"Did you know them? Boys? Girls?"

"Two guys. Seen 'em around. Hanging at Loring, maybe. They didn't go to the Academy."

"What did they look like?"

"One was tall. Ought to play basketball. The other guy, he was shorter. Wore a baseball hat. Light blue. I remember that. Both were wearing those puffy winter jackets."

"Were they white? African-American? Asian?"

"Both white. Tough-looking. One of them had

tattoos. The short one did. Three teardrops by the corner of one eye and this weird lightning bolt above a cross on the back of his hand."

Nice recall. "How old do you think they were?"

"My age, maybe older. Hard to tell."

"Names?"

"No idea."

"Do you think you could identify them?"

"For what?" Confused suspicion fluttered across Mike's face. "What difference does that make?"

"We need to talk to them."

"Why?"

I'd forgotten how many questions kids could ask. "How did the music make you feel when you listened to it?"

Mike tilted his head.

I wasn't sure if he was considering my words or what. "Olivia said she thought you had changed. She felt like you were different after you listened to the music you got from those two."

"When they gave it to me, I forgot all about it—it was on a jump drive. Then one day I found the jump drive again—on my desk buried under some homework. Decided to load it on my iPod, see what it was like. It was some hard shit. Acid. Angry. Made me feel..." His gaze became unfocused. "It made me feel powerful. Fit my mood, somehow."

"What kind of mood was that?"

"Mad. Sad. Dunno. I kinda stopped listening to everything else. It was like—I could finally tune out

Hunter and Billy and the rest of the kids who were bugging me. It was so easy to turn up the volume." He gnawed on his lip. "There was this line. It kept running through my mind." After a few seconds he said, "Defy and stand, protect and defend, hold your ground until the end."

"You were listening to that when you went into the school yesterday?"

"Yeah. The pounding in my ears drowned out everything else."

I hoped they had some good shrinks on the payroll. An overly-receptive kid, angst, music that shrieked hate, and teenage testosterone. All of that was akin to throwing a heavy rock into soft clay. The rock could be removed but the impression would remain.

"Cailin?"

I couldn't remember the last time Mike had used my name. "Yeah?"

"What will happen to me?" The frightened boy was back.

What *were* the authorities going to do with to him? I decided to play it straight, same way I'd always dealt with him. "I'm not sure of the exact details, but I won't sugarcoat what I expect, Mike. They'll have you talk to some people."

The surface of the scarred tabletop now captured Mike's attention. "Shrinks."

"Yes. A lot of people are going to want to understand why you did this. Some of them will try and get you charged as an adult, I imagine. At some point soon there should be a lawyer coming to talk to you, someone who will be on your side to represent your best interests."

"It was my fault. I pulled the trigger." Remorse coated his words.

"I want you to talk to whoever they send. You need to be honest, okay? No more stonewalling."

"Yeah. Okay."

"I have to go for now, but I'll see you again." I put my hand on his shoulder. "Mike, everything seems awful right now. I can see how upset you are. This is going to be a big mess for you for a while, but please, look at me." He met my gaze. "You will get through this. I care about you, and I want you to hang in there. Can you do that for me?"

Wordlessly, he nodded. He had the look of someone on the precipice, unsure whether he should let go and fall or walk away from the edge.

I put my hand behind his head and leaned forward until my forehead touched his briefly. As I pulled away, I said, "You're not alone anymore."

He let out a sigh and looked away.

I called the guard to take Mike back. I gave him a simple nod when I left, and my insides ached with stress and sadness.

After calling in the tattoo lead to Rose for further research, I caught up with Harry, who was hanging outside the front door of the building, an unlit cigarette dangling from the corner of his mouth. He was the image of a down-on-his-luck mid-century PI. A felt fedora and a cigar would have nicely rounded out the cliché.

"Hey." I stuck my hands in my jacket pockets and

rested my shoulder against the brickwork.

"Well?"

A chill worked its way down my spine. "Come on. Let's get warm." I led the way back to the car. "He knows what he did. Accepts responsibility. He's terrified."

"Any info about the people handing out the music?"

I told Harry the bulk of the conversation and ended with, "Got a good description of one of them." I fished out my keys. "He admitted to listening to the hate music. A lot. I can see how it made him feel detached, but empowered. It fed his anger. Maybe it gave him a more righteous anger than the impotent fury he usually felt when he had run-ins with the Bully Boys. This is my own analysis, there. The kid's got a lot of issues."

I was about to back out when a loud bang on the car's roof scared the shit out of me. I hit the brakes hard.

A familiar, dusky-skinned, blue-eyed face peered in my window.

"Jesus Christ." I cranked the window down.

"Hey, sis." My foster brother, Jon, braced an arm on the roof and bent over so he could see in the car.

I slapped my hand to my chest. "You're gonna kill me one of these days."

"Who ya got in there? And why's he pointing a gun at me? You being kidnapped?"

I glanced at Harry, who was indeed in possession of his Glock. It wasn't exactly pointed at Jon, but it could be in a fraction of a second. "Jesus, Harry. It's okay. You can put it away."

Harry reluctantly tucked it into the holster under his arm.

"Jon, Quick Draw McGraw here is Harry Robinson, one of the agents I worked with in Jersey. He's giving me a hand on the school shooting case. Harry, this is my foster brother, Jon McKenna."

Harry thrust an arm in front of my face. I yanked my head back in time to avoid getting popped in the jaw.

"Nice to meet you," Harry said. "Too bad you've had to put up with this one for so long."

Grinning, Jon shook Harry's hand. "She's a pain in the caboose, but sometimes lovable. So you're the infamous Dirty Harry. I've heard a lot about you."

"I'll bet you have. The girl's got a big mouth."

Before they started comparing notes about my past indiscretions, I asked, "What are you doing here, bro?"

"I'm headed into the JDC to see the Lorenzo boy. I was elected to come down and talk to the kid."

My brother was a prosecutor for the Hennepin County Attorney's Office and a children's advocate who bounced between the Adult and Juvenile Divisions of the Attorney's Office.

"I just talked to him."

Jon arched an eyebrow. "Did you, now? I heard he's shut down everyone who comes near him."

"Once Harry left, Mike thawed a bit. Do you remember me telling you about one of the kids I helped get off the street a few years ago, the one whose brother died from ingesting Liquid-Plumr?"

Jon looked blank for a moment. "Maybe. Was the dad too drunk to help and the older brother called 911?"

"Right. Mike is the older brother."

"Oh, no."

"Yeah."

Jon sighed. "Okay. Well, I better be off. You and Alex still coming for dinner at Mom and Dad's next Thursday?"

"Wouldn't miss it." Every month, Gin alternated making a variety of our favorite dishes. This month was my turn, and my mouth watered thinking about her handmade Fettuccini Alfredo, the recipe of which was a closely guarded family secret. So secret, in fact, that even I didn't know it.

Jon ducked lower to peer across me at Harry. "If you're still around, you're welcome to join us."

"Thanks for the offer, man. We'll see."

My brother slapped the roof and backed up. "Later."

Chapter 8

The house was dark when I let myself in the back door. The low drone of the television startled me until I remembered Alex's car was in the shop getting new tires.

I divested myself of my jacket and shoes and entered the living room. Alex was sound asleep on the couch. Flickering light from the TV reflected off a glossy motorcycle-racing magazine that lay on her chest, and one of her hands was splayed across its surface. She was a street-racing, crotch-rocket maniac. I knew she missed the adrenaline hit, the excitement, the danger. The last time she raced, she'd been involved in an accident that nearly killed her. Ultimately, she walked away with only a slew of bruises and a broken arm, but no doubt it could easily have turned deadly. She was a very lucky woman and hadn't been on a bike since. Winter in Minnesota put a damper on that kind of thing, anyway. I didn't know whether later on down the road she'd have the desire to get back in the saddle, so to speak, or not.

At heart, Alex and I were both risk-takers. I totally got it, the need—or maybe compulsion—to feel the blood pound through my veins, to lose myself in the heady rush of riding the razor's edge. I understood the need to embrace life full-tilt. After we'd gotten together, I'd become more mindful of consequences, both good and bad, but that hadn't changed the way I lived my life. Neither had Alex, and I hoped she never did. It was what made us...us, and to mess with that would change who we are at heart.

The carpet felt warm under my feet. I crossed to Alex and dropped to my knees beside her. She didn't stir. For a moment I simply watched her chest gently rise and fall. Her face was relaxed, unlined in slumber. Carefully, I pulled the magazine free, set it on the floor, and brushed my lips against the soft skin of her forehead. I kissed her again, and this time the corners of her mouth curled up lazily, and one eyelid cracked opened.

"Hey."

"Hey," Alex echoed, her voice sleep rough. "What time is it?"

I glanced at my watch. "Seven-twenty."

Alex struggled to sit up. I gave her a helpful boost and settled on the couch beside her. She rewrapped the blanket around herself and swung her feet onto the coffee table. After a wide yawn she mumbled, "How was your day?"

"Okay." I raised my arm and Alex sank against me.

She tried without success to stifle another yawn. "I talked to Mike."

"Tough?"

"He is so messed up. Gonna need a shitload of therapy. Fucking heartbreaking. For everyone."

Alex squeezed my knee.

"He talked to me about the music."

"Who's checking that out?"

"What?"

"The music mess."

"Oh. Cirilli and Bryan Peterson are working that specific angle." I yawned, and we sat in silence for a few moments, half-mesmerized by the drone of the television. "Saw Jon. He wanted to make sure we're still on for dinner at Gin and Thomas's Thursday."

I felt Alex nod.

"Cailin?"

"Hmm?"

"You need to listen to the answering machine."

"Why?"

"Another message from your friendly neighborhood stalker."

"Oh, for God's sake." I unwound myself, stood, and stretched my hands toward the ceiling. "You want anything?"

"Nope. Cailin?"

I half-turned to face Alex.

"I love you."

My heart momentarily stopped, as it did every time she uttered those words. The intensity of our emotions shimmered between us almost tangibly.

"When you come back there's something else you need to know."

In the kitchen, I warily retrieved the message.

"Cailin, I'm tired of waiting for you to get rid that thing you call a girlfriend. Don't make me have to take things into my own hands. If you know what's good for you, and for her, you'll send her packing. I love you, and I will have you." Her voice mellowed. "Please. Stop shutting me out. You know I can give you everything you ever wanted. Please, Cailin."

The line went dead. Amazed at the audacity of my ex, I saved the voicemail. Now I had a two-message tally. I closed my eyes and rested my head against the wall. What did I ever see in her? When I returned to the living room, Alex gazed expectantly at me but didn't say anything. I sat back down beside her. "She's getting ruder."

Alex pulled my hand into her lap and traced my fingers with hers. "She came into the Gallery today."

"What?" I jolted upright and tried to jerk my hand away, but Alex held on tight.

"It's okay. Your mom was there. We handled it."

I felt fury racing through my veins, and my next words came out louder than I intended. "What exactly did that—she say?"

"She..." Alex trailed off. She pressed her lips together hard enough to make a white line around them.

"What?" Again, the word came out more sharply than I intended.

"She told me I better get out of Minnesota, or, to

quote her, I'd be 'one sorry bitch.'"

I tried to get up, but Alex yanked me back down onto the couch.

"Cailin. *Cailin!*"

I blinked.

Alex shifted to face me. "You listen to me." Her voice was low, almost menacing. She lifted my chin with her fingers and forced me to meet her eyes. "I can take care of myself—" I inhaled and she put a finger on my lips. "I'm no stranger to shitheads trying, and let me emphasize *trying*, to fuck with me. I *will* be fine." Her finger pressed harder against my lips. "You now have to be proactive so that if there's more vandalism, we can prove it to the insurance company. You need to get a restraining order. It's time. Talk to Jon."

I nodded mutely. Eli had completely lost her grip on reality, simple as that.

Alex tossed off the blanket and pulled me up from the couch. "Cailin," she whispered, "it's going to be okay. We'll be fine. She won't hurt me. You can worry about me hurting her."

That forced a laugh and I relaxed. I hugged Alex, searched her eyes, and absorbed the affection I saw. My fingers gently traced the contours of her face. My mouth found hers and her lips parted, accepting me, accepting all of me. The whole and the broken.

Chapter 9

I was about to take a bite of a TGI Friday's Mocha Mud Pie when I was ripped from my dreams by an irritating buzzing. The back of my hand banged against a sharp edge. I finally woke up enough to recognize the sound was coming from my cell phone vibrating against the nightstand. I grabbed it and peered blearily at the alarm clock. 4:17.

My mouth felt like a cotton plantation. "McKenna."

"Wake up, girlfriend," Rosie said. "Cirilli found the kids who were distributing the music and got a description of the dude who paid them twenty-five bucks a pop to dole them out."

My brain was still knee-deep in dessert. "What?"

"The kids, Cailin. Cirilli found the kids."

The pie was fading fast. I propped myself on an elbow. "No shit."

"He called Tony and me in, and we've been running all kinds of search strings."

That sat me up. "Based on what?"

"Tattoos. It appears we have a chronic inker."

Alex sleepily wrapped herself around me, warm and oh-so-goddamn inviting. I regretfully kissed the crown of her head.

"Cailin," Rosie said," you there?"

"Yeah, sorry." I gently shifted away from Alex and stood. She curled around my pillow without opening her eyes and mumbled, "Love you."

I tucked the covers around her and trailed the backs of my fingers over her temple. "Love you, too, babe," I whispered.

The phone was away from my ear, but I heard the scratchy sound of Rosie's intended sarcasm. "I love you, too, Cailin. Get your shit in here."

"Yeah, yeah. See you in a few."

★ ★ ★

Half an hour later, I dragged myself into the National Protective and Investigation Unit offices and threaded my way toward the set of cubes Tony worked in.

Four figures huddled around two monitors. A number of additional monitors were stacked on each side and above the two main screens, and keyboards lay scattered across the work surface. Depending on the situation, some or all could be in use at the same time. The setup reminded me of Penelope Garcia's command center on the TV show *Criminal Minds*.

Tony and Rosie pounded away at their respective keyboards. Behind them, SSA Weatherspoon and Dirty Harry watched the screens populate with information.

"Nice you could make it, McKenna." Weatherspoon's hair was still shower damp, evidence he, too, had been rousted from bed.

"Yeah," Harry said, "About time you put in an appearance." His cheeks had moved well past five o'clock shadow into four a.m. scruff. Half his shirt was tucked into his jeans, and the other half hung crookedly outside the waistband.

I ignored them both. "What do we have?"

Without peeling his eyes away from a monitor display rapidly rolling mug shots, Tony said, "After Peterson and Cirilli tracked the kids down and got a description, we popped it into Max. Now we're profiling possible hits."

Tony was a devotee of a short-lived, late 80's sci-fi series called *Max Headroom*. Although the show only lasted eleven episodes, the idea of a computer-generated personality, a precursor to artificial intelligence, fascinated Tony. He'd started calling the NPIU's Criminal Justice Integrated Interface—or CJII—Max, and the nickname stuck. Rosie and Tony had been on the team who initially created and continued to tweak Max.

Good old Max was supposed to be user-friendly, allowing cops to easily input and extract information on criminals and criminal activity by tapping into the FBI's

Criminal Justice Information Services Division records. The creation of Max followed the NPIU's mandate to improve cooperation and to meet the all-important, yet biggest sticking point, among law enforcement officers: freely sharing information between agencies and jurisdictions. In concept, it was a great idea. In action, Max was a time-sucking work-in-progress, and a lot of cops still landed on the "fuck the Feds" side of the fence. One day, if the kinks could actually be worked out, the program would be implemented nationally.

I asked, "Where's Cirilli?"

"Juvie." Rosie scanned the information in front of her. "The kids Mike Lorenzo described were caught breaking into a liquor store. Minneapolis nabbed 'em. They matched the descriptions we put out, and MPD notified us. We played the kids against each other, and they gave up a description of their hate music contact."

"Information-sharing in action." Weatherspoon was only half-sarcastic this time. He stepped back and motioned for me to take his place. "I'll be in my office. If you get anything, let me know. The director will be in about seven-thirty, and I'll update him then."

Weatherspoon left and I stifled a yawn. "What exactly are we looking for?"

"Tattoos, of course," Rosie said. "I already told you that. Isn't it always tattoos these days? The guy is tall, bald, and has a shit-ton of ink. The twerps who gave him up only know him by the name of Hate Man. One of the guy's tats is supposed to be a red flag with a swastika on the inside of one of his biceps. We're specifically running records of known criminals with swastika tattoos. The current list is narrowing quite nicely. If we get a hit, we'll try to crosscheck last known locations and see if anyone is in or near Minneapolis."

Harry moved over to the counter next to Rosie and propped a hip against it. "That's if the man has a record. If not, it'll be a whole different ballgame."

"Hold your taters." Rosie hunched closer to the screen, the glow from the monitor bathing her face in its ghostly light.

The current mug shot showed an angry man with a crew cut and a round, heavy face glaring at the photographer. His lips were turned down, and his forehead was deeply grooved. A barbed-wire tattoo ran from his neck around his jaw and ended at the outside corner of his eye. If you looked up the term "thug" in the dictionary, you'd probably find this joker's picture.

"Name's Edward Norris North, aged thirty-four," Rosie said. "He's a big boy. Six-three, two-ninety." She scrolled down the page. "Known aliases: Enno, Ed North, Ward Norris, Ed Norris. Okay, here we go. The boy's got serious tats. One on his neck and face, double lightning bolt on his right shoulder, Hate Is Truth on the left. Dagger on left calf. HATE tattooed on the knuckles of his left hand, and LOVE on the knuckles on the right. That had to hurt." Rosie scanned down the list. "Bingo. Red flag with a swastika and two lightning bolts on his right inside biceps."

I leaned closer. "What's that scar by his wrist?"

"Looks like a cross. Probably carved while he was in

jail. File says he found religion in the clink." Rosie's eyes roved down the screen. "This upstanding citizen has been convicted of assault, assault with a deadly weapon, auto theft, robbery, home invasion. DWI once, twice, three times. Trifecta! Oh, wait, there's a fourth. Is there a quadfecta? Also arrested for spray-painting racial slurs on the garage door of a Hmong family. What a fucking peach. Known associations—let's see what this says. He's a member of an underground Neo-Nazi organization based out of Mankato. Group disbanded. After that there's a long gap. Probably locked up somewhere. Then there's another home invasion. Nabbed for DWI and fleeing the scene. Back to prison. Was released from Stillwater eight months ago."

"Last known address?" Harry asked.

"Minneapolis. He's supposed to be staying in a halfway house as part of the sentence for his most recent DWI. Address is 745 Gerard. Gotcha, asshole."

Chapter 10

At approximately 8:05 a.m., the MPD pulled Edward North out of his halfway house bed. At 8:35, a disheveled Detective Bryan Peterson and Agent Chris Cirilli occupied one of the Fifth Precinct's interview rooms with Mr. North.

Harry, Martinez, SSA Weatherspoon, and I waited behind the one-way glass window. In the stark, ten-by-twelve, puke-green, interview room, North sat slumped in an old wooden chair, while his nervous fingers beat a silent rhythm on the scarred tabletop.

Peterson sat across from him, shirtsleeves rolled to his elbows. He asked North if he wanted something to drink. North settled on a Pepsi, and Cirilli disappeared, presumably to fetch the soda.

Once the door closed, Peterson said, "Hello, Ed. May I call you Ed?"

North didn't even glance at the detective. "Whatever. I didn't fucking do nothing." His voice was so deep it sounded like it emanated from a cavern.

"We just want to ask you a few questions, Ed." Peterson paused. "Word on the street is a few weeks ago you gave some kids money to hand out thumb drives loaded with music."

North glanced up sharply and returned his gaze to the tabletop. "That's not illegal."

"Technically, no. It's where the kids were handing out the music that might be a problem." Peterson let the words hang. "You heard about the shooting at Gray Academy?"

"Yeah." Now North met Peterson's gaze. "So?"

"The music on the drives those kids distributed played a role in the shooting."

We still weren't sure that was a fact, but our friend Ed didn't need to know that.

Ed's fingers stilled. "What are you talking about?"

"The shooter. Had the music loaded onto his player. Apparently listened to it all the time. Became obsessed with it, even. Might be proven he was influenced by the lyrics. Influenced enough to kill." Peterson leaned forward and laced his fingers together. "Kind of seems like the person who was floating that music around could be held responsible. As an accomplice, you might say. To what happened."

North shifted. Sweat beaded on his forehead. He

stretched his thick neck from one side to the other. "Thought you said I wasn't in trouble."

"I'm just asking a few simple questions."

The door opened and Cirilli entered, can in hand. He set it on the table in front of North and retreated without a word. A moment later the door to our observation room opened. Cirilli came to a stop beside me to watch the unfolding drama.

Peterson was saying, "You might be able to help us out, and we might be able to help you." He had North's undivided attention. "This time you've been doing a good job keeping yourself clean since you've been out, haven't you?"

"Yeah." North squinted at Peterson. "Doin' real good this time."

"We sure don't want all that hard work going down the toilet, do we?"

The squint grew into a glare.

Peterson leaned back in his chair, his hands spread flat on the table. "Now, Ed, you didn't make that music, did you?"

Ed shook his head, which was growing shinier by the minute. Drips of sweat migrated down stubbly cheeks. "No, I didn't make those fuckers. Weren't mine. I was told to dole 'em out by the schools, see? I didn't want to hang around any school. I'm not a fucking perv. I got standards. Found some dopers to do it."

"I can see you wouldn't do anything to hurt children."

North entirely missed the sarcasm behind the detective's comment. Then Peterson cast the hook. "If the thumb drives weren't yours, maybe the responsibility would fall on whoever gave them to you."

North's face transformed from slack to calculating in a split second. No honor among thieves, or among equal opportunity hate mongers. He exhaled noisily. "What do you want?"

The detective again leaned forward. "Who gave them to you?"

"I been doin' right." North regarded Peterson earnestly. "I got religion. I go to church. It was one of the congregation members gave them to me. Told me it was God's will to help spread the word."

"What congregation? What denomination?"

"Denomination? Dunno. They have retreats and shit. Don't allow booze or drugs."

"Where is this church?"

"West. Off Lake Minnetonka."

That matched up with where Third Reich Records was located, and I started to feel a tingle of excitement. Maybe we had a viable lead after all.

"What's the church called?"

"Soldiers of Christ. SOC for short. Like the sock you put on your foot."

Casually, Peterson said, "So what's the word they want to spread?"

Peterson didn't move. I don't think any of us did. I know I was holding my breath.

North leaned forward to speak down to Peterson, as though the cop was a moron and North had to school him in the ways of the church. "SOC wants to protect the proper way of life and keep things pure. Untainted. Fire up the youngsters. Make them understand they need to be with their own kind. None of this mixing shit. Keep people the way God intended."

And there it was. The connection. All of us in the room exhaled with relief.

Once the detective cracked the wall, North became a veritable font of information, though I'm not sure he realized the significance of what he divulged. SOC was holding something called a Jubilee up near Crosby weekend after next. Crosby was somewhere past Brainerd, but beyond that I had no idea.

Peterson stared at North for a long moment. "You know how to help yourself here, Ed?

Ed eyes narrowed in suspicion. "How?"

"You're going to get us into a Soldiers of Christ meeting and stake your rep on how much hate we hold in our hearts for blacks, for Jews, whatever it takes to get us inside."

"If I don't?"

"Well, then." Peterson leaned back in his chair and crossed his arms. "You're going down as an accessory after the fact. The NPIU's involved, Ed. You know what that means?"

"No."

"Fifteen to life in a federal pen. That's some fucking hard time. It'll probably get you tagged on the higher end of the sentence since you targeted juveniles."

North's cheek twitched. "I didn't target nobody. I did what I was asked, and it weren't illegal."

Peterson laughed coldly. "That's what you think. Who was the fool who coordinated the disbursement?"

More sweat popped out on North's forehead and he was silent.

Peterson watched and waited—we all did—while North contemplated his fate. After a couple of painfully long minutes, North heaved a sigh. "Fine. I'll do it."

"I thought you'd see it my way. Now, tell us all about the people in charge."

After securing the names of some low-level players, including that of the man who'd put North up to the music distribution gig, Peterson asked Ed who was ultimately in charge of the Soldiers of Christ.

"Dunno. He hardly ever comes to the meetings, but we all hear his word."

"How does a preacher preach if he's not there?"

"Deacons take turns sharing the word. They carry out whatever he wants. No question. It's all about The Coming."

"The coming?"

"Yeah. Coming with a capital C. The Coming's been coming for a long time." North made a greasy sound I supposed was a laugh. "The Coming's been coming. Get it?"

Detective Peterson pointedly ignored North. "Tell me more about The Coming."

After a bit of spluttering and a noisy slurp of Pepsi, North said, "The Coming is...it's *it*, man. The ultimate." North leaned forward, his eyes shining from the fervor that the thought of The Coming brought him. "If we can get more of the little bastards, see, the church will grow. More people will be saved. Besides, we clean them kids up, get them off drugs and shit. And then they'll be saved in the end, too. Just like I will."

Chapter 11

Cirilli, Harry, and I grabbed an early lunch before following a directive to reconvene in the NPIU conference room. On the way in I stopped to use the facilities, then I swung into a small nook only large enough to hold a couple of padded armchairs. Looking out on a view of the faded brick of the next building, I settled into one of the chairs and called Alex.

"Northstar."

"Hey, babe."

"Cailin. Hi. How's it going?"

I could hear the smile in Alex's voice, and it helped ease the underlying tension that made my shoulders ache. "Long day. Any word from Eli?"

"No. Been quiet so far. Got my car back, and the tires

were still intact when I checked a bit ago."

"Good." Gin's voice filtered indistinctly through the receiver.

"What'd she say?" I asked.

"She wants to make sure you don't forget about Thursday night."

"I won't." It wasn't that I didn't have a good memory, but when I was wrapped up in a case, it was easy for details to get away from me, and Gin knew that.

"How's it going?" Alex asked. "Really?"

"We're making some progress." I sighed. "I'm about to head into a meeting where I'm sure we'll be asked to accomplish the impossible. But better to have a plan than go in with guns blazing and no target in sight. I think we're on the right track, though. We'll see."

I heard more mumbling in the background. Alex laughed. "Gin says to tell you she's making slush cake Thursday."

Slush cake was a personal favorite and a device to ensure my attendance. "Tell her I won't forget, but bribery never hurts." I glanced at my watch. "Sorry to run, but duty calls and all that. Love you."

"I love you too, Cailin. Don't forget that."

"I won't." I disconnected, stretched the kinks out, and headed for the conference room.

Martinez and Peterson had already arrived, along with MPD Chief Helling, SSA Weatherspoon, Director Singleton, and Rosie. Singleton was on his phone, the deep tones of his low voice resonating through the room.

Weatherspoon and Helling had their heads together

over a thick file, and Cirilli, Harry, and Rosie were discussing the various attributes of hate groups.

I settled myself between Rosie and Cirilli and half-listened to their chatter while I thought about Eli. I never would have pegged Eli as a true nut job, but I suppose that's what everyone in a situation like mine might say. When I had a free moment, that come-to-Jesus chat was in our future.

Tony hustled in with his arms full of manila folders and effectively pulled me out of my Eli fixation.

"Sorry I'm late." He sank into a chair and dumped the files on the table.

The director ended his conversation. "That was the governor. I assured him we've got this under control. We have two diverging issues here. First and foremost, two unconnected young men in different schools have killed and injured their targets and innocent bystanders in this last week. Motivation? We understand a bit of that now, although I fear it may be the tip of the iceberg. You know the shrinks are already knee deep in this with both shooters." Singleton paused and drew a breath. "Secondly, we have a situation where a hate group is distributing materials to minors and probably to others in an attempt to recruit fresh blood. Perhaps related is the fact that the Soldiers of Christ are brewing up something called The Coming. At this point we have no idea what this might encompass. Whatever it is, it probably won't be good."

Someone had been quick to update Singleton on the outcome of this morning's interview with Ed North.

He continued, "Agents Smith and Nakamura have

been working to find any information they can on the Soldiers of Christ. At this point, I'll turn it over to you, Agent Smith."

Tony fumbled through one of his folders and extracted a sheaf of papers. "The Soldiers of Christ appear to be an amalgam of both Christian Identity and Neo-Nazi hate groups." He flipped a page. "The Soldiers of Christ have approximately forty-five known members, but it's speculated that number may more likely be between seventy-five and one-fifty. The numbers bounce around depending on which source the information is culled from." Tony scanned farther down the sheet. "We have some names of low-ranking members and some ideas on the identities of a few of the higher ups, but no one can pin down exactly who the backbone behind the operation is. Word has it this mystery person, or maybe persons, has a lot of money. Whoever it is keeps an extremely low profile."

Helling asked, "What about this Jubilee?"

"That's Rosie's department." Tony sat back in his seat.

"The gathering they call the Jubilee with a capital J," Rosie said, "takes place up north near Crosby on privately held land. I'm still trying to trace ownership. For some reason there's a problem with the records, and I'm working to get to the bottom of that.

"Regarding the Jubilees, the Soldiers of Christ hold one of these shindigs every three months or so. Not sure why they call it that when they do them quarterly. A jubilee is supposed to be a special anniversary celebrating twenty-five or fifty years of a reign or some special event. I can't figure out how that applies to these yokels."

"Yeah," Tony said, "I did some further digging. Originally a jubilee was a Jewish event held every fifty years celebrating the emancipation of Hebrew slaves. It's totally ironic that they're having Jubilee retreats using a term that originated with a group they profess to hate."

"In my culture," Singleton said, "the religious songs of black American slaves usually referred to a jubilee as a time of future happiness and jubilation. No special party or year was attached."

Martinez said, "Catholics celebrate meaningful shit every twenty-five years. The pope establishes a time of jubilee with special indulgences and responsibilities. Have to admit I'm happy to be a recovering Catholic."

Who knew there were so many meanings and so much symbolism attached to a word I typically gave zero thought to? I said, "Sounds like a jubilee is many things in many cultures. Leave it to these Neo-Nazi bastards to co-opt the term and turn it into something dangerous and discriminatory."

Rosie shuffled through the pages before her. "I wish I'd been able to turn up some danger and discrimination with these whack jobs. I called the local sheriff. He told me the group actually causes very little trouble, although there have been occasional calls from concerned citizens. For the most part, the SOC has managed to keep their noses as clean as a hate group can."

I asked, "What happens at this festival?"

"From what we've been able to pull together, it's a

weekend-long retreat"—Rosie did the air quote thing—
"to strengthen bonds and court fresh faces. Indoctrinate
them to the philosophy of the Soldiers of Christ. In other
words, a hate-filled family picnic. Pass the hot dish and
nooses, please."

"Chief Helling and I," Singleton said, "have been
discussing the best way to get inside this group. Edward
North has agreed to play matchmaker. We want to find
the people behind the music distribution and, as a larger
objective, figure out what this group is up to. The Coming.
Jesus. The last thing we need is another youth getting their
hands on the music these people are handing out."

"I'll do the infiltration," Cirilli said.

"Agent Cirilli," Weatherspoon said, "we appreciate
your offer, but because of that bust a few months ago with
the Hennepin County Sheriff's Office, you've gained too
much exposure."

The bust in question involved a meth-manufacturing
lab in Dayton, a lot of cash, and a group of illegal
Mexicans. The NPIU hadn't been mentioned in the news
reports as an assisting agency, but Cirilli had been in the
wrong place at the wrong time, and his mug was plastered
across the local TV channels when he inadvertently
strolled by rolling cameras while conversing with two
sheriff's deputies.

"Maybe two of us should go in as a team," Tony
suggested.

That idea ignited some fast dialogue, everyone talking
at once.

"Hold it!" Singleton bellowed. "I do like the prospect

of two agents going in instead of one."

"Peterson and Robinson could do it," Martinez said.

"No." Helling glanced at Singleton. "But what about Agent Nakamura or Agent McKenna and your New Jersey man."

Weatherspoon said, "Robinson, if he's willing, would be an excellent choice. No offense, Nakamura, but you might not be the best candidate to send in to a meeting of racist nutjobs."

Rosie snorted in a rather unladylike fashion. "This Asian agent kind of likes the skin she's in."

Singleton leaned back and narrowed speculative eyes first at Rosie, then at me. "Agent Robinson isn't known at all here, and McKenna, I think your public notoriety is low. How would you two feel about stepping into the role of a loving but hate-filled husband and wife?"

Gender roles probably applied to hate groups, and I wasn't feeling particularly overjoyed at the prospect of playing the meek little woman to Harry's macho shtick. Harry, on the other hand, appeared to have no compunction about the prospect, if his smug grin meant anything. He lived to work undercover.

"Agent Robinson and Agent McKenna," Cirilli intoned, "I now pronounce you mean man and vicious wife. May you live long enough to stop hate and prosper."

Singleton stood. "Robinson, you and McKenna in my office in fifteen. The rest of you, back to work."

★ ★ ★

Near the end of the day, Harry and I spent a couple of hours in Singleton's office deciding how to best use Edward North to worm our way inside the Jesus posse. The first act of service North would do for us would be to get Harry into a get-together at the Minnetonka location. We had eleven days to convince the SOC that Harry—and his wife—were the real deal. That meant I needed to maintain a low profile until go time. Welcome to Paperwork Mountain. From home. If I were made in the next eleven days, it would blow the entire operation, and simply walking into the offices of the National Protection and Investigation Unit provided an easy way for that to happen. Harry was ordered away, too. We hoped the school shooting sprees had come to an end, and we could concentrate on stopping hate. If another incident occurred, the entire case would have to be refocused.

Singleton decided as long as Harry could pull off the meet-and-greet in Minnetonka and get to know a few of the good old boys, we'd try the "stroll right into a mean-old-hate-group's lair" approach and crash the Jubilee. We got our stories straight about how we found out about the Jubilee: Harry ran into Ed North at a bar on yet another drunken binge and they started hanging out. Our story was that we'd never been involved in a group like theirs before but had the same kind of philosophies on race and religion. We would both have to practice our lines regarding how dedicated we were to further the cause and that we were devoted because it was up to people like us—small-minded, nasty, mean-spirited, and bigoted—to save the United States of America. Somehow, with a straight face, I would have to convince a bunch of ignorant skinhead-types that I truly believed The Soldiers of Christ was the vehicle to make it happen.

Just before six I pulled out of the NPIU parking ramp, and I wondered if Eli was still at work. During the four-year span of our doomed relationship, Eli, being the power-hungry woman she was, spent long hours at the office. She often wouldn't come home until well into the late evening. After I kicked her out, I wondered if she'd been working late on projects, or if she'd actually been working late on her boss. Or on whoever might further her career at any given moment.

I decided to swing by her office and see if she was still there before I was locked down under house arrest.

Eli worked for the Great Lakes Advertising Agency, an award-winning group noted for high-end, high-result projects. Located in the IDS tower, Great Lakes was very prestigious, very classy, and very expensive.

I parked in a nearby ramp and walked a block and a half to the IDS Building. No matter how many times I entered the Crystal Court, the glass ceiling and the numerous shops that ringed the center of the space still impressed me. Before I entered the elevator, I quickly scanned the tenant listing. Great Lakes now encompassed the entire floor. The last time I'd been here they'd shared the floor with another firm. Evidently things were going very well for the company.

The ride up didn't take long, and the elevator doors slid open to reveal a roomy, well-appointed lobby. Walls were shades of orange and gold and red. Thick pile carpet

covered the floor. A mahogany reception desk sat in front
of an enormous, ceiling-high TV screen that showcased
various Great Lakes success stories. Every couple of
minutes, the screen changed to feature a different
advertising campaign, each complete with a listing of
awards and commendations.

A woman wearing a headset looked up at my
approach. "Can I help you?" She gave me a half-smile.

"Is Elisa Knight in?"

"Do you have an appointment?"

Uh-oh. Gatekeeper alert. "No, I don't."

Her smile faded.

"I was in the neighborhood. She's an old friend." I
leaned in closer to the woman, who in turn leaned slightly
back. "Trust me. She'll want to see me. Tell her Cailin is
here."

A darkly penciled eyebrow arched.

"Cailin," she said, drawing my name out. "I'll see if
Ms. Knight has time to see you. She's a very busy
woman." With that, she dismissed me and pushed buttons
on a complicated black console. She turned around and
spoke in low tones. Eventually she swiveled back. "Have a
seat. Ms. Knight will be out momentarily."

"Thank you." I stepped away from the desk and
stuffed my hands in my pockets, looking down at my worn
jeans and scuffed black boots. I was underdressed, and the
good thing was I didn't care one damn bit.

I didn't have long to wait before Eli appeared from
behind the screen. She was petite, fine-boned, and oozed
sex. Her red hair touched the small of her back. She wore

a tailored navy power suit like armor. Pumps made her a bit taller, but I still towered over her by close to four inches.

My heart rate picked up and my mouth went dry. My increased respiration used to come from infatuation. These days it was due to barely restrained fury. I hadn't spoken to Eli aside from calling her to tell her to back off a few weeks ago, and I hadn't seen her since she unexpectedly dropped in on me while I was in the hospital recovering from the gunshot wound I'd sustained in Jersey a year ago.

I didn't understand why she still had the power to make my stomach quiver. For a moment, I fell back in time, recalled meeting her in this same lobby, pulling her into my arms and kissing her in front of a different receptionist. The memory was almost visceral and made me feel sick to my stomach.

Eli's ice-blue eyes met mine. Her face showed a familiar, infuriating look of satisfaction.

"Cailin," she practically purred. "I'm so happy you stopped. I told Karen you might be coming by soon to see me." Eli threw a grin over her shoulder at Karen the Gatekeeper.

"Eli," I said, "we need to talk. Do you have a few minutes?"

"Of course, Cailin. Anything for you. Come on back to my office." She turned, expecting me to follow, which I did. I felt like nothing more than an obedient pet, and I hated myself for it.

The space opened onto a wide area dotted with

drafting tables, desks, plants, and various pieces of electronic equipment. Glass-walled offices with honey-colored wood blinds lined the sides of the huge room. Most of the blinds were open. At this late hour, a number of harried-looking employees still scurried around the work floor. Eli's over-work ethic was infectious.

I followed her into, of course, the largest of the offices. The view allowed her to see every nook and cranny of the main floor.

Recessed office lighting softened the harsh glare from the fluorescent light on the main floor. Two leather chairs faced a futuristic onyx desk, its surface shiny-slick. The wall of glass that faced outside was inky with night.

Two framed pictures sat on a credenza behind the desk. One was a smiling Eli accepting an award, and the other was a picture of us, taken not long after we'd first gotten together. I couldn't believe she still had it on display.

"Cailin."

I ripped my gaze away from the photograph, and pressure built behind my eyes. My heart was doing a painful double thump.

"Sit down." She indicated one of the chairs and leaned her curvy behind on the edge of the desk.

"No, thanks. I'll stand."

Eli canted her head to the side. "I like the short hair. It's a big change."

I gave a hard smile and took a step toward her. The scent of Jessica McClintock washed over me like an invisible touch and stirred memories I hated myself for recalling.

"Eli. You have got to stop with the bullshit."

"What are you talking about?"

"This crap you're pulling. The phone calls, the letters. The flowers." My hackles were coming around, and thankfully, memories of the past were falling away. I grounded myself in the here and now. "How could you stoop to slashing Alex's tires?"

"Someone slashed Alex's tires?"

"Don't play me." My blood was finally at a righteous boil, and I felt more in control. I took another half step forward and loomed over her.

She had to tilt her head to peer up at me. The beginnings of a smirk hovered at the corners of her mouth. "I didn't do anything."

"Knock off the shit. We're through. Do you understand? Done. Over."

"That's what you think."

She came away from the desk, and I didn't back away. I moved closer, close enough that I felt her heat radiate against me. She reached to trail a manicured finger down my neck and stopped at the fluttering pulse at my throat. Then she slowly continued downward, past the unbuttoned collar of my shirt to the junction where skin and cloth met. Where my heart pounded wildly inside my chest.

This raw, physical reaction wasn't something I was prepared for. I countered the Eli Effect by unleashing the anger I'd been struggling to hold at bay. "You stay away." My voice was deadly quiet. I gave her a shove. "Stay away from me." I pushed her again and advanced.

"Stay away from Alex."

Eli came to a stop when her butt hit the desk, and she used it to shift her momentum into me. Her breasts were warm and soft. I fought the urge to step away, but this time I was not backing down.

She tipped her face up, her lips scarcely an inch from my own. "I know what you want, baby."

Her breath caressed my face. She slid her hands down my back and onto my ass and pulled me against her.

I dragged in a shuddering breath. My lips were now centimeters from hers, my eyes locked onto her unfathomable blues. I blinked, then blinked again, and jerked away from temptation. "No, Eli. Stop it." How could a woman be so goddamn beguiling? I grabbed her shoulders, and my fingers bit into her soft skin. "You stay away from Alex. Stay away from me." I gave her a hard shake.

Her face twisted. She snarled, "What do you see in that woman? I can give you exactly what you need, Cailin. You know it. You're mine."

"No!" I still had hold of her shoulders, and I pushed her backward over her desk. The movement would have been erotic if it hadn't been driven by furious desperation.

Eli's eyes widened. "Come on, Cailin, hurt me. You know you want to. You need to. You know I like it rough." The tip of her tongue darted out and moistened her upper lip.

"Shut up. Just shut the fuck up." I hated that I knew

it was true. Eli did like sex rough. In the past, I'd given her exactly what she wanted, and I'd satisfied her well. But that was then.

"Maybe Alex will have an unexpected accident. Maybe I'll be there to comfort you."

"You so much as hurt a hair on her head and I'll kill you, Eli. I. Will. Kill. You." I shook her hard with each word. "Do you understand?"

A deep voice interrupted us. "Elisa, everything okay in here?"

I dropped my hands from Eli's shoulders and spun to face a thin man with short blond hair and a manicured goatee, dressed in silk and twill.

Eli's voice was breathy. "Yes, Randall, everything is fine. You can go."

Casting a doubtful glance my way, he backed slowly out of the office. At least three other people stared at us from the work floor. Goddamn glass walls. I turned back to Eli and willed my voice not to shake. "Stay the fuck away from us."

I abruptly exited her office and stalked past the curious onlookers without a backward glance.

Chapter 12

The next day, after Alex left for work, I wandered around the house for ten minutes. Two weeks of this was going to drive me nuts. I finally made myself toast and settled at the table in front of my laptop and the two-foot stack of paperwork Singleton sent home with me.

My phone buzzed. Brian Peterson and FaceTime. He was probably calling to rub in my house-arrest status. When his face filled the screen I had to laugh. He held half a donut in one hand and a large McDonald's coffee in the other. His lips and cheeks were coated with powdered sugar that puffed from his mouth onto the front of his shirt. "How goes it?"

"Aren't you a talking cliché."

"We're all one big goddamn cliché, McKenna. You

know that. Donut?" He held out a white box.

"You're a funny man. What's up? I have work to do."

"Yeah, right. You know you're gonna crash on your couch, and when you wake up, you'll turn on one of those God-awful judge shows and play prosecuting attorney until Alex comes home."

"I've been found out."

Martinez's voice echoed from the background. "Ignore the idiot with the white-powder beard. Peterson, let me see her." In a second Martinez appeared on the screen with his feet on his desk and a bear claw in hand. "Campbell's lit the fuse to charge the kid as an adult."

"Figured. The shrinks done with Mike yet?"

"No," Peterson said. "But you know good old Quenton and his rep for hitting early and hitting hard."

I did know his propensity for calling attention to his political self, but I'd never met Campbell in person. He was the rather obnoxious, yet painfully competent, Hennepin County Attorney, who was always angling for more publicity. This case could put him on the national political map. If these two shootings weren't enough to fire up the Twin Cities—hell, even the entire nation—to remind people that bullying, and now hate groups, could be nothing less than deadly, I didn't know what would.

"Thanks for the heads up," I said. "I wish I could see the kid again, but that's not possible until this is over."

Peterson's less powdery mug reappeared. "We'll check in again soon. Make sure you didn't shoot the television or something."

"Thanks for having my back. I feel so comforted

knowing you two are out there protecting me and the citizens of this lovely city."

"That's what we're here for, McKenna."

The screen went black and I went to work.

★ ★ ★

At five-thirty on the nose I pulled into the driveway of my foster parent's story-and-a-half Cape Cod and parked behind Alex's silver Grand Am. Director Singleton had given me the nod to go home as long as I kept my nose clean and stayed far away from cops and television cameras.

The house's wood siding had long been covered with canary-yellow vinyl. The windows were trimmed in dark brown. The front of the house reminded me of a jaundiced face with black eyes. Gin was always talking about packing up and selling, moving into something a little less Fifties, but hadn't yet found the motivation to follow through. Thomas just smiled when she brought it up and kept his nose stuck in one of his psych journals, which was important reading for a professor of psychology at the U of M.

The days were getting longer. I hit the porch where the setting sun reflected off the windows. Any sliver of light was a welcome sight after what had been a long, cold winter.

The door was unlocked. I entered and yelled, "Hey, anyone home?" I caught the aroma of Alfredo and was amazed how fast a scent could conjure memories. In this case the memory was a happy one.

"Hello," I called again, and headed for the dining-which-also-served-as-a-living room, the designation depending on what was going on at any given time. A dining room table was parked in an alcove, and across the room, a 20-inch TV sat on a low stand.

Alex stood to one side of the table, her hands full of plates. She looked up from her task, her eyes hungry, and not for food. Someone was in a mood.

I tamped down the urge to drag her to my old bedroom and curb that particular hunger. "Where is everyone?"

Gin popped out of the kitchen, a steaming dish in each hand.

"Hi, honey. Thomas is upstairs trying to fix a leak under the bathroom sink, and your brother's running late." Gin McKenna was petite with a salt-and-pepper bob. She had a quick smile and a dry sense of humor. She thumped the bowls onto the table. "Why don't you go see if you can get him to come down?"

In counterpoint, a loud bang echoed from above.

Gin sighed. "You know how Thomas gets when he thinks he can fix something."

The last time Thomas attempted to take on home repair, he'd tried to install a new toilet in the same upstairs bath. Somehow, he'd accidentally reassembled the plumbing wrong. Before long, the kitchen ceiling below the bathroom was dripping and Thomas had to make a very panicked call to a neighbor-plumber friend who wound up spending the better part of two evenings putting things back in working order. The ceiling still needed to be repainted.

I bounded up the steps and stuck my head in the bathroom door. The room was claustrophobic. Thomas had managed to wedge his upper body in the cabinet under the sink and his legs hung over the edge of the tub. He looked like an upside down turtle. When vertical, he stood six-one in his stocking feet and still carried a lot of muscle under the layer of chub he'd accumulated from Gin's cooking. Trying to squeeze his body into the small space was like trying to cram a size eleven foot into a size five shoe. He was never getting out of there without a shoehorn.

"Hey, Thomas."

"Cailin. Good thing you came up. Can you hand me the wrench there on the floor?"

I hefted the tool into his waiting palm and tried to see what was going on under the sink. A flashlight was propped on his chest, the beam shining right in his face. Another loud bang issued from the interior of the cabinet, and Thomas swore, something he rarely did.

I gave up trying to see what was going on and tried not to laugh. "You sure you know what you're doing?"

"Oh, yeah, this is a piece of cake—" A hiss cut off his reply. He yelped. A stream of water spurted out of the cabinet, across the tub, and hit the far wall like a sideways geyser.

Gin yelled something up the stairs, and I scrambled for towels. Poor Thomas. His heart was always in the right place, even if his skills weren't.

The sound of spraying water stopped abruptly, and Thomas wiggled out of the cabinet. His face, beard, head, and shirt were sopping wet. The flashlight rolled off his chest and hit the floor.

I tossed him a towel.

"Pull me up, will you please?"

Between the two of us, he eventually made it to his feet. "It was going fine there for a while. I'll have another go at it after we eat."

Oh, boy. Gin should tie him to the couch before letting him at the leak again.

I said, "You're always great entertainment, Mr. Fixit."

He playfully cuffed the back of my head, and he escaped to the bedroom to change shirts. Then we tromped down the stairs.

Gin and Alex were at the table with my brother, Jon, who'd arrived during the tussle with the plumbing.

Jon was a good-looking guy, as far as guys go. He had toffee-colored skin, big hands, big feet, and a square jaw. The scruffy, not-quite-a-beard on his face matched the close-cut, black hair on the top of his head. When he was younger, he could really rock an Afro, but these days his appearance was pretty conservative. Eyebrows any woman would love to have arched over clear, light-brown eyes. Jon had the wiry build of a runner, which he was, heedless of summer heat or winter cold.

Unlike me, Jon had no problem referring to the McKennas as mom and dad. He came to Gin and Thomas not long after I did. He was a skinny, gun-shy kid who turned out all right despite his rough childhood.

Thomas plopped into a chair with a sigh. Gin stepped up behind him and tried to tame the worst of his mussed, damp hair. "I called Arvin and he said he'd drop by this evening."

Arvin was the next-door neighbor and emergency plumber. I imagined Gin was praying Arvin showed up before Thomas finished eating.

Thomas grumbled good-naturedly and Gin pulled out a chair to sit by him.

I elbowed Jon and planted myself in a chair between him and Alex.

"Long time no see, bro. What's up?" I dragged a bowl of scalloped potatoes closer and scooped some on my plate.

"Please hand me the Alfredo, Jon," Gin said. "I haven't talked to either of you for days. I see more of Alex than you kids."

A serious look replaced Jon's usual happy-go-lucky expression. "I'm caught up in the second school shooting prosecution. Campbell's breathing down my neck. Wants the case wrapped up."

"Is he taking into account the bullying?" I asked. "The music, the hate group? Mike's motivations?"

"Nope. He feels it's pretty cut and dry. Kid wigs out, pulls the trigger, gets certified, and is planted in the poky for the rest of his life. You can't accuse Quenton Campbell of dragging his feet."

Thomas wiped at his beard-shrouded lips with a napkin. "How old is this boy?"

Jon broke a bun in half and reached for the butter.

"Just turned sixteen."

"He was brainwashed." I pulled my own bun apart. "I know the governor is all fired up and wants this resolved immediately, but Jesus, the hate music could be an extenuating factor."

"I know," Jon said. "Believe me, I know. I brought it up to Campbell again today. Blew me off. His one-track mind is too busy plotting how he can slam-dunk this case. He thinks he's on a one-way train to the governor's mansion. So I'm left digging into it on my own."

Thomas asked, "What did the therapists have to say?"

"They're not done yet." Jon shrugged. "And until there's a trial—if there is a trial—I can't reveal anything about his state of mind."

Gin glanced over my shoulder at the TV. "There's the man himself."

The remote was lying on a side table. Thomas grabbed it and unmuted the sound.

Hennepin County Attorney Quenton Campbell filled the screen, dressed in his Sunday finest. Short blond hair waved rakishly across his too-tanned-for-April forehead.

Minneapolis Police Chief Helling stood next to him. Helling's face had a pained, morose expression. The camera panned backward. They were on the stairs of the Hennepin County courthouse, microphones pointed at them from every angle.

Campbell was saying, "Those who kill will be properly adjudicated. Rest assured, we are aggressively working this case, and I hope to certify the accused as an adult by early next week. That's all I have to say at this point. Thank you."

The crowd of reporters shouted questions on deaf ears. Campbell and Helling ignored them and made their way down the courthouse steps.

"He's sure moving quickly on the certification." Thomas glanced at Jon. "Do you know which prosecution psychiatrist interviewed the boy?"

"Connie Tango. And I believe the Nordquists hired Skip Riley to defend him. He brought in his own guy to assess the kid."

"Holy Hannah." Thomas muted the television again and set the remote next to his plate. "Where did they find the money for the likes of Skip Riley?"

Riley had become something of a local celebrity after he'd gotten the Mickey Mouse Bandit off on a mental defect technicality. The Bandit spent a year robbing banks around the metro area by politely asking for money to be placed in an insulated Mickey Mouse lunch bag. He never threatened anyone, and it turned out, he gave the money to a number of minor charities in Minneapolis and St. Paul. Cheers filled the courtroom when he walked out a free man.

I shoved the food in my mouth to one side. "Larry Nordquist is an architect. His wife is E. A. McGregor, the romance writer. They have bucks."

Gin pushed a bowl of fruit salad at me. "I think I've read a couple of her books. They weren't bad."

Thomas made gagging sounds, and Gin tossed a napkin at him. "You should try a romance novel sometime, Thomas. You might learn a thing or two about women that those head-case journals you always read don't tell you."

"Point taken, honey." Thomas patted Gin's arm.

"This certification," Alex said, "why is it happening fast? Is that an advantage for the prosecution?"

I narrowed my eyes. "A big advantage. Of course Campbell is ready to certify Mike before all the results are in."

"That's the extent of it," Jon said. "In fact, at the end of our meeting today, when I mentioned a few avenues we ought to explore before moving so swiftly, Campbell told me to back off. He's convinced that he's got the whole case signed, sealed, and delivered. But I don't give up easy."

Jon detested loose ends, and that might be Mike's saving grace. I wanted to tell everyone about the plan Dirty Harry and I had to crash the Jubilee up north, but I didn't want Gin and Thomas to worry. Some things are best left on a need-to-know basis.

Conversation drifted to more mundane subjects. The Gallery was hosting a showing of Alex's work the following week, and Alex and my mother chatted about their plans while Jon, Thomas, and I offered suggestions that varied in degree of helpfulness.

We were interrupted by a knock on the door. Hiding her relief, Gin let in Arvin from next door to do battle with the errant plumbing. The men trooped upstairs in a show of do-it-yourself testosterone while Alex and I took the opportunity to make our exit and head for home.

Chapter 13

Promptly at five a.m. Saturday morning of Jubilee weekend, Harry tooted the horn of the blue Ford Focus rental car he'd parked in front of my house.

Forty minutes later the "Battle of Evermore" reverberated through the car for the third time as Harry and I cruised north on 169. The hood on my hoodie was pulled up tight over my head, which was pressed against the headrest in an attempt to stave off the ache that was close to gaining migraine status. "Harry. Mercy, man. It's too early for Zeppelin." Thank God I wasn't hung over.

Blissfully ignoring my state of discomfort, Harry thumb-tapped the steering wheel to the beat. He yelled over the din, "This is fightin' music. Gets me all fired up."

I groaned.

Ten minutes later, I ejected the CD from the player.

"Hey, what are you doing?"

"I'm saving you." I rolled down the window, flung the disc outside, and rolled the window back up.

Harry let out a girly-shriek, which he quickly stifled. He pressed his back deep into the seat and dangled a wrist over the edge of the steering wheel. "That was low."

"It was prudent."

"You're going to pay for a new one."

"That was almost as bad as the hate music."

Harry literally grunted. "Find something we can agree on, then."

I tried a pop station, light rock, and classical. All were met with a glare. When I tuned into Lite FM, "Witchy Woman" was ending. Harry glanced pointedly at me. We finally agreed to disagree and settled on the WCCO early agriculture report.

I propped my feet on the dashboard and watched the sign for Onamia as we flew by.

"You know"—another unlit cigarette bounced in the corner of Harry's mouth—"we crash and your knees will meet your backbone."

"I'll take my chances. Besides, if we do crash in this tin can, we'll both be dead anyway." I shifted uncomfortably. Ford needed to add padding to their seats. "You're sure you know how to get there?"

Harry pulled his phone out and waved it at me. "Mapped it."

"That's great, until you lose the signal."

"It'll be okay. North wrote the directions down, too.

It's amazing how cooperative people are when they want to stay out of jail."

During our two-week sabbatical, Edward North had been good on his word. He got Harry into a few SOC gatherings and coughed up all kinds of information about the compound where the Jubilee was held. Harry managed to ingratiate himself with a number of the other members, and more than one had offered up an invite to the Jubilee, so we were covered. I hadn't accompanied Harry to any of these get-togethers, but he'd talked up his hard-ass wife plenty.

WCCO faded out and was replaced by a country station broken up by long periods of static. The buzzing seeped into my brain, and I must have dozed off because the next thing I knew, we were stopping at an old gas station in Garrison, a town that bordered Lake Mille Lacs.

The wind was biting, and I was glad I'd worn a heavy gray jacket under my flannel coat.

Harry was good at dressing the part—whichever part he was playing at any given time. That's what made him so effective undercover. A black motorcycle jacket covered his white T-shirt.

He was in the middle of inserting the nozzle into the tank when a gust of wind caught one side of his jacket and whipped it open. I hadn't seen the words on the shirt: PRAY FOR WHITE POWER, in black letters that were about ten feet tall. "Stop!" I scrambled to extricate myself from the confines of the car. "What are you doing? Zip your jacket!"

Harry flipped me the bird but snapped the bottom

button. The jacket still gaped, but not as much.

"I'm getting something to drink," I called over my shoulder. At the front door of the rundown shop, I called back, "Want anything?"

"Red Bull."

Inside, a white, grease-stained, pegboard counter held an ancient cash register. A tin can with a flyer attached sought donations for six-year-old Holly Johnson, who was stricken with leukemia. I scanned the rest of the place. The shop held the usual assortment of snacks, gum, a lottery stand, and a silver, stand-up cooler.

The unmistakable redolence of gas and oil hung heavy in the air. I wandered over to the cooler and pulled out a bottle of Mello Yello and a can of Red Bull. I snagged a bag of corn chips for me and a Snickers for Harry and set the goods down on the counter. A silver bell sat next to the register so I gave it a whack.

A moment later a door between the convenience store and the shop bays opened. An old man with gray hair in a 1920s cut stepped into the room. A welcoming smile lit his weathered face. He was dressed in heavy blue coveralls with a DX patch sewn on the breast pocket.

"Chilly day." He rang me up. "Where you headed?"

I watched in fascination as the plunger-type buttons on the register activated dials that spun to show the prices in the cracked rectangular display window.

"Crosby. I need to pay for gas outside, too."

He humphed, squinted out the window, and punched more buttons. "Not much to see up there this time of year."

"We're meeting some people."

His eyes caught mine. "You be careful up that way. There's some not-so-friendly folk staying round there."

That was interesting. "What do you mean?"

Something I couldn't define crossed his face. "A nice girl like you—" He stopped. "You just be careful up there. Watch yourself."

"We'll do that." I stuck a five in the tin for the girl with leukemia. "Thanks for the advice."

"Anytime."

I walked out, glad he hadn't seen Harry's T-shirt. Harry was back in the car. He had the heater blowing full force and hummed along to Neil Sedaka. I sank into the low seat and handed him his Red Bull and candy bar. "You're going to kill me before we even get there."

Harry gave me a smug smile and pulled out.

I was right. Cell service crapped out not long after we left the gas station. By the time we hit Crosby my phone showed two bars, and those disappeared again once we were a mile outside of town. After taking a few wrong turns and driving down three dead-end logging roads, we finally found the entrance into The Soldiers of Christ compound.

Huge trees crowded both sides of the gravel entrance. A seven-foot, barbed-wire-topped fence paralleled the road for more than a quarter mile both ways and was connected to a looming log gate. No Trespassing signs were attached to the fence at twenty-foot intervals.

A hut barely large enough for four people sat immediately inside the fence next to the entrance.

"I count two heads," Harry said. "You?"

"Copy that."

"Locked and loaded?"

I was packing a subcompact Glock strapped to my ankle, a Smith & Wesson Compact 9 tucked into a conceal-carry holster at my waistband, and a three-inch Gerber Torch folding knife snug in the pocket of my jeans. Harry was probably armed similarly, and I suspected he'd have even more firepower than I did.

"Yes, I am. Let's give 'em hell."

As adrenaline ramped up, so did my pulse. Every sense was on high alert, and I welcomed the rush. I always forgot how much I loved this shit until I was in the middle of it.

Harry pulled up to the gate. One of the guards came out of the building and unlocked a nearly invisible door next to the main gate. He was maybe six feet tall, muscular, and probably in his twenties. A military-style black sweater with leather elbow patches hugged his torso, and camo cargos were tucked into shiny black boots. The man's head was shaved smooth, and his face was pockmarked from what must have been a raging case of teenage acne. A walkie hung from his hip, the cord stretched tautly across his chest to a hand mike secured to one of the epaulets on his shoulder.

Harry rolled the window down. The guard put a meaty hand on the roof and leaned over to peer in.

"Something I can help you with?"

Harry said, "Ed North should have me on the list. The wife and I decided to come on up and see what this is all about."

The guard frowned. "See what's all about what?"

"You know," Harry made a face that was more leer than smile. "The Jubilee. We come to celebrate the way of things."

"It's invitation only."

"North invited us, like I said. So did Simon Day. Both of 'em told me about it. Said we should drive on up, check it out." Harry shifted so his jacket gaped and exposed the screen-printing on his chest.

Guard Boy glanced down. "What's your name?"

"Ralph Madden. This here's my wife, Alice."

"Hang on." He stepped away from the car and spoke into his shoulder mic.

I whispered, "You make a decent corn-fed skinhead for a guy from New Jersey."

Eyes on the guard, Harry muttered, "You have no idea."

The guard gave his partner thumbs up and returned, his demeanor less brusque.

"Go on in. There's parking at the end of the driveway to the right. Everyone's gathered in Kingdom Hall."

The other man emerged from the shack, unlocked the gate, and swung it open.

We drove into the compound. It appeared our greeters were the only two watchdogs in sight, unless other eyes were hiding in the thick woods that pushed up against the long, curving drive. The trees were so close together they looked like a solid, dark wall.

After a half-mile, the driveway opened into a clearing. About twenty vehicles were parked in a dirt lot. A building with unfinished wood siding, maybe double the size of a typical barn, occupied a great deal of the space, while six smaller outbuildings clustered around it. A navy-colored, two-story pole barn stood on the far side of the parking area.

Harry cut the engine next to a rusty van. "According to North, that's Kingdom Hall." He nodded toward the enormous wood edifice.

I scanned the grounds. "Where is everyone?"

"In Kingdom Hall, Alice. Weren't you listening?" Harry flipped a cigarette to his lips.

"Right-o, Ralph. Let's go."

We headed toward the wood-clad building and made our way around the side to the front door. Above the doorframe, a black sign read KINGDOM HALL.

"Gee whiz, Alice, we found it. Shall we knock?"

"No."

Harry tucked the unlit smoke behind his ear and pushed the door open.

Ochre-colored tiles covered a ten-by-twenty entry. To the left was a closed door. A door on the right stood partially open, the edge of a sink visible through the opening. Probably a bathroom. Beside it, a half-filled, built-in coatrack ran the length of the windowless, rough-hewn plank wall. Dim lamplight from wall sconces left much of the room in shadow.

Dead ahead, a set of double doors was propped open with chunks of firewood. The room beyond was abuzz with voices.

I glanced at Harry. He shrugged and we made for the double doors. As we were about to cross the threshold of the spacious room, a man dressed in the same uniform as the two guards at the front gate stopped us. He raised his arm above his shoulder, snapped it down, and slapped his hand against his thigh. "You the Maddens?"

"We are." Harry returned the salute.

"Come with me."

We followed him into Kingdom Hall proper, a windowless room roughly the size of three racquetball courts. The hardwood flooring reflected light thrown from more of the same wall-mounted fixtures as well as two chandeliers that hung from exposed beams that crossed the ceiling.

A buffet was set up along the farthest wall. Twenty card tables, each with four folding chairs tucked under, sat in front of it. About half of the seats were occupied by an impressive array of extremely white and oft-tattooed people. Several of our new, soon-to-be-best pals milled around the food. In one corner, a tall man with a beer belly and a shaved head preached loudly about the moral decay of white culture. I tried to do a surreptitious head count and came up with forty-three people. The men outnumbered the women two to one.

Camo pants, jeans, combat boots, and T-shirts or military jackets appeared to be the dress code du jour. These people probably shopped en masse at army surplus stores.

Our guide led us toward a cluster of men standing off to the side. He stopped a few feet away, held up a hand, and said, "Wait here." He approached and spoke in low tones to a Hells Angel escapee in an army jacket and jeans. The man said something to our guide, executed a sharp about-turn, and exited through a side door.

The hairs on the back of my neck had been at half-staff since we drove in. I scanned the room and caught sight of a door with a hand-printed Exit sign tacked above it.

The bearded man approached and held out a hand to Harry. "Madden, good to see you again. Welcome to our quarterly Jubilee." He turned to me. "You must be Alice. I'm Simon Day, one of SOC's council members. I've heard all about you."

I wondered what bullshit Harry had fed this man's contact. I smiled like a good wife and shook his hand. "I've heard about you, too, Mr. Day."

Yeah, Harry had filled me in about him, all right. In talking to Day, Harry had unofficially solved an attempted terror attack in Minneapolis. Six years earlier, someone tried to blow up a van in a parking lot not far from the Metrodome after a Vikings football game when hundreds of fans were leaving the sports venue. Fortunately, the van's interior filled with smoke instead of exploding into a million pieces. Passersby alerted the police who found the vehicle stocked with blocks of C-4 that had been packed in cardboard boxes filled with nails. What a lethal combo.

Day bragged to Harry that he'd been the mastermind behind the plot. Now, as I looked at Day, it was hard to sit on the knowledge that he'd set that up. Here he was, standing in front of me, free to plan more death and destruction. The itch to pull my gun and shoot him was a hard one not to scratch.

Unaware of the murderous thoughts running through my mind, Day said, "Have you made a decision?"

Harry gave Day a glimpse of the shirt he wore. "We were hoping we might find folks like us. Looks like we have."

Day grinned, a cold grimace that didn't reach his eyes. I had a feeling we'd better duck fast when he found out who we really were.

"Ralph, why don't you come with me, and your lady can grab some food and meet some of the other women." He waved a hand toward the tables.

"Go on and eat something, Alice." Harry leaned over and nuzzled my cheek while he whispered, "Yell if you need me, sugar."

Sugar? I snapped my teeth next to his ear.

Harry snatched his head back. "She's a frisky one, my Alice." He grabbed my shoulders, spun me around, and swatted my ass. "Go on, honey."

My foot was going to land so deep up Harry's butt he wasn't going to walk for a week. The things I did for my job. I smiled stiffly, muttered, "Yes, dear," and wandered over to sample the buffet. I scooped green Jell-O salad onto a paper plate and thought about how normal some of this scene appeared, if you left out all of the military wear and snippets of hate speech floating around. I could be at any gathering in Minneapolis, about to devour some

Midwest hors d'oeuvres, steeling myself to make small talk with narrow-minded—although probably not deadly—women.

After adding to my plate a couple slabs of herring, some green olives, and a few scrawny pickle spears wrapped in cream cheese and ham, I grabbed a cup of some kind of punch and looked for an open seat.

A table nearby held three women and an unoccupied chair. I approached and asked, "May I join you?"

A middle-aged woman with curly gray hair, a wrinkled face, and WHITE POWER tattooed across the top of one hand shrugged. "Sure."

I set my plate and cup on the table and pulled out the chair. "Thanks." I tried not to be too obvious as I attempted to see what pearls of wisdom she had tattooed on her other hand.

Another woman, probably in her mid-twenties, wore a black, long-sleeved shirt that proclaimed *Those Afraid of Pain Will Never Know Glory*. "I'm Leanna."

"And I'm Paula." The girl sitting beside Leanna looked like she was barely into her teens. She scooped something onto her fork and slid it into her mouth. Then she pointed the fork at the woman who initially spoke to me. "That's my mom, Doreen."

"Nice to meet all of you. I'm Alice."

Leanna took a sip of her punch. "Haven't seen you before."

I popped a chunk of pork-wrapped pickle in my mouth. "Just joined. My husband and I have been looking for a long time for others who reflect our views."

Doreen said, "It's hard to find those who are committed to the Lord and our race. Jews poisoning our very existence, those damn wetbacks spilling across our borders, Japs and their rude, evil ways coming to this great country, black bastards mixing with our white women. Homos trying to get married, screaming all that 'we got rights' bullshit. Someone has to put a stop to it."

Holy cow. Talk about being right up-front with the hate. Pauline and Leanna nodded gravely. I forced my own head to bob up and down with theirs. What would they think if they knew I was a full-blooded lesbian with a Puerto Rican lover, whose friends included a black woman, a feisty Asian, and a Mexican cop. I'd probably be shot on sight. I stuffed some herring in my mouth so I wouldn't have to say anything.

Leanna said, "That's one of the reasons we're so happy the new Augustus Primus has stepped in and pulled everyone together."

We knew the leader of the SOC, this Augustus Primus, was powerful, very charismatic, and extremely secretive about his identity, even among his followers. According to information that Tony and Rosie had dredged up and confirmed with Edward North, any time the man appeared, he was encased in purple robes with his face obscured by a red, peaked hood. He kept his most trusted advisors around him, and armed guards accompanied him in public.

"Who is the Augustus Primus?" I asked.

Paula leaned toward me, her brown eyes wide. "He's coming tomorrow. He's the closest thing we have to God

Almighty. God speaks right through the Primus. And they say he's cute, besides."

"They" did, huh? I wondered who "they" were. I scooped up some green Jell-O. A hate group's green Jell-O tasted just like the green Jell-O the little old church ladies served at lunch after a funeral.

"Cute, huh?" I repeated and casually scanned the hall for Harry. Always good to know where backup was. Said backup was with a group of men, and from the gestures he was making and the reactions from the others, Harry was doing a good job talking smack. I refocused on Paula. "What does this cutie look like?"

Leanna poked Paula. "Don't listen to her. No one here's ever seen him without his robes. She's repeating what all the kids are saying."

"That's right," Doreen said. "The girls are all crazy over the Primus."

"What's his real name?"

"The Augustus Primus is our secret, our protector, and our savior." Leanna pushed the remains of her food away. "That's all we need to know."

The intensity of their devotion was unnerving.

I asked, "The Augustus Primus doesn't come to all the Jubilees?"

"No." Doreen wiped the back of her hand across her lips. "We never know until right before if he'll be here or not. When he does show, he updates us about the latest recruitment numbers, what the plans are to keep spreading the word, other stuff. Heard that the latest news is something big. Don't know what. You heard anything, Leanna?"

"Nothing," Leanna said. "My husband's brother-in-law mentioned the Primus is revealing something important soon. This Augustus Primus will be the one to make things happen for the SOC. Unlike the last one."

"What happened with the last one?" I asked.

Doreen thumped her coffee cup on the table. "Angel Saxon was the last Primus. He was a loudmouth, foul bastard. He about ran the Soldiers of Christ into the ground. Nearly wiped us out."

I vaguely recalled the name. If I remembered right, Saxon dropped out of sight maybe a year and a half ago. I wasn't aware of anything linking him to a hate group in general or to the Soldiers of Christ in particular. Why had his name even been in the news? I refocused. "What happened?"

"Saxon vanished," Leanna said, "along with a lot of money. A real lot. No one knows where he is. You can bet they're still hunting the fool. There's talk the new Primus took care of him." She gave me a you-know-what-I'm-talking-about look. "We finally got a place to call our own, and Saxon nearly destroyed everything."

"No one knows what the Primus's real name is? Really?" Couldn't hurt to try a second time.

Leanna clasped her hands on the table in front of her. "No. No one cares as long as he can lead us into righteousness."

"Now you tell us a little about yourself." Doreen looked at me expectantly.

And we're off. "I'm a long-time believer, and my husband over there," I pointed to Harry, who was laughing obnoxiously, "is Ralph."

Paula said, "He's a nice looking guy."

"Yes," I said through a gritted smile. "We're lucky to have one another."

The next few hours sucked ass. Telling lies and listening to hate-filled talk spew from the mouths of two women and one teenage girl was not the way I wanted to spend my day.

I didn't relax until we were in the rental car headed toward a motel that had been recommended by one of the crazies. Clearly, Harry had run through a boatload of energy, too, because we both had little to say.

Cell service kicked in once we neared Crosby. I called Rosie and had her run a check on Angel Saxon. All that came back was a rap sheet consisting of various drug charges, a couple of assault charges that were later dropped, and one charge of indecent exposure. He had an outstanding two-year-old bench warrant for failure to pay some parking tickets in Hennepin County, but that's where his trail ended. Saxon had apparently gone to ground after the brouhaha with SOC.

I relayed the information to Harry.

"Interesting," he said, "but not particularly helpful."

"They tell you the Primus might come tomorrow?"

"That's all any of them talked about. Sounds like your typical cult leader. No one knows his name, where he lives, what he does outside of his sporadic appearances, but he's charismatic."

"One of the women mentioned a big deal event sometime in the maybe-near future that's supposed to spread the word of the Soldiers of Christ, but she didn't know what specifically. I don't like the sound of that."

"No." Harry was silent a moment. "I'll prod around tomorrow while you entertain your new friends. Maybe you can get the recipe for those wrapped-up pickles."

"Very funny."

We found the motel and checked in. The room was a Sixties throwback, complete with orange-vinyl easy chairs, stained, red shag carpet, and two dinky, saggy full-size beds generously referred to as queen-sized by the manager. At least it was clean and bedbug free. I thoroughly checked before crawling between the white-gray sheets.

The last thought I had before sleep overtook me was to wonder when Austin Powers would burst through the door yelling, "Groovy, baby!"

Chapter 14

Harry and I hit the road back to the compound by nine-thirty the next morning. This time the guards simply waved us through, and we parked among four dozen vehicles in a spot near the blue barn-like structure. Harry killed the engine and I grabbed my jacket.

Harry didn't move. He had an odd look on his face. I'd seen that expression on him before, and it didn't bode anything good. I asked warily, "What?"

"I want to check out this building." He pointed dead ahead at the blue sheet metal that filled the front window. "Go in and cover for me for a few minutes. I won't be long." Harry pulled the keys out of the ignition and bolted. Before I was out of the car he'd disappeared around the corner of the building.

I slammed the car door shut and scanned the area. One person walked briskly toward the front of Kingdom Hall, but otherwise it looked like Harry and I were the only ones out and about.

The big blue building we'd parked in front of looked shut up tight. A chain threaded between the handles of white double doors at one end, and a heavy padlock secured the links. Windows were set up high enough it would be difficult, although not impossible, to access. There very well could be additional entrances on the other side, and maybe Harry could get in that way.

I made a beeline toward the front door of Kingdom Hall. As I rounded the corner, I ran into Leanna. Literally.

"Sorry about that." I put a steadying hand on her arm. "You okay?"

"Alice—hey! Yeah, fine. Glad you made it back." We resumed the short trek to the front door. "Where's the man?"

Good question. "My bladder isn't what it used to be. He was taking his sweet time organizing his stuff in the car so I left him. I swear the man takes forever to get himself together."

"Been there. Between my husband and the boys I'm always waiting. It's like a dog catching sight of a squirrel. There goes the attention span." Leanna opened the door of Kingdom Hall and we joined a foyer full of people whose voices filled the space with white noise. The hall was charged with an anticipatory, edgy energy.

"Go on." Leanna stepped out of my way and sent me toward the restroom with a sweep of her arm.

The restroom was unoccupied so I locked the door. I stalled a couple of minutes by checking my cell phone. Still no signal and texts wouldn't even go through. I wondered if they had a jammer—or maybe they'd picked this spot because it was outside the range of a cell tower. I washed my hands and exited to survey the crowd, but no Harry. Should I be worried yet?

Leanna was leaning against the wall next to the entrance to the hall. I headed toward her, picking up bits of conversation as I went.

"Primus is going to..."

"...kicked my kid out of school for wearing a swas..."

"...got a Ruger 10/22 rifle and that fucker'll take out..."

Everything was said with the calm certainty of a terrifying brand of righteousness. When I reached Leanna, she gave me an excited push toward the main hall. "I just heard. The Primus is definitely going to be here today. You lucked out."

I hesitated, then I decided Harry would find me wherever I was. While he'd only been gone a few minutes, it felt like forever. It was much easier to be the one taking the risks than the person who had to figuratively sit on their hands and wait for the risk-taker to return.

The hall had been transformed from last night's reception into an auditorium that held rows of folding chairs. A walnut-colored wooden lectern faced the sea of them, and to the right of the lectern, six chairs parked in a row faced the audience.

I chose a spot close to the entrance doors and sat.

"Oh, no." Leanna pulled me back to my feet. "When it begins, you have to be up front."

"Why?"

She jerked a thumb toward the lectern. "You want to join the Soldiers of Christ? You have to sit up there, in the hot seat. Everyone starts there. We all did." She looked at me sharply. "If you're ready."

Things were about to shift from two miles an hour to a hundred. "Oh, we're ready," I assured her. Where the hell was Harry? We needed a confab. Now.

"New people are only brought into the organization when the Augustus Primus attends. You and Ralph are lucky. Most wind up waiting a while before they can go through the induction ceremony. You got him first time out."

Lucky us. "What happens at the ceremony?"

"You pledge your life to advance the cause. Complete White Unity. That's where it started and that's where it ends."

Before I had a chance to ask anything else, someone wrapped arms around me from behind. "Hey babe, who's your friend?"

"Ralph." I heaved a mental breath of relief and put a hand on Harry's arm. "This is Leanna."

"Oh, that's right. Leanna. You told me about her."

Leanna smiled. "Nice to meet you, Ralph."

"Honey," I said, "Leanna was telling me about today's induction ceremony."

"Yeah?" Harry kept his arm possessively around my neck.

"As I was explaining to your wife," Leanna said, "to join the Soldiers of Christ, you pledge yourself to the cause. It doesn't take long, and the marking doesn't hurt to bad. It's over before you know it."

My mind was too busy processing the reference to me as Harry's wife to fully comprehend what she'd said. Before I could coherently ask what the "marking" was, a woman approached and whispered something in Leanna's ear. "Okay," Leanna told her and turned to us. "Gotta run. The kids are acting up in the playroom again. I'll see you later. Good luck."

Leanna disappeared into the crowd. I eyed Harry. "Won't hurt too bad? What marking won't hurt too bad?"

"I have no idea. North didn't tell me anything about a physical piece of the initiation."

"Great." I took a deep breath. I hoped it didn't entail having a giant swastika tattooed to my forehead or anything like that. We couldn't do anything about it now except toe the line without blowing our cover. "Find anything on your ill-advised spy mission?"

Harry tugged me closer and whispered, "Unlocked side door. Lots of nooks and crannies. Main area is a garage. A couple of snowmobiles, three trucks—one mostly disassembled—and a four-wheeler. Four rooms off the main area. Two were locked up tight. Of the other two, one was filled with a bunch of chemicals and six fifty-pound bags of what I think is ammonium nitrate in fertilizer form."

"Oh, shit." That was a lot of fertilizer for an organization that didn't farm. It shrieked bomb. "The other?"

"Packed with enough survival supplies to last a horde of people at least a few months. They're set for a siege." Harry casually scanned the room. "We need to get this to Weatherspoon and Helling."

Simon Day came up and slapped Harry on the shoulder. "Glad you could both make it. I'm thrilled to say the Augustus Primus is here. He's very happy to bring more people into our community. There's another couple besides yourselves who are joining, along with two men. What you need to do now is head up to those chairs beside the pulpit that are facing the audience. The address will begin shortly." He nodded, patted my shoulder, and strode toward the foyer.

Harry and I slowly made our way to the front of the room and picked the two chairs farthest from the podium. A moment later, a man and a woman took the two chairs next to us. I introduced us, and we found out our co-rite-takers were Phil and Bree Bendak of Appleton. Both were computer programmers. Phil was a slight man with light brown hair, and Bree was a brittle-looking woman with platinum blonde locks and boobs she hadn't been born with. They didn't appear to be the hate-loving type, but you can't always judge the inside by the out.

Another five minutes and the majority of the crowd had settled. The lights dimmed and stragglers hustled to find a chair. The rumble of the crowd quieted.

The doors closed, and the lights switched from dim to nonexistent. I couldn't see a hand in front of my face, and I knew, because I tried. I felt Harry's hand press along the side of my leg, and then it came to rest on my thigh. His touch was comforting. The inky blackness heightened anticipation, and it felt like the very air vibrated with expectation. Everyone seemed to be holding their breaths, and then a bright spotlight hit the lectern. Suddenly, out of nowhere, a figure appeared beside it. Nice mystical touch. I wondered if the man used a trap door to enter the room. The light bathed his purple robes, and he wore a red, two-foot high, cone-shaped headpiece. Red cloth draped from the brim of the hat and covered his face. Two holes were cut in the cloth, presumably so he could see. This could be no one but the Augustus Primus himself.

A huge, stylized cross hung from the man's neck, shiny against the matte finish of his robe. He waited until people began to clap, then he moved behind the lectern and raised his arms. "Thank you. Thank you." He had a thick, southern accent. He waved a hand, and the fervent clapping cut off just like that.

"It's good to see you, my brothers and sisters. Welcome to the Jubilee. This day we are celebrating many things. We've been blessed by God to gather at this place and affirm our path to rectitude."

The crowd enthusiastically applauded. I wondered how many of them even knew what "rectitude" meant.

The Primus gave the crowd a moment to release some pent-up energy. "Today we're pleased to welcome new members to our flock." His voice boomed through the space like a verbal cannon. He looked toward us. Two men had filled the empty chairs closest to the Primus while I'd been mesmerized by the introductory theatrics. Another spotlight hit us, and I squinted against the glare.

"Brothers and sisters," the Primus said, "we have six disciples. Six who wish to become Soldiers of Christ. Shall we allow it?"

"Yes!" The crowd responded as one.

The hair on my arms stood on end.

"Shall we," the Primus said, "allow these lambs to be saved?"

The cat calls, stomping, and clapping grew so loud the floor vibrated beneath my feet.

"Brothers and Sisters," the Primus bellowed over the cacophony, "I said, do we want to allow these people discipleship in the greatest cause of all time?"

The roar became truly deafening. The Primus's shout of "It is time!" was almost drowned out, but with those words the audience fell silent.

The Primus faced us once more. "One by one, approach the altar." He pointed at the inductee in the chair closest to the podium. I was glad I was in the seat farthest away from His Hateness. "You. Come forward."

A bearded man with a formidable paunch and numerous tattoos on thick forearms moved to the spot indicated by the Primus.

"Raise your left hand and repeat after me."

The man raised his hand.

The Primus said, "I do swear that by giving myself to the Soldiers of Christ..."

The Primus's words were echoed.

"I will do everything in my power to further the cause..."

And so it went.

Finally the man repeated the last line. "I will pursue justice, vanquish evil, preserve our race, and spread the word of our Lord. I will honor the code, I will honor God, and I will obey the Augustus Primus."

The Primus put a hand on his shoulder. "I bestow upon you sacred membership into the Soldiers of Christ."

The audience exploded in cheers.

"Silence, y'all!" the Primus said sharply and raised both arms into the air again. I was surprised at how fast the crowd responded. The Primus pointed at the empty chair and the newest member of the Soldiers of Christ returned to his seat. "Next."

One by one, each of us stood before this man, who was dressed in a ridiculous costume, and vowed allegiance to a group that went against every moral fiber I had.

Once I finished my own recitation and returned to my spot beside Harry, the Primus said, "It's time for the final act of truth." He swung an arm to encompass the six of us. "This will seal your place within the Soldiers of Christ. Please bring me the strike brand."

What the hell was that? Was this for the marking Leanna had mentioned? I shot Harry a quick glance. His jaw was clenched, but he kept his slightly widened eyes focused on the Primus. Bree had leaned into Phil, and he was whispering furiously in her ear.

The side door opened, and a brief spark of daylight flashed into the dark cavern of Kingdom Hall. Two people who wore white robes and white hoods carried a rectangular, six-foot table with thick, rough-hewn legs and an unfinished plank top. They placed it in front of the podium. Two additional men followed, lugging something between them.

The door closed and extinguished the brightness. The spotlight still lit the lectern, and I saw that the men each carried one end of a white cooler. They placed it on the floor next to the table and faded into the darkness.

The Primus opened the cooler and pulled out what appeared to be a coffee-can-sized metal container wrapped in red and purple cloth. A two-foot-long metal rod rested against the rim of the canister, and a white substance covered half of the visible portion of the rod.

"The first will go last and the last will go first. With this brand you will forever be known as a fighter for truth and justice. A true and righteous Soldier of Christ." He leveled his hooded stare at me. "Stand and receive."

Holy shit. He was literally branding us? With what? Where was the fire? The red-hot iron? I wanted nothing to do with this, but it was real and it was go-time. If I hesitated, I would look weak and uncommitted. If I said no, would our cover be blown?

Harry glanced sharply at me, his eyes unreadable. This was light years beyond my job description.

The Primus waited. Time to bite the proverbial bullet. I drew a breath, exhaled loudly, and sidled toward him.

"Stop right there, child." The Primus put up a hand, I halted before him. Two of the white-robed men came to stand on either side of me, while another waited behind the Primus.

The Primus said, "Remove your jacket and bare your left arm." I shrugged out of my hoodie. I'd worn only a

T-shirt beneath it this morning, and the caress of cool air over my exposed flesh made me shiver. One of the men took the jacket. The Primus reached to grasp my left wrist. The skin of his fingers was surprisingly soft. He turned my hand over, palm facing up. Whatever he was about to do would likely be a permanent fixture. I fought against instinct that howled at me to punch him between the eyeholes in his hood and run like hell.

"This won't take long, little lady." He'd set the can on the table within arm's reach, and he grasped the rod and withdrew it. "Think of pain as purity, and purity is the objective of the Soldiers of Christ." I felt like I'd fallen into a vat of cotton. Everything sounded muffled and time passed in slow motion.

The Primus tightened his hold on me and before I could react, pressed the business end of the rod against the inside of my forearm, halfway between my wrist and elbow.

For a fraction of a second, my skin sizzled, and then pain exploded through my arm like the brilliance of fireworks in the night sky, enveloping all my senses. Reflexively, I jerked back, but firm hands clamped around my upper arms. I may have screamed. I have no idea how long the iron was against my skin or how many seconds it took me to realize the Primus had disengaged and stepped away. He held the iron triumphantly above his head. "You are now a true, pure Soldier of Christ."

I fought to stop my eyes from rolling back in my head. I couldn't quite draw a full breath. My heart beat like a snare drum. The men who'd held me up duck-walked me back to my seat. I collapsed onto the hard chair and gingerly cradled my arm against my chest. One of them shook out my jacket and draped it across my back.

The skin of my forearm felt shredded and burned like nothing I'd ever experienced before. I could make out a tiny indentation in my skin that looked like the outline of a cross. For such a diminutive burn, the pain level was excruciating, as if I'd held the inside of my arm against the edge of a white-hot oven. I met Harry's wide, wild eyes and muttered through gritted teeth, "Your turn."

Soon enough, it was all over. No one passed out, but none of the inductees looked very happy. I learned later that the brand was a two-inch replica of the cross the Primus wore. One of the minions went down the row and applied a grease-like substance that dulled the pain far more rapidly than I expected. While it still hurt, I could at least focus again.

"Please," the Primus said, "when y'all have a chance, I hope you'll make your new brothers and sisters welcome. Now, sit back and listen to the glory we have to share."

Harry squeezed my knee with his right hand, and we listened obediently to the Augustus Primus orate about the vices of a world gone awry and how the Soldiers of Christ were preparing to make an impact. Something would soon rock the free world and let it be known the Soldiers of Christ was an organization to fear.

Buzzing static increased in volume in the back of my mind. Before I lost total focus, Harry nudged me. I wondered if what they smeared on us contained something more than numbing gel. The fiery burn had subsided to a dull but constant throbbing. Initially the skin was indented with the outline of the cross, but now the indentation had disappeared into a mass of swelling. I kept gazing from my arm to Harry's. What did we just do? I couldn't believe we'd followed through. The NPIU owed us fucking hazard pay, and they damn well better find someone to do something about this brand when the case was done.

Adrenaline eventually ebbed, and I was in pain, agitated, and ready to get out of there. I was occupying myself by considering inventive ways of taking out the Primus when he finally wrapped it up.

"My flock, please join your hands together and bend your heads in prayer for the success of our mission. The mission to retake our identity. The mission to reclaim our status in the White Power New Order. That mission is upon us." The slow, Southern cadence of his voice was hypnotic.

After a moment of silence, the Primus lifted his arms like the pope blessing the crowd from his balcony at the Vatican.

The spotlight extinguished and plunged us into complete darkness. After maybe a full minute, the house lights came up. The Primus had vanished, along with his lackeys, the cooler, and the table. I wondered how I'd missed the side door opening and closing. Maybe the place held a secret entrance after all.

Simon Day now stood at the lectern. "The Word of the Augustus Primus. Blessed be the Augustus Primus."

The crowd went nuts clapping.

"Thank you," Simon said, several times. "Blessed be you all, bless you." He waited for the audience to calm again. "Please take a few minutes to stretch your legs. I will speak shortly, followed by a couple of the other council members."

✵ ✵ ✵

The hum of tires against the pavement lulled me into a hypnotic state, and I didn't argue when Harry found a country station on the radio.

Between the amount of hate that spewed from the councilmen who addressed the congregation and the burning pain in my forearm that was slowly ramping up, I was exhausted. I imagined Harry had to be, too.

We escaped just past the six o'clock hour and now were burning rubber back to the city. The ringing of my phone jolted me into consciousness, and I snapped to attention. Harry reached over and turned the tunes down.

I didn't recognize the number. "McKenna."

"Cailin, where are you?" Gin's voice trembled on the edge of hysteria. Gin was never hysterical. Dire thoughts of Alex and then Eli flashed through my mind.

I jerked upright. "Gin, what's wrong?"

"It's Jon."

"What?" I was having a hard time recalibrating. Jon. Something wrong with Jon? Fear ballooned in my stomach.

"Jon's in ICU. You need to come."

"What?" Even I could hear how panic raised the pitch

of my voice. Harry glanced at me with wide, what's-going-on eyes.

"He's at HCMC. Someone stabbed him on the light rail on his way home from work this afternoon." Her voice was now steady, her near-hysteria back under control.

"What was he doing at work? It's Sunday."

"I don't know."

I glanced at Harry. He'd caught the gist of Gin's words. His face hardened, and the hands gripping the steering wheel tightened.

"We're on the way. We're—" I had no idea where we were.

Harry said, "Just coming into Elk River."

I did a fast calculation. "We'll be there in forty minutes. Don't worry, Gin. I'm on my way."

✯ ✯ ✯

Harry dropped me at the emergency entrance of the Hennepin County Medical Center and went to find a place to park. I fisted my hands in an attempt to stop shaking, charged through the ER entrance, and approached the reception window. "Excuse me, where is patient Jon McKenna?"

The receptionist, a kind-eyed woman with chocolate brown skin, punched something into the computer. "McKenna. Here we go. Up on four. Take the elevator, and when you get to four, make a right. There's a waiting room at the end of the hall. You can check in with the nurse's station there."

I thanked her and went swiftly in the direction she indicated. I saw rows of ailing people waiting to be seen, and the terrible, antiseptic stink of the place almost made me gag.

Everything came into hyper-focus. Cold, fluorescent light rained down from above and made the shiny floor glow. My shoes squeaked against the linoleum. At the elevators, I pressed the button repeatedly. It wouldn't come any faster, but it gave me a meager sense of control over an entirely uncontrollable situation. As the doors finally, finally slid open, I caught sight of Harry coming into the ER. I stuck one hand on the elevator door to hold it and waved with the other. He hustled toward me. "What's his status?"

I hit the button for the fourth floor. "Don't know yet." I was amazed my voice didn't shake.

We rode the rest of the way in silence. Of course, the elevator had to stop at every floor. After what felt like an eon, we arrived, and I steered Harry to the right. A sign on the door at the end of the hall read, "Waiting Room," and I thrust it open.

Gin stood by the window, her back ramrod stiff, staring out into the darkness. Thomas sat on the edge of one of the couches. He was so pale he looked like he might pass out any moment. Alex had a leg propped on the arm of the couch, and her hand rested on my foster dad's shoulder.

Gin spun around. When she saw me, she gasped, and in two fast steps pulled me hard against her.

Tremors shook her body.

"What's going on?" I whispered.

She shook her head, clearly unable to speak. I tightened my hold and looked over at Thomas.

Thomas had aged years in three days. "He's in surgery. The ER doctor said they'd know more once they opened him up. The knife collapsed his right lung. They're worried about his liver. I don't know what else."

Alex approached and put her arms around both Gin and me. I brushed my lips against hers, gave Gin a final squeeze, and stepped away. A part of me screamed that I was the one who was supposed to get hurt, not the family that had taken me in as their own. I was the expendable one, not Jon. Then I locked my thoughts down like I used to when I was on the streets and slipped into the familiar, welcome numbness of survival. "How long has he been in surgery?"

Gin looked at her watch. "Thomas, they took him in about seven-fifteen?"

"Something like that." He stood to pace the waiting room.

Harry silently watched our interactions. I'd forgotten Gin and Thomas had not yet met him and made quick introductions.

Two armchairs stood on either side of a couch, and a coffee table sat between them. Alex tugged me toward the couch and pulled me down beside her. The heat of her thigh on mine felt comforting.

Harry sank into one of the side chairs and swung his feet up onto the coffee table. "Did they get the person who did it?"

Gin had returned to her post by the window. "The police got a description from some of the witnesses."

The door to the waiting room opened, and I looked up, expecting to see a doctor. Instead we got a six-foot, blond-haired man in a wool overcoat and a pinstriped, three-piece suit. He glanced around the room, and then said, "Mr. and Mrs. McKenna?"

"Yes," Thomas answered reluctantly.

"Quenton Campbell, Hennepin County Attorney. Jon works for my office."

Now I recognized Campbell and his clipped, precise speech. He spoke carefully, enunciating his words clearly, probably so used to public speaking he no longer thought twice about it.

My father held a hand out and shook with him. "I'm Thomas, and this is my wife, Virginia." He put his hand on my arm. "This is my daughter, Cailin, her partner, Alex, and Harry Robinson."

Campbell went to my mother and shook her hand, murmuring something I couldn't hear. Then he turned to face the rest of us, every part of him positioned appropriately to radiate compassion. "I'm so sorry. I came as soon as I heard. I'm glad they brought you to a semiprivate waiting room. Is there any news about Jon?"

"Nothing." Thomas didn't bother to hide the strain in his voice. "Jon was in critical condition when they brought him into surgery."

"I want you to know I've got the police, the sheriff's department, and our offices doing everything that can be done. I promise you we will bring whoever dared to hurt one of my people to swift and sure justice."

He sounded like a television ad.

Gin hugged herself and looked out the window again. "Are there any leads?"

"Not yet, but rest assured, I'll personally let you know as soon as I hear anything."

The door opened again, and this time a doctor dressed in light-green scrubs came in. "Are you the family of Jonathan McKenna?"

"Yes," Thomas said.

Alex grabbed my hand.

"I'm Doctor Landry. Jonathan's out of surgery and in recovery. He's still in critical condition, but he's a fighter."

"How bad is it?" Gin asked.

The doctor stretched his neck. "There's only one stab wound, from Jonathan's lower abdomen and going up." He traced a finger across his own belly. "One kidney was nicked, and his lung collapsed. We repaired the lung, although we'll keep him on a ventilator for a while. Had to do a minor repair on the kidney. Now it's wait and see."

"What about his liver?" Thomas's voice was low. "They seemed to be concerned about that."

"Liver's fine. It wasn't damaged."

Gin inhaled sharply, and for a moment I wondered if she was going to lose it.

Dr. Landry said, "We'll keep you updated. Once Jonathan is settled in ICU, he can have two visitors at a time. He'll be sedated for now, so he won't be able to respond, but talk to him, let him know you're there. That always helps."

After fielding a few more questions, the doctor left, and Quenton Campbell bid his own goodbyes.

Gin gazed blankly around the room, exhaustion shadowing her eyes. "Why don't you kids go home and get some sleep. We'll call if there's any change."

I opened my mouth to argue, but Alex stopped me with a hand on my forearm. "I think Gin is right, Cailin. Your cell is always on." Alex sometimes knew me better than I knew myself. I didn't do well in hospitals, worse if I was the patient.

Alex squeezed my forearm reassuringly. I bit off a gasp and jerked my arm away. Alarmed, Alex glanced sharply at me. I caught her eyes and minutely shook my head. She gave me a confused nod but said nothing. I'd have some explaining to do when we got home. After a visit to the freezer for some ice.

We hugged Gin and Thomas and made our exit, taking Harry with us. As we descended to the first floor in silence, the question hit me that should have popped into my mind when Gin first called.

Why?

Why would someone do this? Was it random? Revenge from someone Jon had prosecuted? Who were my brother's enemies?

Harry broke off to find his car while I followed Alex to hers. As we made our way through the parking ramp, I pulled out my phone and dialed a number. I said a few words to the person on the other end and hung up.

Alex gave me a questioning glance. "What's gotten into you today?"

"Confidential informants are good to have," I told her. "If anyone can find out what's going on, Crab can."

"Crab?"

"Don't ask."

$$\star\ \star\ \star$$

Half an hour later, Alex and I sat at the kitchen table while she furiously Googled cold versus hot branding. Who knew such a thing even existed. Apparently cold branding wasn't all that common, but some information was available online. With a cold brand, I could anticipate pain equivalent to that of a hot burn, and both took about the same amount of time to simmer down. Eventually the area would scab and flake, and if I were a furred creature, my fur would most likely grow back white. My forearm was fairly hairless, so I didn't expect to see that phenomenon.

Alex said, "The brand won't be too big once the swelling goes down." She pulled something from her pocket and made a quick move toward my arm. I flinched and jerked away.

"Trust, Cailin. Stay still." She put her hand out. I gingerly gave her my wrist, and she held a coin near the raised cross. "I think it'll be no bigger than a quarter. Jesus. I can't believe they actually branded you."

"I can't imagine what my face must have looked like

when the Grand Poobah came at me. When that iron thing hit my skin, I was debating whether to pretend to pass out, do it for real, or just let it happen." I shuddered. "For a second I didn't feel anything, but I heard the sizzle. The fucking sizzle was loud, and it felt like my entire arm was on fire. It's amazing how something so small can hurt so goddamn much."

Alex made a sympathetic noise. "I wonder if anyone specializes in brand removal."

I studied my arm. "Doubt it. Maybe I could tattoo something over it. After I sue the NPIU." I yawned and checked my phone. No calls, no texts.

"Come on." Alex stood. "Let's try to get some sleep."

Chapter 15

Early the next morning, sun shone in a bright blue sky, a stark contrast to the darkness that hovered in my chest like a physical thing. We'd received no word from Gin or Thomas, so I hoped the night had been uneventful. I tried Gin's cell, and when she didn't answer, I called the hospital. Jon was still sedated, but he'd been upgraded to serious but stable condition.

Per Gin's direction, Alex left for the Gallery. I headed over to the hospital to give my foster parents a break.

A bored security guard at the information desk told me where to go, and I moved like a mouse in a maze through the hallways to Jon's room. I slowly pushed open his door, but there was no need. He was out for the count.

Tubes and wires protruded from his body like alien

weeds. He was so still. The only movement was the even rise and fall of his chest. His brown skin contrasted starkly to the whiteness of the sheets and blankets that covered his body. I fought back tears. He did not belong here.

I slid my fingers over his oh-so-still ones. I'd always protected him when we were young, when kids picked on him because of his mixed race or because he was prone to geekiness. I'd had my share of fights on his behalf. This time I hadn't been there, and while I knew it didn't make sense, I felt like I should have been.

I leaned in and stroked his forehead. He looked impossibly young. "Jon," I whispered, "I'll find whoever did this to you. I swear." I put two fingers to my lips and pressed them lightly against the tip of his nose. "I love you."

✳ ✳ ✳

A few hours later, Gin relieved my vigil, and I headed to work. A part of me wondered if that was a good idea, but a larger part didn't care, and I hadn't had any word from on high to stay away. The moment I stepped into my cube, I was paged to the director's office. Once my boss ascertained I was coherent, and that my branded arm wasn't going to fall off, he sent me packing. Harry had told both Singleton and Weatherspoon what had happened and filled them in on our last forty-eight hours. Unless something serious came up, I wasn't needed. So much for that.

I got back into the car and drove aimlessly, crossing

the light rail tracks on one street and again on another, looking for anything and coming up with nothing. My cell remained silent. No word from the hospital and no word from my CI.

The question of who would stab my brother continued to haunt me. Was it a coincidence? Or could it possibly have something to do with his stance on the school shooting case? Would I ever know?

Eventually I called it quits and drove home. My arm ached, and my head pounded. I threw myself on the couch and one-armed a throw pillow against my chest. My mind bounced from the Jubilee to Jon. I was on overload, and I knew it. They say meditation is good for stress, so I tried to focus on my breathing.

The next thing I knew, something touched my face.

I pried an eye open.

Alex knelt next to me, cupping my cheek with her palm. "Hey, baby. You okay?"

I must have slept hard. For a moment, blissful mindlessness surrounded me...and then reality blew that feeling away. I peeled my tongue off the roof of my mouth and tried to swallow. "Yeah. What time is it?" I rolled onto my back. Alex settled on the edge of the couch next to my leg.

"Almost seven. How long have you been out?"

I blinked. Blinked again. "Couple hours."

Alex ruffled the hair on the top of my head. "Pick called on the way home. Invited us to a party at Jada's tonight. Want to go? Might do you some good." A smile deepened the dimple in her cheek.

I pushed myself up and rubbed my eyes. "I don't know. Wouldn't feel right with Jon injured so badly. I should run over to the hospital."

"I called Gin after I talked to Pick. Jon's the same. The doc said things are looking good. I told Gin about the party, and she said you should go if you felt like it. Told me all you'd do at the hospital is sit and stew and make her crazy. She's got both our cell numbers, and she'll call right away if anything changes."

I didn't feel like doing anything but going back to sleep. Alex caught the expression of refusal I was sure was written all over my face. "Come on. We only have to stay for a while. We can leave whenever you want."

"The only reason you want to go is to get your hands on some of Jada's appetizers."

Alex smiled. "Guilty. Pick said she thought Jada would serve her Mexican-chocolate mousse, too."

I had to admit, Jada's Mexican-chocolate mousse was amazing. "You drive a hard bargain, sister. What time's the party?"

★ ★ ★

An hour later we pulled up a block away from Jada's place, which wasn't far from Lake of the Isles. Parking in Uptown is usually a nightmare, but Monday nights are quiet, and we found a spot without much trouble. Jada lived in a rehabbed fire station. The upstairs and the main floor were still connected by the brass pole. I loved that damn pole, the feel of the smooth metal sliding through the crook of my arm, and the fun ride down. Jada herself never used it, but it was a great conversation starter.

I knocked.

Muffled music seeped outside. A moment later Jada opened the door. She was dressed in swaths of lavender and pink chiffon. She looked like an overgrown lava lamp. I was smart enough to keep that comment to myself and settled on something between snark and truth. "You're looking rather floaty tonight."

Jada did a pirouette, her cornrows and their multicolored ribbons swinging wildly. The colors set off the rich burnt umber hue of her skin.

"Wow," Alex said. "We could set you up in the center of the show floor at the Gallery."

"Thank you, Alex. I'll take that as a compliment. Don't just stand there. Get inside. The party's full-steam ahead, and in a little while, Bronwyn Calais is doing some readings."

"Bronwyn Calais, the psychic?" I asked. Calais was a semi-famous local personality who had, on occasion, assisted the police on different cases. Word had it she might be the real deal. I'd never met her, but I had seen ads for her readings at the Eye of Horus in Minneapolis.

"One and the same. Now in you go." Jada gave my butt a healthy swat.

"Come on, before she beats you into submission." Alex grabbed my elbow, careful to avoid my sore forearm, and pulled me through the door.

The interior decorating was similar to the way Jada adorned herself. Gauzy, pastel curtains hung over the windows, and her furniture was over-sized, primary colored, and surprisingly comfortable. The walls in the living room were scarlet and cinnamon. Candles burned in holders on the walls, setting a cozy, glam-medieval tone.

The music playing was DrumHeart, a Minneapolis-based drumming group. The infectious rhythms came through speakers strategically placed throughout the house.

In the living room, groups of women sat in clusters on chairs or relaxed on huge pillows scattered on the floor. I recognized some of the faces from previous parties and a few from past clandestine hookups. Before Alex, and after Eli, I'd decided that I wasn't cut out for long-term relationships. I created a two-day rule—no more than two days with the same girl. Figured that would protect us both. I gained a reputation as a player but not a stayer, and I made sure the women I went home with understood that. I'd successfully followed my two-day stipulation until Alex came along. Then, my rule flew right out the window, along with my non-monogamous ways.

Fabulous aromas permeated the place. Alex made a beeline for the kitchen and I followed.

Crossing the threshold from Jada's living room into her kitchen was like walking from one world into another. In contrast to the richness of the living room, the kitchen was a study in light. Pale green walls, cream ceramic tile floor, Empress green marble countertops. Gleaming silver pots and pans hung from an overhead grid and screamed "chef."

The counters held every kitchen accouterment known to humankind as well as a few that weren't. A freestanding butcher-block counter was littered with an assortment of palate-tempting goodies. Bright pink punch, known as Jada's Happy Juice, filled a crystal bowl. The very-alcoholic concoction was legendary for its kick. Looked like Barbie, knocked you out like Xena.

Women milled around the butcher block snagging hors d'oevres. Pick leaned against one of the counters, deep in conversation with a cute tomboy I recognized from parties past.

Alex grabbed a plate and started loading up as she fell into conversation with another woman. I scooped a ginormous portion of chocolate mousse onto my plate.

Pick caught sight of us and came over. "Look what the Jersey girl dragged in." She swiped some mousse off my plate with a finger and stuck it in her mouth.

I gave her a warning glare.

She ignored me and licked her finger clean. "How's Jon? Alex told me what happened."

My mouth was full, so I nodded and swallowed. "Stable."

"They get the bastard who did it?" Pick ladled herself some punch and leaned against the wall next to me.

"Not yet."

"I'm going to the hospital tomorrow. Thought it would be good to check in." Pick had hung around the McKenna household plenty while we'd been in high school. Gin and Thomas viewed her as another daughter.

Alex came back with a full plate. "They'd like that. Thomas has taken the next couple days off from school, and I'm covering the Gallery for Gin."

The kitchen door opened and Jada sashayed in. "Five minutes, ladies. Five minutes and Bronwyn Calais starts doing readings free of charge, so come and get it while you can." She dramatically clapped twice and flounced off.

Bronwyn Calais was tiny. She couldn't have been more than five feet tall, with sharp features and an aquiline nose. She was dressed in black, her movements graceful and controlled. She sat cross-legged on the couch, her cards before her on the coffee table. A number of pillows had been rearranged in front of the table.

A tall woman with ash-brown hair pulled back in a messy French braid sat across from Bronwyn. Her name was Kat, and I recalled a pleasurably brief fling I'd had with her. She had some issues with multiple sclerosis but was managing it well. Graphic design was her thing, and she illustrated Manga comic books.

Bronwyn spread a black velvet cloth across the coffee table and shuffled her Tarot cards. She then offered the deck up to Kat to cut.

The only sound came from the drumming music in the background that someone had turned way down. Kat cut the deck, and Bronwyn laid the cards out in a classic Celtic Cross spread. When she was done, Bronwyn said in a smooth voice, "Kat, are you ready?"

Kat nodded.

Leaning forward, Bronwyn studied the spread, then she sat back and took a deep breath. "The main issue is about your life and how it will play out. The Sun indicates contentment, freedom, creative inspiration. It's a positive card." She closed her eyes and began to sway slightly, her palms facing up as her hands rested on her knees.

"The center card, in this case the Wheel of Fortune, represents an obstacle, something you need to get around, or through. You're on your destiny's path." Bronwyn reached out to touch the edge of the card in question. She went on to explain the meanings of the rest of the cards. When she arrived at the last card, Bronwyn said, "This is the ultimate outcome. The Tower indicates a major change in your life, perhaps a new lifestyle, an entirely new direction." She looked squarely at Kat. "Aside from the reading, I feel pain you hold, pain deep inside. I feel this pain diminish as you focus on the final outcome."

"Thanks," Kat said with a rather patronizing smile. I didn't blame her.

Jada, the cheery cheerleader you secretly wanted to punch, said, "Okay, who's next?"

Pick elbowed me. "You should do it."

I shook my head.

"Come on, Cailin," she said, "it'll be fun."

"No thanks." The last thing I wanted was to have the fortune-teller inform me my future was in question.

Alex leaned against the wall next to me, an amused smile on her face as she watched the scene play itself out.

"Come on, Cailin. Sit down." Jada propelled me to the coffee table and, with a heavy hand, pushed me onto the floor. "Don't be a party pooper."

Bronwyn reshuffled her deck, and I cut it. With a few fast snaps of her wrist, she dealt the spread and stared at the cards with narrowed eyes. "Your first card, Temperance, represents balance, harmony. However, there is a quest in the offing. Something is not as it appears."

Here we go.

"Next, the Queen of Coins is your obstacle. Something sounds good, but in the end does not benefit you."

Was she talking about Eli? I shifted uncomfortably.

"The Five of Cups indicates your goal, your outcome without a change in your priorities. There will be a mistake, a betrayal, but it can be overcome."

Who would betray whom? For God's sake, why was I even thinking that? I didn't believe in this crap anyway.

"Your foundation is the Ten of Cups. You have much love, happiness. Balance." She closed her eyes and rocked slightly from side to side.

Now that sounded more like it. I glanced at Alex, and she grinned at me.

"Justice represents a release, an ending, vindication." Maybe I'd find whoever knifed Jon and give him his. Or maybe this was the indicator that we'd stop the Soldiers of Christ. If both happened, I might have to start believing in this hooey.

"The Queen of Staves represents something to be embraced, a person, perhaps. Sunny and brave, accomplished."

That would be my Alex.

"The base of your cross is the Wheel of Fortune. You must grab what you want before it goes by. There will be an unlikely coincidence. Care must be exercised." Bronwyn swayed faster and opened her eyes to look up at the ceiling. I was afraid she might rock herself right off the couch.

"The Ten of Staves indicates there will be a trial, a final trial before there can be a reward. A great struggle, a great reward. Or a great loss." Bronwyn's eyes slid shut, then she opened them and bent her head to the table again. "The Fool brings in unexpected elements, willfulness. Impulse. Instinct will guide you safely."

Now this was getting weird.

"Your last card..." She studied the spread and then looked at me, her eyes wild and intent. "The Devil. If you continue on the course of action you have chosen, there will be wickedness and danger. Life is challenged, death is on the precipice. Yours or someone else's. Soon."

Holy shit. Was she talking about Jon? This was bullshit. This was exactly why I didn't believe in this smoke-and-mirrors production.

Bronwyn broke eye contact and slowly gathered up the tarot cards. I saw that she was sweating and looked a little shaky. Weird.

As the next psychic victim eagerly sat, I went to Alex, who stood with Pick and Jada. I leaned close to Jada and whispered, "You fed her information, didn't you?"

"No." Jada held a hand up. "I swear. I didn't tell her a thing. Not about anyone. That was all her."

"Come on." Alex rolled her eyes as she took my hand. "You can't believe that. They play off your reactions. They're masters of reading people's emotions. It's a con."

I shook myself like a dog flinging off excess water. "That was creepy."

"You need a drink. Allow me." Pick headed for the punch bowl and returned moments later with two red plastic glasses that she handed to Alex and me.

Alex raised her glass. "Bottoms up."

I clinked plastic glasses with her and proceeded to down the entire contents. "What in God's name," I wheezed, "is in this?"

Jada let out a big, rolling laugh. "Everything but the kitchen sink, honey."

Chapter 16

My brain felt like it no longer fit in my skull. I cracked open an eye, and carefully raised my head to assess the situation. I was fully dressed, lying on the bed in one of Jada's spare bedrooms. Alex was on her stomach, asleep, next to me. A comforter lay over us. Designer shades covered the windows and blocked out most of the light trying to invade the room.

I cautiously rolled onto my side, took slow, deep breaths, and willed the contents of my stomach to stay where they belonged. My head throbbed a slow cadence, pounding with each thump of my heart.

I lay still and let my mind drift. The memory of the past evening washed over me in startling clarity. I remembered Pick and the huge glass of punch she had given me after my reading. I thought I recalled downing a few more while we played "50 Shades of Grey, the Party Game."

My mind floated aimlessly for a while until Jon popped into my head.

Oh, my God.

I jolted into a sitting position, breathed through a wave of nausea, and felt for my cell phone. It wasn't on my person, or on the bedside table. I was contemplating my chances of standing without throwing up when Alex stirred. She groaned and slowly propped herself on her elbows. A curtain of black hair shielded her face. "What the hell was in that punch?"

"Ancient Jada Secret. It's thinking about making a encore."

Alex cut her eyes toward me without moving her head. "Easy does it. Can't handle that right now." She wrapped her hands around her forehead. "Time?"

I held my watch up close to my eyes. "7:30. I need to check on Jon."

Very gingerly, Alex sat up. "God." She cradled her head in her hands again. "Most of last night is a big fat blur." She took a slow, even breath. "Someone would've called if anything changed."

Intellectually I knew that, but my guilt factor was in fine form. "I know. Doesn't make me feel much better about the fact I'm hung over and he's on a ventilator. Besides, I don't know where my phone is."

"You needed to blow off some steam. You know Gin and Thomas will understand."

I brought my fingers to my temples. Even my hair follicles hurt. On the bright side, the slightly-less-angry-looking cross on my arm wasn't throbbing. "Any idea where my phone is?"

"I think I put it on the nightstand next to you." I didn't find it there, so I gingerly stretched my arm toward the floor and felt around. The phone was partially under the bed, and it was vibrating when I wrapped my fingers around it. I brought it up to my face. Martinez's name filled the screen.

I hit accept and held it a few inches away from my ear. "What."

"Morning, chica," Martinez said. "You awake?"

"No. What's up?"

"We picked up Markus Simonson, small-time thief and minor league drug pusher. Was bragging to his friends about sticking it to some lawyer, and one of the friends happens to be a CI on Peterson's payroll."

"No shit." I carefully swung my legs to the side of the bed and levered myself up into sitting position. Alex laid a steadying hand on my back. "This guy talked?"

"Cried like a baby when we threatened to give his name to the drug lord whose territory he was jumping. He wouldn't be worth squat once Dice Man got hold of him."

Dice Man, whose real name was Marvin Busky, was well known to both police and the media. He was the controversial owner of Neon Lights, a semi-seedy strip club downtown. Somehow Dice managed to keep Neon Lights legit, the money clean, and the clientele hooked. For years, Minneapolis police suspected Dice was a drug kingpin, but he kept his above-the-table business dealings clean enough to stay out of trouble, and he'd never been nailed for his below-the-table dirty work. Word on the street was that he ran drugs through intermediaries he never met, but whom he paid well. He was careful and thus kept himself out of prison. He wasn't a man any hustler wanted to be on the wrong side of.

I found my shoes and leaned on the end of the bed to pull them on. I had the phone pinned between my ear and my shoulder. "What'd Simonson say?"

"Claimed he'd been paid by some guy who approached him while he was down with his homies. Gave him five grand to do your bro."

Bile bubbled in the back of my throat. I swallowed it. "Get an ID on that bastard?"

"Not yet. Got a description though."

"Cough it up." The bed dipped as Alex kneeled behind me and put her hands on my shoulders. I gratefully leaned back into her touch.

"Caucasian, thirties. Big guy, like three-fifty big. Pockmarked face, bald. Told Simonson he was working toward his own personal destiny."

"Destiny? What's that supposed to mean?"

"No idea. We got people checking all of Jon's cases to see who's in and who's out of the can. Maybe it's a revenge thing."

"Thanks, Manny. I appreciate the heads up."

"No sweat. Task force met yesterday. Jesus, McKenna. Branded?"

I sighed long and loud. "I know. Things I do for the

job. How's Harry's new decoration looking?"

"Painful. By the way, there's another meeting scheduled day after tomorrow at ten down here at the Fifth."

"Duly noted. Unless something happens with Jon, I'll see you then."

I disconnected, flipped the phone onto the bed, and sank into Alex. She wrapped her arms around me and rested her cheek on the top of my head. "They got him?"

"Yeah. He was approached by some jackass and offered five grand to do the job. We'll find out more as soon as we can." I reluctantly stood and stretched. "How are the preparations for the Gallery showing going?"

Alex crawled off the bed. "Going. There's a lot of things I'm not sure about, and with your mom gone, I'm kind of winging it."

I caught her chin and kissed the corner of her mouth. "Thank you."

★ ★ ★

On the way to work I called Gin. Everything was status quo. I was relieved, but still appalled at myself for getting plowed while Jon lay comatose in the hospital. Way to go, Cailin. Responsibility at its finest.

The morning dragged. Quenton Campbell had put in a request to move back Mike Lorenzo's certification hearing a few days while his office rearranged Jon's case load and court schedules.

I stopped by the Brain Trust to check in with Rosie

and Tony. They had nothing new to report but were dying to lay eyes on my new body decor. Rosie researched tattoo art and gave me a number of suggestions that might work for her but certainly did not for me. Her first idea was to tattoo the outline of a fist with a raised middle finger encompassing the brand. Things went downhill from there.

After that, I hit the paperwork bandwagon and spent the rest of the day drafting a report about the events of Jubilee weekend and filling out the endless injury-on-duty forms.

I wrapped things up after a quick word with Singleton, who claimed he wanted the latest on Jon, but I suspected he wanted to see for himself that I was okay. I relayed the conversation I'd had with Gin earlier in the afternoon. They were talking about removing Jon's ventilator in the morning, so things were improving.

Singleton examined my arm without displaying any emotion and booted me out of his office with an order to get some sleep.

I headed for the hospital and rode the elevator with two doctors and a nurse who looked like she hadn't slept for a week. We all could use a time-out. I made my way to Jon's room and paused outside the partially open door. I heard voices inside, and I didn't want to interrupt if the doctor was in. I listened for a few seconds, enough time to recognize trouble, and I burst into the room.

Jon lay unmoving, the beeping of machinery and the hiss of the ventilator the only indication he was alive.

Eli Knight had Gin herded into a corner of the room.

The expression on Gin's face was one of disbelief. My ex had a vase with flowers in her hands.

I crossed the room in three strides and furiously whispered, "What the hell do you think you're doing here?"

Gin looked relieved to see me, and I could feel anger rolling off her.

"Cailin," Eli said. "I was telling Gin how sorry I was to hear about what happened. I brought flowers to help brighten up the room." She thrust the bouquet at me, but I made no move to take it. After a moment, she pulled it back. "I knew you'd show up sooner or later. I've been patiently waiting. I'm here for you, baby."

Gin warily watched our exchange. She shifted sideways, probably ready to grab me if I made an untoward move at Eli. Gin knew me well—and the itch to wrap my fingers around Eli's throat was nearly impossible to ignore.

The blatant look of ownership on Eli's face infuriated me. "You've been staking out the hospital? You really have turned into a goddamn stalker."

"Cailin," Gin said, "keep it down." She shot a pointed glance at the bed, where Jon lay oblivious to the charged atmosphere.

"I wasn't stalking you," Eli whispered heatedly. "I just stopped by to see one of my employees and thought I'd check in."

Employee, my ass. I none-too-gently grabbed her arm. "And now you can check out." I steered her to the door and called over my shoulder, "I'll be back."

We rounded the corner, nearly taking out a wide-eyed orderly, and I jerked her to a stop in front of the elevators. "We need to talk."

"It's about time." A sanctimonious expression crossed Eli's face. "Let's go to the cafeteria."

I led the way without another word. Eli placed the flowers on the table and sat.

In an attempt to give myself a moment to calm down and think rationally, I filled a to-go cup with Mello Yello from the fountain, put the plastic lid on, and angrily stabbed the straw through the opening. I took a breath and willed myself to chill, but it wasn't working.

I stalked over to Eli and loomed over her. Without preamble I said in a low voice, "What the fuck do you think you're doing? You have no right to be here, no right to barge in on my family while my brother is on the edge of death. I told you to stay away. Permanently."

The tip of Eli's tongue snaked out to moisten her lips. The movement threw me into a visceral memory of what that tongue could do. Jesus Christ. I needed to wash my brain out with soap. I slid into the chair, and I was back in the moment. "I'm taking out a fucking restraining order to have your sorry ass handed to you when you violate the conditions. It obviously won't take long before you do."

Eli sat back in her chair, smug confidence radiating from her like a physical thing. I wanted to plow my fist directly into that confidence and take her down.

She crossed her legs, swinging a heeled foot. A perfectly shaped eyebrow rose. "You don't know what you want, my little lover. But that's okay. I can show you." Her tongue slipped out again, sliding wetly along her bottom lip. "I'm simply here to remind you of who can satisfy your every need."

Jesus. "No, Eli. I don't need anything from you. I never needed you, and I get that now."

She leaned forward and put her hand on my non-branded forearm, lightly running her fingernails toward my wrist. Goosebumps rose and I yanked my arm away, glad she hadn't touched the branded arm. "Stop."

"Poor Cailin. Always trying so hard. Do the right thing this time. We both know I'm the best thing that's ever happened to you."

"Fuck you." I stood abruptly. I needed to get out from under the web she was weaving, mentally and physically. I hated her ability to turn our arguments around until I had no idea which end was up.

Her gaze could only be defined as sultry. "Would you please get me a glass of water since you're up? I'm feeling...hot."

I'd be more than happy to dump a bucket of ice directly over the witch's hot little head. I stomped off, peevish but obedient. A part of me recognized I was sliding back into a habit I thought I'd forever banished. Goddamn it. What kind of hold did she still have over me? I wasn't hers anymore, and from here on, I'd never again ask how high when she told me to jump. This was it. I returned and slammed the glass of water on the table. Liquid sloshed over the rim of the chipped amber plastic cup.

"Thank you." Eli picked up the glass and took a sip,

her ice-blue eyes boring into me. "See? Nothing's changed. I always could make you do whatever I wanted, and I still can."

"Fuck you." I picked up my drink and glugged it down, the burning sensation of carbonation grounding me as it slid down my throat. "I don't ever want to see you near any of the people in my life again. You stay away from me, from Alex, from the McKenna's, from my job, from our cars. Tomorrow I'm filing that restraining order. If you so much as show your face near any of us, you're done."

We argued back and forth, with Eli countering everything I said with her version of reality. She was like a termite, burrowing into the very core of me. Where was a good exterminator when you needed one? The stress of the confrontation made my head ache and my stomach hurt.

I rubbed my temples. "I need to go. We're not getting anywhere. I'm done." I stood, but every muscle in my body suddenly felt loose. Yes, I decided, time to quit. That's what I was going to do, and my body agreed with my decision. My knees gave out and abruptly I sat back down. Somehow gravity had tripled, gluing my ass to the hard plastic seat. I peered curiously down at my legs, which felt distinctly separated from my body, and then gazed back up at Eli. My lips felt stiff, and I was having a hard time focusing on the red-headed devil. "I feel strange." My voice sounded miles away.

"Come on, you need some fresh air." She grabbed my arm and pulled me up. The floor was rolling like a ship in twenty-foot swells. At least I was in the hospital if I fell off the deck. I knew I was supposed to be pissed at Eli, but I was fast forgetting why.

Eli held tight to my undamaged arm, and I allowed her to steer me outside. I pulled in a lungful of air, then another, but it didn't do much to clear my head.

"Let's get you to your car. I think you should go home." Maybe she wanted me to kill myself, since I wasn't sure I was in any condition to drive. But maybe I could drive. I stumbled over nothing. Yeah, I needed to sit down for a couple of minutes.

We made it through the parking lot to the ramp, and my legs only gave out once. Eli jerked me up, so I didn't fall. My mind blurred, and it took every ounce of concentration I had not to slither to the ground like a limp noodle.

Eli's voice swirled around me. In front of me. No, it was coming from somewhere behind. But she was walking along next to me. I was so confused.

"I can drive you to your car. Mine's right over here."

I vaguely felt her push me into her passenger seat and pull the seat belt around me. I inhaled and opened my mouth to speak. Suddenly my vision narrowed, and an inky, strangely comforting blackness enveloped my head and spread like slow-moving lava into my chest and down my limbs, until the black filled every crevice of my being. The lava was everything, and then it became nothing at all.

Chapter 17

I felt warm, languid, and headachy, like I was hung over from a good night of booze and sex. I nuzzled into the soft pillow under my head. Stretching like a cat, I enjoyed the feel of smooth sheets against my skin. I slowly rolled over onto my back, eyes closed, savoring the moment.

I reached out and felt for Alex. It took a few long seconds before it dawned on me she wasn't in bed. She was probably downstairs whipping up some after-love breakfast. I opened my eyes and gazed at the ceiling for a second before allowing gravity to pull the lids shut again.

Something was wrong. I opened both eyes and tried to focus. The ceiling was still there, but it was an unfamiliar light green, not the white it was supposed to be.

I considered the possibility that Alex had grown bored with her artwork and decided to liven up the bedroom in pale mold.

Sleepy. I was so sleepy. My head pounded, and maybe if I went back to sleep, it wouldn't hurt so much. I drifted in and out for a while. Eventually, I figured I should get up and see what was taking Alex so long. I rolled my head to the side to check the time. Where was my alarm clock? In fact, where was my nightstand?

I sat up with a jolt that made my head swim. I wasn't in our bedroom. I was in a bedroom I'd never seen before. I struggled to sit up, my heart racing. Across the room was an unfamiliar dresser, an unfamiliar entertainment center with a flat-screen TV, and mirrored doors leading to an unfamiliar closet.

My panicked gaze caught sight of a small statue of an eagle in flight on top of the dresser. I'd given that statue to Eli on our first anniversary.

Oh, my God. I was in Eli's bed. Which meant I was in Eli's bedroom. Which meant I was in Eli's house.

What the hell was I doing here?

I looked down at myself and saw bare flesh. I slowly picked up the edge of the blanket. I wasn't wearing anything on my bottom half either. I stumbled in my haste to vacate the bed and closed my eyes at the light-headed feeling my abrupt movement caused. Where were my clothes? I spotted them, folded neatly over the back of an armchair. My gun was on the seat, still safely in its holster. I made it to the chair and grabbed my pants.

"Eli!" I shouted. Where was that little shit? I dressed

in a hurry and opened the shade, revealing a bright, sun-filled day. I was many stories above the city. I felt some measure of relief to recognize skyscrapers that I knew belonged in Minneapolis. At least I wasn't somewhere completely unfamiliar.

Slow-burning dread and confusion clouded my still-muzzy brain. The glowing green digits of an alarm clock on the opposite nightstand read 12:45.

I wasn't even sure what day it was. I left the bedroom and crossed into a well-appointed living room. The space was huge, furnished expensively, and void of Eli. A sheet of folded pink paper was taped to the front door. It looked like the same stationery that had been sent to my house. I peeled the sheet off the door and opened it.

Last night was incredible. Better than ever. You were an animal. You couldn't get enough of me. I can't remember the last time you came to me with that much passion, that much raw need.

Speaking of coming, I think five times might be a new record. You cried out my name so sweetly. I loved bringing you to the brink, teasing you, and then driving you over the edge when I decided it was time. You are mine again, and it feels so right.

You returned the favor with a vengeance, my lover. I am so sore in all the right places. You were amazing. Now everything is the way it should be. You will not regret what you've done, what you've said, what you have chosen. I'll see you tonight.

All my love,
Eli

My hands shook so hard I nearly ripped the paper in

half. Did I really do Eli? I closed my eyes, rested my forehead against the doorframe, and tried to eke out any glimmer, any scrap of memory. The last thing I recalled with any clarity was feeling strange at the hospital. The hospital. That bitch.

Eli must have slipped a roofie-type drug into the soda I'd purchased in the cafeteria. I recalled feeling weak and dizzy after I finished the beverage. I vaguely remembered her saying she'd drive me to my car, but I recollected being buckled into hers. Everything after that was a complete blank until I awakened a short time ago.

Could I have slept with Eli? Could I have been responsive enough not only to receive, but give? I shuddered and swallowed an hysterical wail. Nausea rose again, and I whispered aloud, "What am I going to tell Alex?"

"Goddamn it, Eli." I punched the door hard. And did it again. And again. "What did you do to me?" The pain in my hand eclipsed the pounding of my head, and I stopped. "Fucking hell." I shook my bruised hand. Beating the crap out of an inanimate object wouldn't do anyone any good. I backed up and took a couple slow, deep breaths. My head began to clear.

I had no idea what day it was. I searched my pockets for my phone and came up empty. I went back and scoured the bedroom. No luck. What had she done with it? Alex and my family had to be worried sick, and I'd missed the ten o'clock meeting at the Fifth Precinct.

Rage was single-mindedly overshadowing my hysteria. I stuffed the note in my pocket, stomped to the front door, and left, slamming it shut behind me. I found myself in a short, elegant hall that led to a set of elevator doors. Plush beige pile cushioned my footsteps, and the walls were painted sage with darker green trim, in a tasteful kind of sloppy that costs a small fortune. Eli's was apparently the only apartment on the floor.

I didn't see an operating panel to call the elevator to come get me the hell out the devil bitch's lair. Instead, a box was mounted to the right side of the elevator doors that accepted a swipe card of some kind.

Loudly proclaiming my frustration, I went back to the apartment, amazed the door swung open when I turned the knob. To the immediate right was one of those reception-type tables that wasn't big enough for much more than keys and mail. An empty bud vase and a basket took up most of the space. The basket was empty except for a white plastic card. The card itself held no writing, but a magnetic stripe was imbedded on the opposite side.

I snatched it up and stalked back out to the elevator, expecting the worst. I swiped the card, and a green light appeared on the card reader. Well. One move worked out right today. I waited impatiently and was pacing back and forth like a caged cat when the doors of the elevator slid open. I pocketed the card and stepped inside. After another few seconds of figuring out what to do to make the thing descend, I was on the express ride to the ground. When I burst out of the lobby onto the sidewalk, I realized I had no wheels and didn't even know exactly where I was. I went back in and talked to the security guy who informed me it was Wednesday and called me a taxi.

At ten past two, I paid an atrocious amount to retrieve my car from the hospital parking ramp. For about two seconds, I considered a blood test, and then let that thought go. Most often drugs like that disappear from the bloodstream too fast to be detectable, anyway. I felt bad for not going inside to see Jon and the McKennas, but not guilty enough to do anything about it. My mind was locked on one track. Eli was about to get it, and not at all in the way she wanted.

As I drove through the myriad of one-way streets toward the IDS Center, I wracked my brain for any inkling, any scrap of memory between the time I talked to Eli in the cafeteria to waking up naked in her bed. Nothing. Not a fucking thing.

✷ ✷ ✷

The elevator doors slid open to the Great Lakes lobby. I stalked straight past the reception desk and around the partition onto the work floor.

This time the main floor was alive with the din of an ad agency in high gear. Workers conferred, laughed, and argued like it was any other day. I stormed right through the middle of the huge room. The buzz ceased as people caught sight of me charging through their midst. Eli was in her office with Randall the hamster, the same man who had interrupted us the last time I'd been there.

I barged in without knocking. "Excuse us, Randy. I need to speak to Eli." I grabbed him by the arm, propelled him out of the office, and slammed the door. I spun on

Eli, who was leaning back in her chair, a knowing smirk on her face.

"What the fucking hell." I rounded the desk. "What did you do to me, you little freak?"

"God, you're so hot when you go all commando. Just like last night. You showed me exactly how you feel, sweetheart." The corners of her mouth deepened into a lewd smile. "I knew you'd finally see the light."

I braced my hands on the arms of her chair and went nose to nose. "I should arrest you for drugging and kidnapping a federal agent."

One manicured eyebrow arched. "The sounds you made last night weren't complaining, baby. You begged for more."

Catty fucker. "You're insane." I had never hit anyone except in the line of duty, but I was dangerously close to laying her flat.

"Your body told me how much you missed me. After the first time I got you off, you told me you'd never, never come that hard. You cried out my name. *My* name, Cailin. I'm the one who knows how you like it." Eli gazed out at the work floor. All work had ceased, and everyone stared at the spectacle in their boss's office. "I told my entire staff," she waved an arm toward the window, "that you've finally come back to me. Just like I knew you would. Do you remember how you cried, how you begged for me, Cailin?"

She put a hand on my forearm, and her fingertips grazed the edge of the cross. I hissed in pain and yanked my arm away. That was the last straw. I blew like a geyser.

I grabbed the lapels of Eli's tailored blazer and propelled her to her high-heeled feet. I snarled, "You fucking monster. I will not—ever—come back to your sorry, scheming ass." I shook her. Out of the corner of my eye, I saw movement through the glass as though the cast of "The Walking Dead" was perambulating closer.

Eli's grabbed my wrists for balance and arched into me with a guttural moan. "Oh, yes, I love the new you."

"Eli, I swear to God. This is it. I am through with your bullshit."

She inhaled sharply. "This dom side of you, I can't get enough. Last night was so goddamn good. Truly fucking amazing. I cannot wait to have you again." She ground her hips against me, and I couldn't shove her back into her chair fast enough.

My entire body vibrated with rage, and my head felt like it would split open. I could barely restrain myself from backhanding her. "Listen, you malicious bitch. Whatever happened last night wasn't me. There won't be a next time." I grabbed the front of her jacket again and pulled her closer, my lips a breath from hers. How could I have ever thought they were kissable? "Stay away from me and mine, you crazy fuck. If you don't, I swear to God I'll shoot you dead."

I shoved Eli again, and the chair rolled backward. I had to admit I enjoyed seeing a glimmer of fear reflected in those icy eyes.

I turned my back on her and opened her door. Eli called out, loud enough for her staff to hear, "I'll see you for dinner at six, sweetheart."

"Like hell you will," I bellowed and marched out, feeling eyes bore into me as I beat a hasty retreat.

Back in my car, I gripped the steering wheel with both hands and took slow, deep breaths. If I had any hope of reducing the throbbing in my head, my pulse needed to come out of the red zone.

As I calmed, it occurred to me that the confrontation was the closest I'd ever been to committing homicide.

I waved halfheartedly at our neighbor lady, who was pulling weeds from her lawn, and trudged up to the back door of my house. How could everyone be so fucking cheerful today?

Once inside, I allowed the safety and familiarity of home to surround me. The pain in my head had finally dropped to a tolerable level, but the pain in my heart was nearly unbearable.

I shouted, "Alex?"

Almost immediately, she appeared at the top of the stairs and took the steps down two at a time. I caught her when she reached the bottom.

Alex wrapped her arms around my neck and hugged me ferociously. "Where have you been? Are you okay?"

I buried my head in her neck and burrowed into the softness of her hair. I breathed her in and tried to choke down the gigantic lump that rose in my throat. I had no idea how she would react after I told her what happened.

Alex pushed me gently away. She peered into my eyes

with such a look of concern and fear that it took my breath away. "Cailin, what happened?"

I wondered if she'd still look at me like that once I confessed. I opened my mouth, but I couldn't force any words out. Shame, anger, and disbelief immobilized me. Combined with the traumatic weekend, I simply shut down.

Without another word, Alex led me into the living room to the couch. She sat down and gathered me into her arms, holding on until, eventually, I relaxed into her.

After many long minutes, I straightened. "Okay. I'm sorry. I don't even know how to begin."

She turned to face me and tucked a leg beneath her. Deep, black smudges ringed bloodshot eyes. She looked like she hadn't slept at all. "Jesus, you're scaring me. Start at the beginning. Just tell me what happened."

I wanted to memorize the love that shone so clearly on her face, because I was about to wipe it off, maybe for good. "No matter what, remember how very much I love you. Okay?"

Alex nodded, and I felt both confusion and trepidation pouring off her.

"Yesterday after work I went to the hospital. Eli was there. Right there in the goddamn room with Gin and Jon."

"Gin told me. That was the last she saw of you."

"That was the final fucking straw. I marched Eli downstairs to the cafeteria and let her have it. Told her I was taking out a restraining order."

Keeping my eyes averted from Alex's probing gaze, I

continued, staring at the black screen of the TV. "We got to the cafeteria and I bought myself a pop. Eli wanted some water, so I left the pop on the table and went and got it for her." I closed my eyes in disgust. "Just like it used to be. She spoke and I jumped." I rubbed my face and leaned forward, elbows on my knees. "So I came back to the table with her water and argued and threatened her, but she just sat there like a fucking prima donna."

I went on to describe the rest of the experience, how she must have slipped me a drug, and then I stopped speaking. I wracked my mind to recall something. Anything.

Alex put her arm on my back, and her fingers toyed with my hair. The only change I felt in her relaxed posture was a quickening of breath.

I said, "And...then I have nothing, no memory, until I woke up today." I looked Alex straight in the eye. "I woke up in Eli's apartment, or condo, whatever the fuck it was. I woke up in her bed. Naked."

Alex's eyebrows shot up, her mouth opened, and she snapped it shut.

My breath caught in my throat, but I pushed on, my voice tight. "She wasn't there. I found a note on the door." I pulled out the crumpled sheet from my pocket and thrust it at Alex. She took it, and her eyes skimmed quickly down the page. I had to give her credit. If I'd been in her shoes I would have been fit to be cuffed, storming about, preparing to do something really stupid.

When Alex finished, she slowly folded the note and placed it on the coffee table. Then she brought narrowed eyes up to mine. "That little bitch. Jesus fucking Christ."

"I don't know what happened last night. I can't remember a goddamn thing. I've tried. I can't believe what I might have done with her." I shifted to face Alex. My heart thundered so hard in my chest I was afraid it might burst right out of me. "I don't know what to say. I'm so sorry."

Alex looked at me, her gaze even. "She drugged you."

"Yes." Needing to feel grounded, I reached out my hand and gently touched Alex's cheek with my thumb. "I cheated on you last night."

She turned her face into my palm and kissed it. "Oh, Cailin. Baby. You don't smell like sex. You don't smell like her at all. I don't know what happened last night either, but if you were drugged, isn't that kidnapping or something? And wouldn't it be rape, if she actually did it?"

"Yeah. But I have no proof." My pulse was slowing, and I thought I might be able to breathe again. "Her word against mine."

"Did she hurt you?"

I considered that. My entire body felt stiff and somewhat sore when I woke up, but that could have been from being drugged and then lying in one position for a long time. If we'd had such dominating sex as Eli claimed, wouldn't I feel it a lot more? The only part of me that hurt at the moment was the knuckles on my right hand. They were skinned, and bruises were coming up on the bottom two fingers. I hoped I'd left a dent in her door.

"No," I said, "I don't think she hurt me at all."

Alex studied me speculatively. "I tried to call you

repeatedly. Didn't you get my messages?"

I shrugged. "I don't know where my phone went. Eli might have dumped it. I should probably report it missing."

"Yes. And you need to call your parents and Martinez. Let them know you're okay. I've got to get to the Gallery. Gin's at the hospital, so we didn't open up since I was trying to find you."

"Have you heard how Jon's doing?"

Alex's smile was genuine. "They lowered his knockout medication, and he woke up about ten this morning. He's weak, but okay. Sounds like everything is healing."

I rested my forehead on clasped hands. At least one thing went right today. I allowed my eyes to drift shut. I was so tired. "I'll call Gin, and the Bureau. I missed a meeting this morning."

Alex put her hand under my chin and gently tugged until I looked at her. "Cailin, I love you with every beat of this heart." She grabbed my hand and put it against her chest. "I don't know what happened last night. We might never know. But I do know that I trust you. I know that you wouldn't hurt me if you could help it. You weren't aware, you...it's like you weren't even there."

I reached for her and she held me tight.

After some long minutes, I reluctantly released her and she got ready to leave for the Gallery. Once she left, after another lingering embrace, I picked up the cordless phone and made my calls. Jon was grumpy, which I took as a good sign. Gin was happy I hadn't skipped town with

Eli and furious I hadn't let her know where I was. I didn't think it would be a good idea to tell her I hadn't known where I was, so I blamed my absence on work.

After that, I called Weatherspoon and apologized for missing the meeting. I had a pretty good attendance record so Weatherspoon let it go. Probably figured the trauma of the branding and my brother's stabbing was enough to cause some temporarily erratic behavior. I also told him I accidentally dropped my cell in the toilet and needed a replacement.

After that, I rang Martinez, but the call went to voicemail. I left him a message.

I was starving and headed to the kitchen to remedy that. I hadn't eaten anything since lunch the day before, so while I waited for Martinez to call back, I made myself a ham sandwich. I was halfway through it when the phone rang.

"McKenna," I answered.

"Where the hell have you been?" Martinez was pissed.

"Long story. Can't get into it, it's personal."

Martinez made an unhappy sound. "Is it Eli again? Mrs. McKenna told me that two-timing whore came to the hospital, and you got there in time to stop her from grabbing the flowers out of that bitch's hand and beating her with them. Then you disappeared with the crazy woman. I'll take her out for you."

"Martinez. It's okay. I'm okay. I can handle it." He'd stuck pretty close to my side after I'd kicked Eli out and had watched me drown my sorrows in Jack more than once. When I hit the floor he'd pick me up and bring me home. Nice to have colleagues on my side.

"Fine. Eleven tomorrow. The NPIU field office. Robinson'll bring you up to speed." Martinez hung up before I could say anything else. Clearly he wasn't happy with me, but he'd get over it. I felt moody and angry, completely unsettled. I tried to decide if my body ached in the way it sometimes did after an aggressive round of shaboinking with Alex, and I kept coming around to the feeling that no, it did not.

I trudged into the bedroom and stripped, scrutinizing myself in the mirror for any marks that might've been left on my skin. I didn't see a thing that hadn't already been there. No bruising, no bite marks, nothing.

The specter of what Eli might have done or what I might have done in return wouldn't let go. Was she speaking truth? I was now completely doubtful. It was entirely possible she was blowing smoke, talking big. That was one of her most patented MO's, but it was also within her skill-set to do all of those things she claimed to have done. Without memory, who knows what happened. Rohypnol—the infamous roofie—if that's what she used on me, was a date rape drug, but I'd never been up close and personal. Until now, perhaps. I knew roofies weren't uncommon in the party crowd and plenty of rapists had used the drug with impunity. So I settled on the couch with the laptop and Googled it.

Fast-acting, check. Loss of muscle control, check. Headache, check. Dizziness, check. Loss of memory, check. Eli could lie through her teeth, and I may never know if we did or did not have sex. After ten minutes of surfing and no solid answers, I shut the laptop down and set it on the coffee table.

Sometime later, Alex came home. I'd fallen sound asleep sitting on the couch. The headache had faded into a dull echo in the back of my skull, and I gladly allowed Alex to lead me to bed.

Later, I dreamed I was back on the streets, ruled by desperation and hunger. I was so starved for affection that I was willing to do anything for it. Eli appeared and offered me repentance and rebirth. She reached out, her blue eyes glowing with unholy fire. In a blink, I was running hard but getting nowhere. Suddenly a life-size hamster appeared and dragged me to its den by the scruff of my neck. I struggled to escape, but couldn't. I awoke with a start.

The silence of the bedroom soothed my racing heart, and the alarm clock assured me it was still the middle of the night. I lay back down and tried to slow my breathing.

Alex rolled over and curled into my side. "You okay?" she mumbled.

"Yeah," I whispered, "go back to sleep."

I was thankful to be in my own bed and not stuck in some fucking hamster den, or worse yet, held prisoner in Eli's bed.

Chapter 18

I was at work by eight the next morning. Weatherspoon had left a requisition form on my desk so I could get a new cell phone. I occupied myself with paperwork for numerous other cases I was working and read the recently filed reports about the school shooting cases.

Near eleven, I went to find Harry. I ran into Rosie, who was on a snack run and momentarily separated from her computer. Briefly, I filled her in on what had happened the night before last with Eli. She was, in turn, freaked, then furious.

We stopped at the vending machine, and Rosie fed quarters into the slot. Once the machine swallowed the last coin, she punched in the numbers of her selection. "If

I were you I'd kidnap that stupid shit and let us work her over. What a crazy bitch." A Kit Kat dropped into the retrieval pan and Rosie grabbed it.

I said, "I have no proof anything happened. Well, except for being knocked out and waking up in her apartment."

"Naked and in her bed." Rosie savagely ripped the wrapper open and waved the candy bar at me.

"No, thanks. It's all yours." I couldn't think about this anymore. "What's new in the ether?"

Rosie took a big bite and mumbled, "Less than half the states have Soldiers of Christ chapters. Total membership across the U.S. varies from three thousand to over ten thou, depending on whose numbers you take. Not all chapters are active." She stuffed another chunk of the Kit Kat in her mouth. I was going to be impressed if she polished off the entire thing in three chomps.

She swallowed and cleared her throat. "Here's one interesting item. Only a few of the chapters are involved in Proposition Playground. That's what they're calling their push to recruit kids. The CDs and jump drives are definitely manufactured in Minneapolis, although they may be recorded elsewhere. We're sifting that now."

Harry ambled around the corner. "There you are, Cailin." He was dressed in a sea-blue sweater and tan cargo pants, and his hair was slicked back, shiny with some kind of gel. If things went south with the NPIU, he could take up a second career as a model.

His gaze momentarily focused on me and then zeroed in on Rosie. "Hey, Rosie." Harry propped an arm on the vending machine. "What you got there?"

Rosie looked at the last of the candy bar melting between her fingers. "Kit Kat. Bite?"

"Sure."

He opened his mouth and Rosie deposited the remnants. He chewed slowly, his eyes on hers. She licked her lips, and Harry caught the hand that had held the bar. The corner of his eye twitched as he slowly pulled her hand toward his mouth. No, he wasn't going to do what I thought he was—oh, yes. Yes, he was. He drew her two chocolate-coated fingers into his mouth. Gross.

"Oh, no." I clapped a hand over my eyes. "No, no, no. I'm too young for this."

Rosie actually giggled.

"Are you done?" I asked as I peered through my fingers.

Laughter rumbled through Harry. "Yes."

I dropped my hand and looked from Harry to Rosie. "You two have something to tell me?"

Rosie ducked under Harry's arm. "Sorry to run. Later."

Harry grinned and gave her a two-finger salute. "Later."

"Harry?"

"What?"

"You and Rosie?"

He shrugged. "Don't know."

"What do you mean, you don't know? I could have started my car from the electricity you two just generated."

Harry harrumphed and crossed his arms.

"Come off it, man. That's a classic defensive posture. You like Rosie." I looked closer at the set of his face. "You do like her, don't you?"

A flash of uncertainty flickered over his features. Uncertain wasn't a word I associated with him. "Maybe. She's definitely hot."

"I don't disagree. But if you're sucking her fingers clean, I think the answer's a whole lot more than maybe."

"I don't kiss or, in this case, suck fingers and tell. So where were you yesterday?"

My playful mood dissipated. Harry knew the Eli basics, but since he'd come to town, I hadn't had an opportunity to brief him on my ex-girlfriend-turned-stalker. I told him about the letters, the phone calls, Alex's slashed tires, and finally about Eli bullying Gin in Jon's hospital room and me subsequently finding myself in Eli's bed.

Harry listened quietly. "Let's take this into a con room."

Inside, he pulled the door closed and sat across from me. I put my hands, palms down, on the smooth tabletop. "With Eli—that's where I was yesterday, having the time of my fucking life."

Harry eyed me. "Why didn't you file a restraining order when she slashed the tires?"

That was a good question. Why hadn't I gone ahead and done it? There was something—I couldn't explain it—that still tried to draw me to Eli in a strange sick way. Maybe it was pheromones. Maybe it was a kind of unconscious dysfunction left over from the days on the street. I don't know what it was, but I felt ashamed because of it.

I forced myself to peer into Harry's eyes. They didn't hold judgment, simply concern.

"I don't know why I haven't done the restraining order yet. I thought I could handle her myself." Over Harry's shoulder was a sign posted above the door. "Watch the hands. The hands are what can hurt you." It was never truer than at this moment.

Harry tilted his chair back. "What'll you do now?"

"I'll file the order. I hate for everyone to know my business."

"I know. Do it anyway."

"I will. Now, what's going on?"

Harry rubbed the stubble on his chin. "I got a call yesterday morning from a member of the Soldiers of Christ inviting me and the 'little missus' to a gathering somewhere in St. Paul Sunday afternoon. They said we should get a big bang out of it."

"Big bang. Interesting choice of words."

"At the meeting you conveniently missed—"

I rolled my eyes.

The dimple in his cheek deepened. "As I was saying, at the meeting, I briefed everyone on our adventures 'Up North,' as you Eskimos say."

"Cold noses, warm hearts."

"Then I told them about our invite to Sunday afternoon's get-together. They're gonna wire us."

I nodded. "News on Mike?"

"Nothing." Harry rolled his shoulders. "Your county

attorney is hot to certify the kid. The guy's kind of an asshole, isn't he?"

"Yeah, aggressive and ruthless. Rumors are flying regarding his political aspirations."

"Scary."

"Tell me about it. Where is this shindig going down?"

"I'm supposed to get a call on the exact location Thursday night. Then we can plan it."

"Sounds good."

We bullshitted a few more minutes and then wrapped it up.

I ran into Weatherspoon on the way back to my cube and gave him an edited version of what had happened with Eli. With his blessing I headed over to the courthouse to talk to a lawyer friend I knew who could help me get the restraining order filed.

Having covered what bases I could, I went back to the NPIU offices, worked until after six, packed it up, and headed to the hospital.

Chapter 19

Friday morning gave new meaning to April showers. The way people were driving, one would think six inches of snow had fallen. I called to check on Jon, and things were thumbs up. Thomas told me Jon was having a busy day of tests and scans and kindly told me to stay away. So I did.

The NPIU had its own firing range in the basement of the Amethyst Building, and qualifications were coming up soon, so I worked on my shooting skills for almost three hours. I was cleaning my Glock when the range door opened and Weatherspoon appeared. "McKenna, a couple of Minneapolis detectives are asking for you upstairs."

"Sorry you had to come all the way down here, sir." There was no cell reception in the basement, and it was usually too noisy to hear the phone that was mounted on the wall in the hall outside the range. "Is it Martinez and Peterson?" I pulled the slide back and chambered a round.

"No. I haven't met these two before."

I dropped the magazine, loaded another bullet into it, and jammed the mag back into the gun. "They tell you what they wanted?"

"No. But they look serious."

I holstered my weapon. "Maybe it's about Mike."

We rode up the elevator in companionable silence. When the elevator doors slid open, I caught sight of two men I assumed were the MPD detectives. One was whipcord lean and brown-haired, while the other was stockier and blond. I approached them while Weatherspoon continued on toward his office.

"Cailin McKenna?" The blond held his hand out and I shook it.

"Yes, I am."

"I'm Detective Brad Hutchinson and this is my partner, David DeCamp, MPD Homicide."

"What can I do for you?"

DeCamp came closer, while Hutchinson moved to my flank. DeCamp said, "We have a few questions. Wondered if you'd come down to the precinct."

"About what?"

Hutchinson said, "The death of Elisa Knight."

My mouth literally dropped open. "What?"

"Early this morning," DeCamp said, "a jogger found the body of Elisa Knight on the west bank of the Mississippi not far from the Stone Arch Bridge."

"You've got to be kidding me. She put you up to this?" Now what had that conniving shit done to make my life miserable? I didn't believe for one minute she was dead.

"No, ma'am," DeCamp said. "I'm not kidding. Are you willing to come on down and talk with us?"

On the ride to the station, they showed me a crime scene photo that convinced me the body they'd found was actually Eli's. Next thing I knew, I was on the wrong side of one-way glass in a very small, very bleak First Precinct interrogation room facing DeCamp and Hutchinson across a table that looked like it barely made it out of World War II.

Hutchinson said, "You're not charged with anything at this point. We can stop at any time."

I waved my hand in dismissal. "I have nothing to hide. Can you tell me how she died?"

"We're not at liberty to divulge that at the moment," Hutchinson said. "We also don't have autopsy results yet."

Of course they couldn't tell me a damn thing. But they must have *some* evidence that it was a homicide, otherwise why would they have rounded me up?

A yellow legal pad sat on a manila file folder in front of DeCamp. He slid the folder from under the pad, and opened it. "When was the last time you saw Ms. Knight?"

"Day before yesterday." My insides roiled uneasily. While I was furious with Eli, I'd never hurt her. I maybe *wanted* to hurt her, but I could hold my temper.

DeCamp tapped his pen on the file. "Where?"

"Great Lakes Advertising, where she works.

Worked." Maybe I was having a far too lucid dream.

Hutchinson leaned forward, his sleeves rolled up past his elbows. "What time did you see her?"

"Sometime around five p.m."

Hutchinson gave me a speculative look. "How long were you there?"

An hour? A day? Time was jumbled. "I'm not sure. Maybe ten minutes."

"What did you do after you left the agency?" DeCamp didn't glance up from his folder. I wondered what he was looking at.

"I drove home and fell asleep on the couch."

DeCamp looked up at me. "Do you have anyone who could verify that?"

"Alex, my girlfriend. She was there when I got home."

Hutchinson's eyebrow twitched. I wondered if he had a problem with gay people. He asked, "Was Alex with you all night?"

"Yes—" I frowned. "Well, no. She left for work shortly after I got home."

Decamp asked, "What time did she leave?"

"Six-thirty? I'm not sure exactly."

Hutchinson asked, "What is your relationship to Ms. Knight?"

Truth or dare. I chose truth. "We'd been in a four-and-a-half-year relationship, and we split about two years ago."

DeCamp made a note on the legal pad. "Why did you break up?"

"She cheated on me and I kicked her out." I cringed internally, aware that my report sounded like a "scorned lover gets revenge" scenario. Great.

"Did you," Hutchinson asked, "remain in contact after the break up?"

"No. I hadn't seen her for almost a year and half when she showed up in New Jersey while I was working a case out there."

Hutchinson sat back in his chair. "Why did she travel all the way to the East Coast to see you?"

Oh, God. Did we have to go there? Of course we did. "I'd been hurt and was in the hospital. She heard about it and decided she wanted to get back together. She showed up, and I told her in no uncertain terms that wasn't going to happen. When I came home, she started sending cards and flowers. Left messages on my machine telling me how much she wanted to get back together. I filed a restraining order yesterday."

DeCamp said, "Sounds like she was getting desperate."

"Yeah, I think she is. Was." Jesus. Past tense. I still couldn't wrap my head around the fact that Eli was gone. I was waiting for the disbelief to subside, for it to hurt, to feel like it did the day I kicked her out. That emotion didn't seem to be asserting itself. Mostly I was feeling relief. "We're pretty sure she slashed, or maybe had someone slash, Alex's tires about a couple weeks ago."

"Did you report it?"

"Alex did that day."

DeCamp made another note on the legal pad. "Did

you ever confront her about what she was doing?"

"Yes. I talked to her a number of times. I thought she'd get the message, but nothing I said worked. She didn't stop." I flashed back to waking up in her bedroom and shuddered.

Hutchinson leaned forward again. "What else happened?"

I briefly described the incident at the hospital and awakening with no memory in her penthouse.

"Why didn't you file a restraining order before yesterday?" DeCamp asked.

The question of the fucking hour. "I thought I could handle it. I didn't want to air my dirty laundry in public." That was an excuse often used by victims. I wasn't a victim. Was I? Yeah, I guess I was. A stupid victim, and I knew better. She could have gone after Alex instead of me.

Hutchinson slid the yellow legal pad away from DeCamp, toward himself. He licked his finger, and flipped the top sheet over. "You talked to Ms. Knight the evening of the fifth. A witness says you and Ms. Knight had words. That you threatened to kill her."

Of course that'd come back and chomp me in the ass. "I did threaten her, but just to scare her off. I wouldn't actually do anything." That sounded pathetic. "I'm a cop, for chrissake. And yes, I was mad, but I was fully aware her entire staff was able to see our argument. I did not kill her." I looked at Hutchinson, then at DeCamp. Their faces were smooth as stone, giving nothing away. My pulse did a painful two-step. "Maybe this would be a good time to ask for a lawyer."

Hutchinson said, "No, there's no need for that yet. We aren't charging you with anything, Agent McKenna. We just want to get your side of the story."

I straightened. Might as well get it all out. "Night before last when I talked to her, it wasn't pretty. I confronted her about how I wound up at her place, with no memory of what had occurred, and I think most of the employees of Great Lakes saw the altercation. I stomped out of there, too."

DeCamp nodded. "Yeah, we heard." He looked back down at the file and pulled out a sheaf of papers. He flipped through a few pages, studied one, and looked back up at me. "Were you aware that Ms. Knight has a life insurance policy in excess of $750,000?"

That was a lot of dough. We'd never taken out life insurance while we were together. "No."

DeCamp sighed, and his shoulders dropped. "Were you aware that the primary beneficiary on the policy is you, Agent McKenna?"

"What?" I was so surprised I couldn't articulate a thing for a few long seconds. Both detectives were watching my reaction. Why on earth would Eli have left me any money? Unless she was more delusional than I realized. Maybe she truly believed I'd slink back to her like a whipped puppy. I cleared my throat. "I had no knowledge of this. None."

"Now," Hutchinson said, "I think you understand the gravity of the situation."

No shit. I was prime suspect number one. Eli and I

had history. I had a heated confrontation with her and threatened her life. Then I confronted her in front of even more workers and threatened her again. Now she was dead, and my name was on the insurance policy. What a clusterfuck.

Shortly after that revelation, I was sprung, with the usual warnings not to leave the area. The detectives called for a squad car to return me to the NPIU offices. The sergeant on duty let me use his phone, professional courtesy and all that, and I even had a modicum of privacy. I called Alex's cell. I wanted to tell her what had transpired before someone else did.

I paced the three-foot distance the cord allowed and counted the rings. Outside, the rain had finally given way. A mom and her small son walked past the entrance, and I watched the kid happily jump in the middle of a puddle on the sidewalk. I wished that getting around, or through, a puddle was the biggest worry in my life right now.

"Come on," I muttered under my breath. Finally, Alex picked up.

My voice sounded strange to my own ears. "Where are you?"

"At the Gallery. Why? You sound funny. Are you okay?"

"Not exactly. Can you go somewhere away from people for a minute?"

I heard faint voices in the background, and then they faded. "Yeah, what's up?"

How to even begin?

"Cailin?"

"Yeah." I swallowed. "Alex, Eli is dead."

For a moment, there was complete silence on the other end. "What happened?"

"A jogger found her body this morning on the bank of the Mississippi."

"Oh, my God. What happened?"

"I don't know, but apparently she was murdered, and the detectives who are investigating have some pretty solid reasons for suspecting I did it."

"You? What are you talking about? This makes no sense."

"I sort of threatened to kill her if she came near us again."

"You did *what?*"

I let out a frustrated breath. "I went to talk to her after she slashed your tires. I may have gotten slightly carried away."

"Oh, Cailin."

"Yeah. It gets worse."

"Worse? What can be worse?"

"She has me listed as the primary on her insurance policy."

"So? I can see how she might have done that while you two were together."

"No, Alex. We never took insurance out on each other."

"Never—holy shit. How much?"

"Seven hundred fifty thousand."

"Oh, my God." Alex was starting to repeat herself. "Cailin. You're in a shitload of trouble."

"Tell me about it. I'm going to talk to Singleton now and let him know what's going on."

"Okay. Keep me updated."

"I will."

"Cailin?"

"Yeah?"

"I love you."

"Love you, too."

I hung up, but before I headed upstairs, I called Gin. Jon was fine. He was one worry I didn't need to deal with at the moment.

✯ ✯ ✯

I found Director Singleton in his office. I tapped on the clear glass window in the door. He looked up and waved me in as he listened to someone on the other end of the phone. While I waited for him to finish, I debated how to explain I was a suspect in the death of Elisa Knight.

After a couple of minutes he hung up, folded his hands together, and looked curiously at me.

"I'm sorry to barge in."

"No, Agent McKenna, it's quite all right. In fact, I think I have a good idea why you've stopped by to see me this afternoon."

"You do, sir?"

"I just got off the phone with MPD Chief Helling. He briefed me on your trip downtown."

The words stung.

                                                                                                                                                                                             Jessie Chandler

"We have a predicament here, Agent, as I am sure you can well appreciate."

"Yes, sir." My voice was barely audible.

Singleton sighed and sat back, the leather of his chair creaking. "I have to put you on paid admin leave until this gets cleared up. Helling wants you off the task force."

Son of a bitch. There it was. "No. Please don't. I didn't do it—"

"Cailin, I believe you. But there are considerations."

Yeah. Considerations that I might somehow tarnish Helling's rep. Singleton wearily ran a hand over the top of his head. He looked haggard.

"A couple more days, sir. Please. Harry and I have been invited—"

"I know all about that invitation, Agent McKenna."

"But we're close to getting some solid intel."

Harry chose that moment to enter Singleton's office without knocking.

"Cailin," he said, sounding breathless, "where have you been? Martinez and I have been trying to get hold of you for the last four hours." Harry glanced over at Singleton, and it finally dawned on him he'd crashed the party. "Sir, I'm sorry. I wasn't thinking. I didn't mean to come storming in. I need to talk to McKenna."

Singleton waved off Harry's apology. "What's the fire, Agent Robinson?"

"They moved up the Soldiers of Christ event in Minnetonka to tonight. It's a prime opportunity—"

"Harry, stop," I said.

Harry looked from me to Singleton, who said,

"There's a small problem. An investigation involving the death of an acquaintance of Agent McKenna's has begun. She's been put on leave. Effective immediately."

Harry's gaze shifted from Singleton to me and back again, and he frowned. "Who?"

Singleton said nothing.

"For God's sake," I grumbled. "Eli Knight. Eli's dead."

Harry was quiet for a stunned second. "Dead? Don't tell me you actually—"

"No, I didn't. Christ, Harry. Give me a little credit."

He did have the sense to look sheepish. To Singleton, he said, "Sir, you can't do this right now. We're about to make some real moves into the organization."

"I understand that." Singleton's tone was sharp.

"At least wait until tomorrow."

I'd never seen Harry plead before. "You can have her then. Let us try and see what happens tonight. Besides, it'll take another operation to attempt to infiltrate the group again." Harry held up a hand, thumb and forefinger half an inch apart. "We're this close. I can feel it."

"Agent McKenna," Singleton said, "is placed on administrative leave. Leave is what happens when you're an officer of the law and are investigated in the death of someone. In addition, Chief Helling wants McKenna off the task force so she doesn't compromise the case."

With a heavy heart, I studied a stain in the blue carpet by my feet.

Harry said, "Please, sir. Just give us twenty-four hours."

Singleton studied his clasped hands for a very long moment. Under his breath he muttered, "I can't believe I'm about to do this." Louder, "Okay, Agents. Twenty-four hours. I have not seen either one of you this afternoon, and I certainly have not been able to reach *you*, Agent McKenna."

Harry opened the door and I stood, ready to bolt.

"McKenna, wait. I forgot this." Singleton opened a drawer and handed me a cell phone. "It's charged and loaded with all of your contacts. Now, get out of here."

★ ★ ★

Once we were safely out of the building and cruising west on 394 in my car, Harry said, "What exactly happened?"

I told him about my visit to the First Precinct, how I looked liked a prime-grade suspect in Eli's death, and the damning insurance policy.

"She named you the beneficiary? You sure you didn't do it?"

"Fuck you, Robinson."

"Remind me not to get on your bad side."

I stopped so we could get a bite to eat, and I called Alex and told her I was going on my last assignment before the events of the day caught up with me. She was surprisingly calm when I explained I had barely avoided suspension, and we were on the way to the SOC meeting.

Harry had written down the directions his contact gave him, and he tried to play navigator. The problem was he couldn't read his own writing and was completely unfamiliar with the area. To further complicate things, a heavy fog had rolled in off the lake, making driving a real challenge and seeing road signs nearly impossible.

I finally pulled over and yanked the crumpled sheet of paper out of Harry's hand to decipher it myself. Eventually we pulled up to the curb of a dwelling that would be considered modest for this area.

Lights blazed throughout the house, and the windows took on the look of a Monet: sharp edges fuzzed by the abundant fog made everything appear slightly out of focus. Half a dozen cars were parked on the hilly street in front of the house. The long driveway was steeply banked, and I felt for the poor soul who had to snowblow or shovel that treacherous incline.

The heavy air made it feel like extra work as we climbed the drive. I said, "Get yourself in shape walking this a couple times a day."

At the front door, I raised my hand to ring the doorbell but Harry caught it.

"Ouch." I pulled my hand back. He'd grabbed right where my knuckles were skinned.

"Don't forget, we're rednecks who love to hate. Right, Mrs. Madden?"

I pinched Harry's scruffy cheek. "Indeed, Ralphie, my boy." He let go and I rang the bell. We waited a few seconds, and the door opened to reveal Leanna, the woman from the Jubilee. Her mouse-brown hair dusted her shoulders, and she was neatly dressed in a green blouse, black skirt, and combat boots. "I'm glad you could make it. I was happy to hear that Phil and Bree got hold of you. We have much to discuss and pray about."

We followed our strangely formal hostess through the door into the foyer. Maybe the SOC's new slogan could be "Pray for Hate."

She led us into a spacious, stark-white living room. The overstuffed leather furniture looked glaringly white against the dark green carpet. Six women sat scattered around the room, including Leanna, Bree, and Doreen, sans daughter. The other three chicks were new to me. Harry and I settled on an unoccupied love seat.

Leanna made the introductions to those we hadn't met. "Joanne Parker, Nancy Hall, and Elizabeth Michaels, please meet Ralph and Alice Madden."

Between worrying my pants might dirty her pristine love seat and trying to remember names, I wasn't paying attention until Harry unobtrusively elbowed me. A man had come up behind Leanna and put an arm possessively around her. He was well over six feet and sinewy, with a thick shock of brown hair. Leanna pulled him toward Harry and me.

The man moved with a pronounced limp.

"This is my husband, Dave," Leanna said. "I was telling him how happy I am to meet another woman who has the same high moral values the rest of us do."

If our moral values were similar, I'd eat my undies. "So am I, Leanna."

Leanna smiled in a chilling, Stepford Wives sort of way. "Harry, why don't you go with Dave and join the men in the library. We womenfolk can chat in here."

"Just point the way." Harry stood, shot me an apologetic glance, and followed Dave and Leanna out of the room.

I slid to the edge of the love seat, ready to run if I needed to.

Leanna returned to the room with a bottle of wine in one hand and a tray of vegetables and dip in the other. When her husband was out of sight, her demeanor changed from sort-of-submissive wife to woman on a mission. I had no idea how to process the transformation.

"Okay, girls," she said. "Time to make the plans while our men relax." She set the tray on the coffee table. The rest of the women pulled their chairs closer, which reminded me of circling the wagons.

Leanna disappeared again and quickly returned with wineglasses. She handed one to each of us. After popping the cork and pouring a dollop for each of us, she raised hers.

"To the Soldier's of Christ. If the men only knew the women were the brains behind their brawn. Directed by the Augustus Primus, of course."

What the hell did that even mean?

Glasses clinked and crystal sparkled in the light as the women cheerfully consumed the contents. Leanna set her glass aside and picked up a tube of rolled paper from a desk that sat against the wall. She unrolled the paper and spread it across the coffee table. From a shelf behind her, she picked up four multicolored glass paperweights and set them on the edges to hold it down.

After a moment of study, I realized I was looking at

blueprints for a building.

Leanna sat and rubbed her hands together. "We're within a week of the objective we've worked toward for the last year." She glanced at Bree and me. "Our two new members need to be brought up to speed. Joanne, give them the overview."

Joanne was a heavyset, jowly woman with a bad, trying-to-be-blonde-but-looked-orange dye job. She said, "Welcome. You're now involved in one of the most important events the SOC will ever undertake. This endeavor will cast us into the limelight, and everyone will know our true agenda. It's our mission to plant the seeds of this plan in the minds of our husbands. We must make them think the ideas are their own." She eyed Bree and me. "Just because we women know our place doesn't mean we're stupid. After the last bungled attempt to gain recognition, we decided—or should I say, Nancy, here, decided not to take any more chances." She jerked a thumb at a dark-haired, big-boned woman with pale skin and weird lips like Stephen Tyler from the band Aerosmith. "Nancy came up with this idea to guide our men in the right direction."

With a flourish, Nancy swept her arm over the blueprints. As I looked closer, I saw the words Xcel Center and Saint Paul RiverCentre printed in blue. Sitting on a table in front of me was the entire layout of both facilities, including the inner workings of duct and HVAC systems.

"We'll have plants here and here." Nancy pointed a finger at the blueprints. "Our lookouts will be over here, and there."

One of the women, an older, grandma-type, asked, "Have we prepared all the C-4 we need for the explosive charges?" If I had false teeth, they would have dropped out of my mouth. The words "C-4" and "charges" should not be coming out of Grandma's mouth. It was just wrong.

Leanna said, "I personally made sure the correct quantities were brought down and set up."

I tried to mask the horror I was feeling. They were going to bomb either the X or the RiverCentre. Or maybe both.

"Have we decided on the best time for the cleansing?" Doreen asked.

Leanna glanced at her. "Sunday at two. The school kids will all be there with the performers on stage. We should manage to take out approximately two hundred with several hundred injuries. The Celebration of Nations will become a celebration of cleansing for the Soldiers of Christ."

Oh, my God. These women, these seemingly innocuous women, were planning to blow up the Celebration of Nations. The Celebration was an annual get-together that promoted understanding and tolerance among different ethnicities and celebrated the rich differences from one culture to the next. Harry and I had to get out of there and alert the Task Force. Sunday was only two days away.

Silently, I listened to these murderous women plot the demise of hundreds of children and adults like they were discussing who brought the winning apple pie to the state fair.

I excused myself, claimed I had to use the facilities, and went off in search of Harry. The ladies hardly noticed my absence. Between sips of cheap wine, they were too busy planning death and destruction, studying the blueprints, and arguing about the best places to plant additional explosives. Unbelievable.

I easily identified the library by the cloud of cigar smoke billowing out the open door. I peered inside. The men were gathered around a felt-covered table playing cards. I caught Harry's eye. He folded his hand and excused himself. I dragged him down the hall and pulled him into the bathroom.

"We have to get out of here. They're planning to blow up RiverCentre Sunday afternoon at two. During the Celebration of Nations."

Harry's eyes widened. "You're kidding."

"I wish I was. These women are the masterminds and are feeding the plans to the men. They're crazy, homicidal freaks. We need to get out of here and let the authorities know."

"Go tell them you aren't feeling well, and I'll tell the guys you're sick and we have to leave."

After I informed the murderous maidens, Harry returned and escorted me out the door into the darkness outside.

We hustled down the steep drive, nearly blind in the fog. Sound was muffled, dampened by soupy air that swirled with our footsteps. Harry veered toward the passenger door. I took one more step and somebody grabbed the back of my jacket.

Before I could react, I was bodychecked against the side of the car. I grunted at the impact and tried to twist away. As I moved sideways, my assailant caught my wrist. He twisted my arm behind my back and used his body weight to pin me against the door. A bag—burlap from the smell and rough feel of it—was pulled over my head and yanked tight around my throat. Something poked into the side of my head. I was pretty sure it was a gun.

Heavy breathing filled my ear. "Don't fucking make a sound, or I'll blow your brains to kingdom come." The warning was delivered in a low growl, in a voice I didn't recognize.

From the other side of the car I heard a muffled thump and a moan. That didn't sound good. Not at all.

The pressure on my pretzeled arm lessened, and he wrenched my other arm behind me. I wanted to scream when the guy's careless mitt grazed the brand on my forearm, but I managed to stifle the outcry. Steel bit into my skin, and I heard the familiar zip-click of handcuffs tightening around my wrists.

I hunched forward and lashed out behind with my foot. My boot connected with a satisfying thump.

"Bitch!" A heavy hand wrenched the scratchy hood tight against my face. He jerked my head back and rocketed it forward against the doorframe. My skull bounced off the metal like a giant Super Ball. Pain exploded through me, and white spots danced inside my eyelids. I almost missed feeling the fingers that fumbled with the retention strap of the Glock I had strapped to my belt.

Oh, fuck no.

No way was I going to wind up a cop-killed-by-own-gun statistic. I bucked like a star bronco at the rodeo and thrashed every which way. My captor body-slammed me against the car again. The impact knocked the wind and the fight right out of me.

Stunned, I couldn't move. The man's fingertips dug into the small of my back. He hoisted me up by my belt. Without the use of my arms I pitched forward. He caught me by the back of the hood and choked off what little oxygen I was able to suck. Then I was flying through the air. I landed with a thud on what felt like a bony hip and a sharp elbow.

I heard a bang like a trunk lid slamming shut. It was and I was inside it. The car started up, rolled and bumped along, and picked up speed.

I attempted to wriggle off the sharp parts poking into me. I assumed I was on top of Harry, unless these people made a habit of kidnapping strangers. I finally managed to squirm to the side of the body beneath me.

There was a hoarse, "Thanks."

Harry it was.

"You okay?" I asked.

"Think so. Got a fuckin' robin's egg coming on the back of my fuckin' head, but other than loss of motor function due to lack of fuckin' circulation, I'm fuckin' ducky. You?"

I had no chance of beating Harry's creative use of the f-word. "Got my bell rung when my head got up close and personal with the car. I think I'm all right though." My forehead felt tight, like the skin was stretched across it. "You cuffed?"

I heard a rattle. "Yeah. You?"

"Yes."

"Fuck," he said again.

Then I said, "You got a sack on your head?"

"Yeah."

"You see any of them?"

"No."

My arms were falling asleep. I managed to roll halfway onto my back. For the second time in an hour, I felt like I was going to blow chunks.

"You all right?" Harry asked. "You're breathing funny."

"Just..."—breath—"fine..."—another breath. If I kept breathing deep, maybe I'd be okay. "What now, Ralph?"

"Alice, shut up and let me think."

"You're as dickheaded as the fictional Ralph."

"Har de har. I'll hazard a guess that they're on to us."

"Captain Obvious."

On that note, we went silent. The only sound came from tires humming against pavement. The vehicle periodically slowed and sped up, but eventually the ride smoothed out. Then the vehicle slowed again, and we made more stops and starts.

"Stop signs?" I guessed.

"Could be. Maybe stoplights. Aren't the lights in Minneapolis practically every block?"

"Yeah." My gut was still roiling, but at least I now felt

more in control of the puke factor.

The vehicle braked yet again and came to a stop. The sound of doors slamming set the butterflies in my stomach fluttering again.

A key rattled in the lock, and the trunk popped open. Cold air trickled across my exposed skin, and I shivered. Somebody roughly extracted me, scraping my side raw on the edge of the trunk. There was some DNA evidence to be found if I didn't make it through this.

We were led inside a building. No one would answer any questions I asked, so I couldn't get a bead on how many shitheads were with us.

My location contemplation abruptly halted when they shoved me into a chair. The handcuffs cut into my wrists, and I bit back a yelp.

Someone yanked the hood off my head. I blinked and tried to focus. Harry sat in a chair next to me. Pallets, with various-sized cardboard boxes stacked two and three high, lay near us. Bare bulbs hung from a high ceiling, but the light did little to penetrate the vastness of the interior. The air smelled like the inside of the engine room on a ship— greasy and metallic.

A man stepped in front us. I frowned in confusion at the scowling face of Hennepin County Attorney Quenton Campbell.

What. The. Fuck.

Three men I didn't recognize stood behind him. They were dressed in black, semi-automatic rifles in hand.

I returned my attention to Campbell.

Harry said, "What the hell are you doing?"

Campbell stared at Harry for long seconds. "When I saw you two at the Jubilee, I didn't recognize you." His eyes flicked to me. "But I thought you looked familiar, and I couldn't quite remember where from. I haven't worked closely with any of the scum at the NPIU. Then I saw you at the hospital, and I was shocked to realize you're part of the sick joke that masquerades as law enforcement. You two were getting far too close for comfort. You're too much like your poor, persistent brother."

"You can leave my brother out of this."

"Not really," Campbell said. "But he'll be dealt with at the next available opportunity."

Confusion and fear faded. I went rigid. "What do you mean by that?"

Campbell laughed. "Oh, you three have been leading me on a merry chase, and you'll pay for it with your lives. Your hardheaded brother stuck his nose into business he was better served staying away from, and then you two lying miscreants attempt to infiltrate us." He moved closer and frowned. "It occurs to me now that you had the impertinence to stand before me and swear your allegiance to a group that despises everything you represent. You attempted to make a mockery of solemn, holy proceedings. You've given false testimony in the presence of the Flock, and now you shall be treated like the heretics you are."

Harry sneered at Campbell. "So you're the grand carbunkle on my ass."

"Laugh it up, Mr. Robinson. I am the Augustus Primus of the Soldiers of Christ."

OhMyFuckingGod.

The enormity of the matter wasn't lost on me. Harry and I were sitting at gunpoint in some filthy warehouse, talking to the charismatic head of the Soldiers of Christ, who happened to be a high-powered county attorney with an eye on the governor's mansion.

Campbell's eyes glinted coldly. He dropped his cultured, refined, non-accent and fell into the Southern tones I'd heard at the Jubilee. "We're on the brink of a coup, y'all, and we will stop at nothin' to achieve our goals. I knew it wouldn't be long before your brother would find out more than he bargained for. I told him to back off. But no."

The blood lurched to a stop in my veins. "You ordered a hit. You fucking bastard. You ordered a hit on my brother."

Campbell's eyes bored through me. "I had no choice. It should have come off as a random attack, and that would have been the end of it. But no. He had to live."

"You son of a bitch!" I jerked forward in an attempt to charge Campbell. He backed up a pace, and a heavy hand painfully clamped onto my shoulder and shoved me back into my chair. I hadn't heard anyone behind us.

He continued. "If you hadn't gotten involved, this would have been over. Damage control was just about complete. I'm required to do what I must to protect the Soldiers of Christ and our holy mission."

The man had lost his mind.

"What exactly is it you must do?" Harry asked.

"You'll have an entertaining ride, and it'll be

oh-so-unfortunate that two National Protection and Investigation agents who, I might add, were having a clandestine relationship, decided to run off together. Who better to disappear without a trace than a couple of well-trained feds?"

So that's why the ultra-secretive leader of hate didn't care if we literally saw who he was. One of those leg-aching, chest-hurting hits of adrenaline charged through my system. "You really think you can make two people vanish and no one will ask any questions? I didn't take you for a complete idiot."

Campbell took a step toward me, anger flaring. "I won't be talked to like that."

He backhanded me so hard my head rocketed to one side. I tasted blood where the inside of my cheek had impacted my teeth. Out of the corner of my eye I saw Harry watching me. I knew he was calculating the odds of two handcuffed agents against at least three well-armed men. Not likely a successful scenario.

"You should watch that mouth, Ms. McKenna. You're no better than the black man or the Jew. You have no real family. And you're a disgusting homosexual to boot."

He leaned down into my face. I resisted the urge to sink my teeth into his nose, but I glared at him. Maybe my words might draw another blow, but glares were still pain-free.

"The world will be better off without you and your filth." He drew himself to full height and folded his arms over his chest. "Enough. Take this trash away. Make sure they don't come back."

Campbell turned on his heel and disappeared around a pallet of boxes. Fucking asshole. I hoped he died a hideous death. Karma was a bitch, dickhead.

We were again hauled to our feet, not hooded this time, and marched outside. I could now see our ride had been a late model Lincoln. One of the men unlocked the trunk.

Here we go again.

After a scuffle that was quelled before it really started, Harry and I were once more sardined in the dark. This time, our friendly thugs made sure we couldn't get at the trunk release since, without hoods blinding us, we could actually see the dangling yellow Emergency pull. They made Harry roll on his side and forced me to lay with my back toward him. Then one of the part-time masochists took another handcuff and connected my cuff chain to Harry's, which gave us no way to maneuver into a position to pull the trunk release, and even if we did, we wouldn't be able to get out of the car without a crane.

After a few uncomfortable turns that reminded me of riding the Scrambler at Valleyfair, the car picked up speed.

"Nice ass." Harry goosed me.

"Sexual harassment." I pinched him back, maybe with more enthusiasm than I should have.

"Yeeouch, McKenna."

"You started it. What do you think they'll do with us?"

"Make sure they get rid of us where we'll never be found."

I shuddered, a mixture of dread and cold seeping into me from the metal beneath the thin carpet of the car. I thought about Alex, about Thomas and Gin and Jon. I quickly shut down that line of thought before I bawled like a baby. Eventually I dozed to the hum of rubber on asphalt.

Sometime later I was jolted awake by the change in pitch of the tires. The car lurched, rolled forward to continue on for a short distance, came to a stop, and stayed there.

Harry said, "If there's an opening—"

"I know. We'll take it."

The trunk popped open. One of the men unhooked the cuff linking Harry and me together. Someone hoisted me up like a sack of potatoes and deposited me on my feet. Blood rushed into areas that had been without circulation for far too long, and it hurt like hell.

The other guy dragged Harry out of the trunk and dumped him on the ground, which was still snow covered. We must have come a long way north, since most of the snow in the Twin Cities and to the south had already melted. Harry struggled to get his feet under him, which was a feat because the hard ground was slippery, and he couldn't use his arms for balance.

We were deep in a forest. Towering trees formed a black, oppressive outline. The darkness felt absolute.

"Hey," I said. "You don't have to—"

Before I could get another word out, someone grabbed me from behind and crammed a foul-tasting cloth in my mouth. More cloth was wrapped around my head and tied tightly at the base of my skull. Another hood was pulled over my head. Talk about overkill. Damn, I hated not being able to see my own impending death.

"That'll shut 'em up," one of the gunmen muttered. I didn't recognize his voice, but I wondered if these were the same men who'd carried the cooler of branding supplies into Kingdom Hall at the Jubilee.

A gun barrel to my ribs and a hand on my back propelled me forward. I had a hard time keeping my footing without the benefit of sight, and more than once someone grabbed the scruff of my neck to keep me from falling flat on my face.

Eventually we were led into an area that must have been somehow enclosed. It didn't feel like open forest. The icy wind that had been stinging my uncovered hands faded, but the chill itself remained. I caught a musty smell that lingered in the back of my throat. The hollow silence was unsettling.

After about fifteen minutes, we stopped. A quiet murmur of voices came from off to the side. Then a hand on my shoulder forced me to the ground.

Harry tried to say something, but the gag did its job. All that came out was garbled nonsense.

Then the echo of rapid footsteps faded.

I heard Harry thrashing, and it sounded like he was having a seizure. One of his body parts caught me in the side. I groaned at the pain through the cloth in my mouth.

"You okay?" Harry asked thickly. I wasn't sure how, but he'd managed to get his gag off.

"Agghh," I gasped, the sound all but swallowed by an

eardrum-popping explosion. The concussion tore the breath from my lungs and then I was airborne. The very air shuddered as the blast ripped violently through the chamber like a physical thing.

Sometime later, I was jolted into consciousness. The sudden wakening left me gasping as if three elephants were sitting on my chest.

My head throbbed in time with the pounding of my heart. The ringing in my ears was so loud I could hardly concentrate on anything else. I took inventory of my body parts, and everything felt intact and moveable. The hood was still on my head, but the gag had been shifted half out of my mouth. I worked my jaw in an attempt to dislodge it the rest of the way and tried to straighten. As I shifted, I felt more than heard rocks and debris fall off my legs. I bent my knees and tried to buck off the elephant lying across my chest.

"Wha..." Harry. It was Harry. He was pinning me down.

"Ged ah way!" I struggled beneath him. After a few moments he shifted, eventually rolling himself off. I reflexively sucked in a deep breath, but I still felt like I couldn't get enough air. The fucking hood was making me claustrophobic.

I struggled to sit up, panic overruling control. Something that sounded like rocks and grit tumbled off me as I thrashed. I used my shoulder to rub furiously at my face through the rough cloth of the hood. If we got out of this I was going to have rug burns on my cheeks. The work my shoulder was doing succeeded. The gag was dragged low enough on my chin that I could spit out the soggy ball of cloth.

"Oh, God," I hollered. "The hood. Get this hood off! I—"

"Cailin! Don't move!" The bark in Harry's voice stopped me cold.

"You're okay," he said.

"But I can't br—"

Something bashed the side of my head. It felt like someone was using pliers to rip the skin off my scalp. I yelped, and then the hood was yanked from my head, along with a handful of hair.

I was surrounded by pitch dark. I pulled in a huge lungful of non-cloth-covered oxygen and promptly gagged on the dust in the air. Then I was caught in a cycle of inhaling what felt like solid matter and hacking it out.

"Don't breathe deep. Should've warned you it was worse outside the hood. Sorry."

I followed Harry's directions, feeling dust coat the inside of my mouth. I panted rapidly but shallowly. "Holy shit. Did you get the fucking bag off my head with your teeth?"

"Can't use my hands. The explosion did me the favor of dislodging my hood. My mouth is the only tool I have at the moment."

We lapsed into silence, and I could literally feel the air flow more easily into my lungs. The downside was the dankness became much more apparent.

Eventually I croaked hoarsely, "Where the hell are we?"

"Dunno." I felt Harry move against my side.

"We need to get out of these cuffs." By this point, everything below my elbows had lost all feeling.

"Want me to try to hack one of your hands off?" he asked.

"Harry. Listen. My car keys are in the front pocket of my jeans. I keep an extra cuff key, but I obviously can't reach it. You gotta do it."

We wiggled around until Harry's back was against my front, and after a number of contortions that involved a few curses from me, Harry managed to pull the keys from my pocket.

"Okay," he said after a bit. "Can't reach the keyhole. Let's sit back to back and maybe I can get at yours easier."

We heaved ourselves into position. After Harry dropped the key a few times, I said, "Let me try."

I didn't expect it to be quite so hard to get that tiny key into the lock. On my sixth fumbling attempt, the lock release clicked, and the metal made a ratcheting sound as I pulled the cuff apart.

In less than thirty seconds, the rest of the cuffs were off even though we couldn't see a damn thing. There was something to be said for being forced in training to remove handcuffs after you've been hit with pepper spray.

"My wrists feel like hamburger." I gingerly rubbed first one, then the other. The stinging in my hands as circulation returned hurt like a mother.

"I think I've..." Harry trailed off and grumbled nonsensically. "...got a lighter here somewhere. There we go." A second later a flame flickered to life, illuminating the area around us and casting wavering shadows in to the dark beyond.

We were not in any kind of building I recognized. We were in a tunnel. The dirt floor was strewn with rocks and boulders of varying sizes.

Harry crawled in a slow circle. Fallen rubble blocked one end of the tunnel not far from where we stood. Railroad ties and parallel rails ran down one side of the twenty-foot-wide space. Blackened four-by-four beams blocked up the rock walls at periodic intervals.

Carefully, Harry rose, holding the lighter high. "Okay, you're from Minnesota. Where are we?"

"A mine? We could be in or near the Iron Range in northern Minnesota. I've also heard of some mining in the southern part of the state. That doesn't do much to narrow down our location, does it?"

The flame flickered out, plunging us into blackness so complete it took my breath away.

"No, ma'am, it does not."

"Maybe we should dig—"

Another, more muffled explosion rattled the wooden joists above our heads and thrummed the ground beneath our feet. I grabbed Harry's sleeve and jerked him down, covering my head with my arms. Pebbles and sand from above pelted my back, and I braced for the big one to take me out. After a few long seconds I pushed myself up and stood, shedding sand and rocks. "This is ridiculous. We've gotta get the hell out of here."

Harry grabbed my elbow and I helped him up. "I'd hazard a guess they've blown shut the entrance to the mine, or whatever this place is. An insurance policy, so to speak."

"Fucking A. I wonder if we're going to have an oxygen problem."

Harry flicked his Bic again. The flame burned solid and strong. "I think there's air flow." Harry made his way toward what looked like a big black gaping nothing where the tunnel continued deeper into the ground. Rocks, gravel, boulders of various sizes, and pieces of fallen timber were strewn everywhere. Harry grabbed a few chunks of wood, came back to where I stood, and dumped a couple at my feet.

"What are you doing?"

"Making a fire."

"Oh, no. No way. Oxygen, man. Maybe the air is moving because of the explosions, and before we know it we'll have used it all up, and die a terrible, gasping, supremely painful death."

Harry let the rest of the wood slip out of his hands. "You have a disturbingly poetic way with words."

"Oh, for Christ sake." I pulled my cell from my pocket. "As long as they still work, we can use the lights on our phones. That should help conserve air."

"You're a fucking genius."

"I know. Let's poke around and then tackle the great wall of rubble." I slid my thumb across the bottom of the screen to unlock it. "I still have eighty percent juice, but zip for reception. Not surprising, but disappointing."

Harry withdrew his cell. "Goddamn. The glass is shattered."

"Try it anyway. That's a new thing, you know. Kids think cracked glass on cell phones are a status symbol."

"And that's why they're kids." Harry tinkered with the device. "I'll be damned. It works."

The screen glowed, the backlight fractured from the cracks in the glass. "Twenty-three percent juice. Should have charged it before I left for the Minnetonka meeting."

Some was better than none, but we'd best conserve what we could. "Any service?" I asked.

"No."

"Okay. Shut it down for now." I hit the flashlight function on my phone, and bright light filled the space. They managed to pack some serious lumens in the tiny contraption.

I squinted, allowed my eyes to adjust, and took in the debris field. What a mess.

"Tell you what," Harry said. "You check out the tunnel, and I'll see what I can do to shift some of this shit out of the way."

"Okay. Just don't use up all your battery or your lighter fluid, okay?"

"Deal."

I glanced up at the ceiling of the mine and studied the integrity of the cross-timbers. We might be short-timers no matter what. Metal high above glinted back at me, and I moved closer. An old lantern hung from the center of one of the cross-timbers.

"Harry!" Excitement made my voice rise.

"What?" He came to stand next to me and follow my gaze. "Oh, nice. Very nice, McKenna."

"Boost me up."

I put my boot in the step he made of his hands, and he heaved. I caught the rusty handle and pulled the lantern down, managing not to drop it or smack it against anything. It was square, with a solid metal base and four sooty glass panes. I shook it, but it was bone dry. The spark of hope that I'd had fizzled. "No fuel."

Harry put his hands on his hips, head cocked to the side. "Where there's one, there's another. Come on."

We moved deeper into the blackness of the open shaft, away from the blocked passage and its false sense of security. I suppressed a shivery mix of anticipation and fear.

Resolutely, we made our way through the fallen ruins toward the next set of beams. The good news was they looked solid. Bad news was no lantern hung from it.

We continued along, careful not to trip over the mess or the railroad ties. The tunnel curved gently, and after we passed a third set of beams lacking a light, we found another lantern hanging from the fourth. Harry again boosted me up and I grabbed the handle to lift it off its S-hook.

As Harry lowered me to the ground, liquid sloshed within the metal housing.

"Yes!" I fumbled for the pane of glass that doubled as a tiny door. I unlatched it, and Harry lit his lighter and touched it to the wick. After a second, the cotton ignited, its flame burning weakly. Then the fluid must have somehow been sucked up the wick, because the lantern brightened and the flame stabilized. I dialed down the wick to conserve oil, shut the small opening, and looked triumphantly at Harry.

He graced me with a dimpled grin. "Good girl."

We turned to retrace our steps, and the light caught a partially dislodged railroad tie. An object lay against it. I prodded what looked like an old boot with my foot. Curiosity overruled sense, and I handed the lantern to Harry. I grabbed the boot and pulled. It was caught beneath the tie, so I pulled harder. I felt it give, but didn't get my feet under me in time, stumbled backward a few steps, tripped over some rubble, and landed hard on my ass.

Harry moved the lantern closer. Jutting from the top of the boot was a sock, some weirdly shriveled leather, and two forearm-sized pieces of bleached wood either sawed off or crushed on the end. I held it closer to the light. The wood resembled bone. Oh, my God. What was actually protruding out of the boot was what was left of someone's tibia and fibula. I was holding the lower half of someone's goddamn leg. Usually I was pretty calm in emergencies, but this was the last straw. I howled like a raving banshee.

"Cailin!" Harry hollered over my hysterics. "Let go. Drop it!"

"Can't!" I'd bolted to my feet and danced around as if my pants were on fire, holding the leg as far away from my body as I could.

Harry grabbed my hand and gingerly pried my fingers from the death grip they had on the boot without touching it himself. The boot and skeleton parts hit the ground with a thud.

I panted as if I'd run a marathon and bent over, hands on my knees. "Wonder where"—gasp—"the rest of the poor"—gasp—"bastard is."

"Breathe, Cailin."

I focused on inhaling and exhaling, and eventually straightened up, still warily eyeing my found object. "Jesus. Okay. Let's go find the rest of him."

Harry held the lantern high, its light casting an eight-foot cone around us. We searched the area by the uprooted railroad tie, but we found no additional body parts.

A short distance down the tunnel, we found the other leg, its boot also still attached. The ends of the bones looked similarly severed.

"Over here," Harry called from the other side of the tracks, near the passage wall.

A partially mummified skull lay face-up. Empty, dark orbits kept a ghostly watch. It looked like the neck had been severed from the body, as had the legs. Strands of hair were still attached to the scalp, but I couldn't tell exactly what color they were.

The skin had tightened across bone, and the mouth was frozen in a perpetually surprised "Oh." An animal had nibbled in a few places, but apparently the victim wasn't too appetizing because most of the shriveled head was still intact.

"Ouch," Harry said.

"Come on, let's see if we can find the torso. Maybe we can ID him, and then we need to get out of here." I did not let myself consider failure. Didn't think about the fact we might very well wind up looking like something that could be an attraction in a Ripley's Believe it or Not! museum. Alex was out there, waiting for me to come home, and so was my family. Failure to find our way out of here was not an option.

I followed Harry as he moved away from the decapitated head deeper into the black hole. A stone's throw later, we came across an old ore cart, its metal rusty and tarnished, but intact. It didn't take long to put two and two together. Oh, my God. "Harry, they—"

"Ran the poor bastard over." Harry held the lantern closer, and the flame flickered as he tilted it.

"How much juice is left?"

Harry gently shook it. "Half, maybe. We should keep an eye out for others, siphon the oil, just in case."

The light reflected off the ore cart, and something on the ground below it glittered. "What's that?

Harry crouched and picked it up. "Necklace. Crucifix."

"That didn't help him any." I knelt beside Harry and leaned down far enough to peer under the cart. I could just make out the collar of a jacket. Something white protruded from it. Probably the spine that had been attached to the beheaded skull. "Yeah, that's the rest of him."

Harry pulled me up. "Come on. Let's figure out how to get out of here."

★ ★ ★

For close to an hour Harry and I grunted and

strained, hefted and swore while we tried to make a dent in the pile of rubble blocking the tunnel. We finally stopped, out of breath and more than warmed up. In fact, I was hot. Sweat snaked down between my shoulder blades and made the middle of my back itch.

Harry had propped the lantern on an outcropping of rock off to the side, where it cast weird, sideways shadows. I stretched and assessed our progress, disheartened to see we hadn't made much. I was cranky, thirsty, and hungry.

Sheer stubbornness kept both of us at it. Ever so slowly, we tunneled our way through the mess. A couple of hours later, Harry said, "I need a break." He heaved a chunk of rock toward our growing pile. It hit and clattered noisily down the side of our mini-mountain and came to rest next to my foot. He staggered away and sat on a rock, head in hands.

I shuffled to lean against the wall of the tunnel and sank to the floor. My body felt like I'd gone ten rounds with the "red man," the red suit of padding donned by defensive tactics instructors for unit recertification.

"I'm starving." Maybe that was the way we'd die. What a terrible way to go. Hell, everything about this was terrible.

Harry rummaged through the pockets of his jacket and produced two bite-size candy bars. He tossed me one. I ripped the wrapper off and stuffed it in my mouth. Then I grabbed up my jacket and put a hand in the pocket to triple check no stray snacks were in hiding. My fingers brushed against my cell phone. I pulled it out and fired it up, just in case. Good thing I had low expectations. With a regretful sigh, I shut it down and tucked the phone away. "Ready?"

"Yeah." Harry pulled himself to his feet, a grimace flickering across his features. "I have to give it to the miners back in the day doing this kind of thing. Day after day after day. If we live through this, I'm going to appreciate the easy life."

"You're not kidding. Come on. Let's do this so we can get to the appreciating part."

We climbed back up the debris field and went to town. As we worked, my mind turned over the events that had led us here. I tossed a stone and then a handful of sand and pebbles to the floor of the tunnel. "Why do you think they didn't just shoot us?"

Harry hefted a smallish boulder and tossed it to the side. "Couple of reasons, I suppose. First, if no bullets are found in our dead carcasses, there's no evidence to track back to a weapon and, ultimately, to the Soldiers of Christ."

"I'll buy that. And?"

"Damn it." Harry vigorously shook out his hand. "Pinched my goddamn finger. Secondly, if our poor, dehydrated, animal-scavenged bodies were found, an argument could be made that the mine shaft was a meeting place for the illicit affair we're having, and we got caught in an accidental collapse."

"Yeah, finding us shot or stabbed would knock their ore cart right off the tracks. Maybe we got into a lover's quarrel and I offed you in the heat of the moment."

Harry laughed and the sound was good to hear.

We swapped places periodically so one of us wouldn't be bent over pawing through the mess for too long at any one time. I was about to call another break when my hand broke through a gap I'd been working near the top of the mound, close to the ceiling of the tunnel.

"Holy shit. Harry. We might have done it."

Harry hustled toward me, hunkered down, and worked his own hand through the hole. "Son of a bitch, baby, we're getting out of here!"

We redoubled our efforts and the gap widened. As we worked, I periodically glanced over to check the lantern. The status of our only light haunted me. I was irrationally terrified that the lamp would burn through the oil before we got out or had a chance to find more fuel. But each time I looked, the flame continued to burn steadily.

Once we made enough of a breach, I wiggled through the opening. Furiously, I worked one side and Harry worked the other. In short order the hole was wide enough for Harry to fit, too. He scrambled down the rubble and snagged the lantern, which he handed to me through the gap before he squeezed through the portal.

I held the lantern aloft. We were still trapped in a mineshaft in Bumfuck, Minnesota. This side of the shaft was identical to the one we'd abandoned, but at least the illumination cast by the lamp wasn't blotted out by a cave-in. The blackness in the distance simply swallowed it up, which seemed like a good, though intimidating, sign.

We picked our way to the bottom. I tried to dust myself off, but it was a lost cause. "Okay?"

Harry took the lantern from me. "Let's go."

The lantern swung from its handle with each step, casting oddly shifting shadows. We passed three more lamps dangling from cross-joists. Only one of them had fuel in it, and I poured about a pint into the base of the lantern we'd been using. I felt marginally better in regard to our lighting situation after that.

We'd been going for an eternity when we came to a literal fork in the road. The cart tracks split both ways as well.

Harry scratched at his grimy cheek. "Left or right?"

"Let's flip." I stuck a hand in my pocket and came out with a quarter. "Heads to the right, tails to the left." I flicked the coin into the air, caught it, and slapped it onto my arm. "Here we go."

Harry nodded. I pulled my hand away. Tails. We veered left.

"You know," Harry said, his voice thoughtful, "Campbell was a fucked up jerk when he said you have no real family. You have the McKennas, you have Alex." He stopped and turned toward me, the flame from the lamp playing over one side of his face. "And you'll always have me."

I was taken aback. I ran my teeth over the raw skin on the inside of my cheek and digested his words. "Harry." I looked carefully at him. He was dead serious. "Thank you."

He gave my shoulder a friendly swat and we resumed forward motion. "Is it strange not knowing your past?"

I thought about that. "Guess I've never paid much attention. Too busy trying to survive. Then I landed at the McKennas."

"As a kid," Harry asked, his tone tentative, "what happened?"

Stumbling along in an inky dark mine, not knowing whether or not we'd find a way out, was a good motivator to make confessions. "When I was young, I was dumped at the emergency entrance at North Memorial, a hospital in a suburb adjacent to Minneapolis."

Harry caught a knee on an outcropping of rock and grunted. I grabbed his shirt to help stabilize him before he took a header. "Good reflexes," he said. "So, you were a baby in a basket. Like Moses floating down the river."

"Something like that, only I was older."

"How old?"

"Three."

"Shit. They ever catch who left you?"

"No one saw the person that I know of. Now that I think about it, I never bothered to ask any details."

"I can understand that. Maybe it's better not to know."

"Maybe." I thought about that as we tramped through the passage. My parentage was not something I cared to dwell on, but there were some definite advantages of knowing where you came from. Medical and psychological histories, for instance. A sense of place. But whoever gave me up obviously didn't have the capacity to care for me. Or maybe they simply didn't want me. Who would dump a three-year-old kid on the steps of a hospital anyway? Yeah, there went my monkey mind. Exactly why I tried to steer clear of the topic. I could consider all of those chaotic thoughts after this horrible adventure was finished.

Harry said, "Foster homes after that?"

"For as long as they lasted. Then on to the next crappy situation until I was done with that at fourteen."

"You've made a good life for yourself, considering the rough start in the world."

"Maybe I have."

We rounded a curve, and the lamplight cast its dim glow on another wall of rubble entirely plugging the shaft. This must have come from the second explosion. "Not again." Every muscle in my body screamed for mercy.

Harry wedged the lamp into a safe crevice, and we dove in.

An hour later, it looked like we'd barely done a thing. Our hands and various other body parts oozed blood. My legs and back ached from trying to balance on a surface that kept shifting. I braced my arms against a boulder and tried to catch my breath.

Harry scrambled to a stop beside me. "What time is it?"

I reached for my phone and powered it up. I knew reception wouldn't magically appear, but the time function should still work. After a few seconds, the screen populated. 6:23 in the morning. No wonder we were done in. Then dots in the upper left corner of the screen caught my attention. "Harry!" I grabbed his shirt in my fist. "Harry, I've got a signal." There were only two dots, but it was two more than we'd had earlier.

Not holding much hope the call would actually go through, I dialed the direct number to the office. After ten rings, I hung up. With a trembling finger, I ended the call and tried Rosie's cell. To my surprise, it was answered almost instantaneously before the first ring was through.

"Cailin." Rosie's voice was high-pitched. "Where the hell are you? Is Harry with you?"

I literally sagged against Harry. "Yeah, he is. Right here. Listen, Rosie. I don't know how long this signal will hold, and I don't know where we are. You need to trace the tower this call is coming from. Now."

"Hang on." Rosie repeated my words, then she was back. "Tony's on it. What happened? You guys hurt?"

I told her what had occurred at the meeting, the subsequent ride in the trunk, and then the death march into the bowels of a mine. Beside me, Harry stamped his feet. Since we'd stopped moving, the cold seeped in, relentlessly. I tried unsuccessfully to suppress a shiver.

"The director's here. He wants to talk to you."

"Cailin, thank God." Singleton's tone was grave. "What's going on?" He rarely used first names. It was the first indication our absence had been taken seriously. I gave him a more thorough rundown of the night's events.

He said, "I think Campbell's headlining a fundraiser at the Minneapolis Convention Center this evening. I'll contact Chief Helling immediately. Hang on." The sound of garbled voices came through the receiver, and then he was back. "We have you tracked to a tower south of Mountain Iron. Agent Smith is looking for plat maps. We'll have your location in no time."

"Thank you, sir. If you don't mind, I want to call home before I run out of juice."

"By all means, but try to conserve your cell power.

We'll call when we know more."

I disconnected and dialed Alex, and Harry moved away from me.

"Cailin! Where the hell are you?" Those words were becoming a familiar refrain. From the strain evident in her voice, she might have post-traumatic stress disorder before this business was over. Maybe we all would.

"Somewhere up north."

"You okay?"

"Aside from a few bruises, I'm fine. Harry's with me." I didn't want to tell her the entirety of what had gone down, so I glossed over the details. She didn't buy it. So I came clean and for the third time spit out the entire story. Before she could move into meltdown mode, I explained I needed to save battery life.

"I need to go, baby. I love you."

"I love you too, Cailin. You get your ass back to me."

"I will. I promise." Reluctantly, I hit the end button. At least this time the promise felt like a much better bet than it might have a few hours ago.

Harry had been wandering around while I'd been on the phone with Alex. I shivered again and hoped the NPIU would find us before we froze. To get to us, they would need a seriously badass backhoe or some other ginormous earth-moving equipment.

After two more hours and another phone call from Singleton, we heard the distant sounds of rescue. Two hours and forty-five minutes more passed before they cleared enough space to get access, and then it took more time for engineers to come in and ensure the shaft was stable. If it'd been left up to me I would have crawled right out, but the operation had become official and with that came redundancy and red tape. As it turned out, Harry and I were actually only about fifty feet from the entrance of the mine. Campbell's lackeys must have tripled the explosive charge when they took out the entrance.

Once we got the thumbs up, we made our way along a narrow passage that appeared as if it might collapse on itself at any moment. Fresh air had never smelled so good. I stepped into the sunlight and turned my face into the sun's warmth.

Then medics were on us like bears to honey. They wrapped us in blankets, checked our vitals and various injuries, and patched up whatever needed patching. As they did their thing, I took my first real look at the mine. Another set of chills wracked me when I saw we were on the side of a steep hill, in the middle of the forest, and the area looked nothing like the entrance to a mine. We were lucky to have been found.

Chapter 20

Almost a full twenty-four hours after Harry's and my fateful meeting with the SOC in Minnetonka, an NPIU helicopter lifted off from the Range Regional Airport en route to the Twin Cities. I must have fallen asleep, because the next thing I felt was the jolt of the skids hitting tarmac at Crystal Airport, aptly named after the city of Crystal, a suburb outside Minneapolis.

Rosie and Tony were waiting a hundred feet away beside a black Chevy Tahoe. Even at that distance, they were buffeted by the wash of the helicopter rotors. It took a couple of minutes for the rotors to still, and then we were allowed to exit.

After my quick reunion with the joy of indoor plumbing, I checked in with Alex to let her know we were back in one piece, and then called Gin. Alex had touched base with Gin after we'd spoken immediately after the mine extraction to let her know I was okay, so some of the heat was off. I hated to make the McKennas worry, and my career path did nothing to alleviate that. Gin tried to downplay her concern, but it wasn't always easy for her to hide her feelings. She was with Thomas at the hospital, and after some parental interrogation, they handed the cell over to Jon.

My throat closed when I heard him speak. His voice sounded so strong and steady, and the knowledge we'd nearly lost him rendered me inarticulate. He knew I wasn't one to display much in the way of deep emotion and must have sensed I was on the edge, because he joked around until I was able to return his banter. Then I told him we were after his boss, who'd ordered a hit on him. From the disbelief in his voice, I could imagine the surprised expression on his face. Jon promised to make sure Gin and Thomas kept that bit of news under their hats, and we disconnected.

On the way to the NPIU field office, Tony and Rosie explained how they found us. Tony had gotten hold of a plat map of the area and a number of potentially relevant mine maps, thanks to the Minnesota Department of Natural Resources Underground Mine Mapping Project. He concentrated on the area surrounding the cell tower that my signal had bounced off. Rosie did some complicated math and statistically figured out the probability of our location. Tony then confirmed the existence of an abandoned mine within spitting distance of her calculations. They contacted the St. Louis County authorities and the rest was living history.

I was never so thankful for nerds in my life.

Exhaustion pulled hard at my very core. More than once I startled myself awake. Tony must have seen my head drop and then bounce up in the rearview mirror. He said something to Rosie, and a second later, she thrust a box of protein bars and four bottles of water through the gap in the seats. Harry and I fell on the bars like rabid dogs and drank all the water in ten minutes flat.

By the time we arrived at the NPIU offices, Harry and I both bolted for our respective locker rooms. I couldn't stand one more minute in my sweat-stained, ripped, filthy clothes, and my scalp itched from the dust and debris that had taken up residence. I hoped a fast, hot shower might revive me.

Rosie went for the go-bag I kept under my desk, so I knew a fresh set of clothes would be waiting when I finished.

I stripped and deposited the remnants of my wardrobe in evidence bags. I wasn't sure any trace elements or DNA would be found on my clothing and shoes, but they were still evidence.

As I pivoted toward the shower, I caught sight of my reflection in the mirror. I braced my arms against the sink and leaned into my reflection. The right side of my face was puffy and bruised, and the outer edge of my eye was going black from Campbell's backhand. Seven stitches held the skin on my forehead together. The rest of me was covered with too many cuts, scrapes, and bruises to catalog.

I shuffled to the showers. The delicious feeling of hot water raining over my body was exquisite. If only I could stay forever...but we were burning time.

"Cailin," Rosie called from the locker room, "your clothes are out here."

"Can you grab the shampoo and body wash for me? In the right-hand side pocket."

"Got 'em." Her voice grew louder. "Here you go." She handed me the requested items through the curtain. "Towel's hanging on the hook right beside the stall."

"Thanks, Rosie."

Her shadow stilled. "Wasn't sure we'd find you, McKenna. You scared me."

"I know. It wouldn't have happened without you and Tony."

Gruffly, she said, "Fifteen minutes, and we're meeting in the main conference room."

I squeezed body wash into my hand. "I'll be there."

I gave myself three latherings before I felt like I was even close to human. With a final rinse and a resigned sigh, I shut off the water and groped between the plastic curtain and the tile-covered wall for the towel.

"Here," a very familiar voice said. The terrycloth was thrust into my hand.

I ripped the curtain open.

Alex stood before me, the expression on her face at first relieved and then aghast as her eyes raked me from head to foot. She uttered a stunned, "Oh, my God," and then I was out of the stall, in her arms. She didn't care that I was soaking wet, and I didn't care how bad I hurt. I crushed her to me. I'd almost lost this. Lost her.

My hands cupped her warm face and then I was kissing her with a desperation I could barely contain. I lost myself in the taste, the texture, the smell that was my lover. Many moments later Alex gently pulled away. If we were anywhere but the locker room of the NPIU, I would have taken her—not with mindless passion—but with careful intention. The base need, the instinctual drive to reaffirm life in the arms of the person who meant everything to me, was almost impossible to deny. I whimpered in frustration.

Alex wrapped the towel around me and held her palm to the undamaged side of my face. "I'm sorry, baby. Rosie let me in with the understanding I was to deliver you in"—she glanced at her watch—"uh-oh, we're late. Shit."

Between the two of us, I was redressed and ready to go in under three minutes. With another swift kiss, Alex took off for the elevator and I headed for the gathering.

I stood before the closed door of the conference room and took a centering breath. I had no idea what awaited me on the other side, especially since I'd been unofficially suspended before any of this latest insanity started.

Time to face the music, Cailin, with all the dignity your battered body can muster. I thrust the door open and strode in, shoulders back, head high.

We were a sight to behold, Harry and me. With all our stitches, bruises, cuts, and scrapes, we were the walking wounded. Harry, too, had cleaned himself up and was dressed in designer jeans and a fancy-brand shirt that could only belong to Clotheshorse Cirilli.

Rosie was the first to voice what I was sure the rest were thinking. "When you got off the helicopter, I was all ready to give you both crap about looking like you'd been on a hell of a bender, but man, all you look like is shit."

Harry glanced at me, and I could read the strain in his eyes. The protein bar buzz was wearing off, and all my body parts hurt. He wasn't in any better shape

After a long moment, Martinez said, "McKenna's like a bad penny. You can try to get rid of her, but she still keeps popping up. Looks like Robinson has the same kind of luck." He paused, then added in a gruffer voice, "I'm glad you're both okay."

Singleton said, "Okay. Now that we have our people back, we need to focus. Here's what we know. First, the man behind the Twin Cities chapter of the Soldiers of Christ is Hennepin County Attorney Quenton Campbell. That'll cause one hell of a ruckus when it comes out to the public. Agents McKenna and Robinson can both place him at the warehouse. We're running the records right now to link him to any properties fitting the warehouse profile they provided." He nodded at Harry and me. "We have enough probable cause to arrest him on kidnapping and assault on a peace officer, and that's only scratching the surface."

Singleton leaned back in his chair and tugged at his already loosened tie. I couldn't remember a time I'd ever witnessed him so disheveled.

"Right now," he continued, "Chief Helling and I both feel very strongly about keeping this information to ourselves. It would be far too easy for a leak to occur, and alert Campbell we're onto him, before we have a plan to bring him into custody."

"Chief?" Singleton nodded at Helling and ceded the floor.

"Thank you," Helling said. "Ironically enough, Campbell is scheduled to address the ACLU on the subject of neighborhood diversity and safety at a charity fundraiser at seven this evening at the Minneapolis Convention Center. I can't stress enough the fallout that will occur when it comes out Campbell is, among other things, a leader of a hate group. What I propose is we move in and apprehend him before he has a chance to make his appearance, but while he's at the convention center. I agree that we can't allow anyone to let something slip." Helling glanced at his notepad. "We're waiting, because, as of this moment, he's AWOL from his office and has been unreachable. We're hoping the pull of a high-profile speech will be too much for his power-hungry ego to give up. Agent Weatherspoon?"

All eyes now turned on the SSA.

Weatherspoon said, "We've drawn up teams, and the divisions are as follows. Agent Cirilli, Officer Martinez, and I will make direct contact and proceed with the arrest.

"Agents Robinson and Nakamura, along with Officer Peterson, will coordinate escape route coverage. Chief Helling will call out the SRT team an hour ahead and have them placed before we arrive. We're not moving on Campbell until he's backstage.

"Security's already high, and extra uniforms will be on

scene in case something goes awry."

Singleton muttered, "As these things are bound to."

"True," Weatherspoon said. "The extra law-enforcement presence shouldn't appear too suspicious since Campbell tends to travel with a large security contingent anyway. He routinely asks for additional officers when he makes public appearances."

"Yeah," Cirilli said. "Now we know why."

Weatherspoon looked at Tony. "Agent Smith will be in our communications vehicle, coordinating the NPIU and SRT, and will maintain communication with MPD dispatch. Any questions?"

With a sinking feeling, I asked, "What can I do?"

Weatherspoon shot a quick glance at Singleton, who regarded me with eyes that were at once kind, yet resolute. "I'm sorry, Agent McKenna, but the second you walk out of this room, you're on paid administrative leave."

Goddamn it. I knew I was in trouble, but I didn't expect that.

A jumble of voices, including my own, erupted.

Singleton let the rumble continue for a few seconds and then bellowed, "Stop!"

The silence was instantaneous.

"There will be no discussion on this point." Singleton pinned me in place with his gaze. "Agent McKenna, I leave it up to you to inform the rest of the team of what has occurred in the past forty-eight hours." He scanned the faces in the room. "If no one has any other questions, we will reconvene at the BatMobile in the parking garage at five sharp."

"Wait a minute," I said. "What about tomorrow's bombing in Saint Paul? Even if Campbell and his cronies are arrested, it's the women who are carrying out the planning and execution."

Singleton nodded. "You're exactly right, and we've turned that operation over to the FBI. They've got it well in hand. Meanwhile, we've got our own operation to accomplish.

"McKenna, I'm sorry. When you're finished in here, I need you in my office. This meeting is adjourned."

Helling, Singleton, and SSA Weatherspoon filed out of the room. Six pairs of eyes stared at me in obvious confusion. Harry slumped back in his seat, disgust on his face.

"Okay." Ripping the Band-Aid off was probably the easiest way to get this over with. "I'm the suspect in a homicide." I never, ever, thought those words would come out of my mouth.

The unanimous widening of eyes would have been comical under other circumstances. I explained the basics of Eli's death.

"Fuck this." Martinez slammed a hand on the table. "Complete and utter bullshit."

"I concur." Tony said. "If McKenna wanted someone dead, all she'd have to do is come to us and no one would ever find the body."

Although I was furious, Tony's comment made me smile. "I understand the position Singleton's in. Kick some ass for me, guys." I stood, walked out, and shut the door quietly behind me.

Before I'd taken four steps, Harry came out of the conference room and grabbed my arm. "Cailin, wait. You're not going to stand down, are you?"

While I had absolutely no intention of backing off, I wasn't about to involve my coworkers in disobeying a direct order from the boss. "After the shit that asshole did to us? After what he did to Jon? No way. But I don't want you involved."

Harry glanced away, then he met my eyes again. His intensity nearly scorched a hole through me. "You're a stubborn woman, McKenna."

"Whatever." I tried to pull away, but Harry tightened his grip and leaned close.

"Listen to me."

"What?"

"You know Singleton will make you turn in your badge and weapon, and when you can't give him your gun, he'll make you fill out endless missing service pistol paperwork."

I knew.

"Here." He let go of me, rummaged in his pocket, and pulled out his keys. "Take my car. In the trunk you'll find something that'll work. I don't know where we'll be set up, and I probably won't be able to contact you. It's on you to get yourself in."

"Harry, I—"

"Don't even say it. Just be safe. And don't crash the fuckin' rental car because you're not listed as a legal driver." With that he spun around to reenter the conference room.

I didn't care what this would mean to my career, what this could do to my reputation. I made a beeline for the back stairwell and the asylum of Harry's car.

Chapter 21

Safely buckled behind the wheel of Agent Robinson's rental, I headed down Hennepin and watched the day slowly give way to twilight. I flipped the headlights on and drove without a plan. I wasn't sure where to go, but I'd better come up with something fast. I crossed the Mississippi Bridge and headed east.

The glow of the huge Old Milwaukee sign on the east bank of the river looked like an obnoxious North Star. I pulled into the parking lot of Surdyk's, a landmark liquor store that was always busy. The lot was nearly full but I found an open space. What was I thinking? I'd be in some seriously deep trouble if I followed through with this non-plan. I switched the car off and scanned the area. The traffic on Hennepin moved steadily, and no one was in my immediate vicinity. Might as well see what surprises Harry had in his trunk.

Another quick glance around assured me I was still alone in the lot. I popped the lock and slowly raised the lid. Two black plastic cases sat side by side on the trunk floor. I grabbed them and got back in the car and checked the time. The in-dash clock read 5:05. By now my disappearance would be obvious. There was no going back.

I laid one of the cases on the passenger seat and propped the other between the steering wheel and my stomach. Adrenaline was once again rushing through my system, and I fumbled with the latch. A Glock .40 nestled inside with two additional loaded magazines, two boxes of ammo, and a silencer. Maybe our East Coast agent really was Hit Man Harry.

The weapon felt cold against my skin. I racked it and a bullet ejected and bounced off the passenger seat to the floor while another slid into the chamber. I dropped the magazine from the butt of the gun, picked up the wayward bullet, reloaded it, and replaced the magazine.

After holstering the gun, I took the other two magazines and slid them into the back pocket of my jeans. Then I checked the other case. Another Glock. Subcompact this time. I repeated the same procedure and tucked it in the pocket of my hoodie.

I replaced the two gun cases in the trunk and headed into the liquor store, feeling stiffness all through my body, but especially in my legs, neck, and shoulders. If I made it through this night, I was going to need a very stiff drink. I bought a bottle of Effen vodka and stowed it in the trunk. Properly prepared, I headed for the convention center.

By the time I found a parking space, it was almost six o'clock. I locked the car and bolted. My feet flew two steps at a time down the parking ramp stairs, but I slowed my pace when I crossed the street to the entrance. No need to attract undue attention. I flashed my NPIU badge at the security guards hovering near the entrance and kept moving. It was a good thing I'd gotten the chance to wash up and change out of the filthy clothing I'd been wearing. Better I didn't look like some homeless person trying to crash the party.

A huge sign directed people to a scrapbooking convention in one auditorium and to the ACLU fundraiser in another. I kept my head down and tried not to break into a run. The place truly was swarming with security and cops. It was critical no one recognize me, or I was done before I got anything started.

A number of entrances led into the auditorium that held the fundraiser. I picked one with the shortest line, which was growing longer by the second. As the line crept forward, I realized I had dual problems. The line was backed up because security was wanding everyone, and secondly, each person had a ticket that was scanned at the door. I was in trouble on both fronts. I shielded myself behind an African-American couple excitedly talking about the event. They were enthralled about Campbell's appearance.

If they only knew.

Think, Cailin. Maybe someone I knew was working

the detail and would let me in. Yeah, right. There had to be a way to get inside without a ticket. At this point, maybe fifteen people were ahead of me. Jesus Christ.

Behind me, a tall, hulking man held a cell phone two inches from his ear and spoke so loudly everyone in a twenty-foot radius could hear his half of the conversation.

Obnoxious Cell Guy said, "But I—You said you wanted to come. I already bought the tickets."

I glanced back at him in mild alarm.

He barked, "Fine!" and ended the call. A second later he growled, "To hell with it," and stomped out of line, accidentally clipping me as he blew by.

"Oh!" Spinning around, he reached out a hand to steady me. "You okay? Sorry about that."

"I'm fine, no problem." Take the chance, Cailin. "It was, ah, a little hard not to hear...did you just get stood up?"

"Yeah." His face was a mask of anger. "I wasted good money on these tickets and she tells me she got a better offer. Screw it. I'm outta here."

"Wait." My hand was in my pocket feeling for cash when a man behind Obnoxious Cell Guy called, "Hey! Can I take those tickets off your hands?"

"Gladly." Obnoxious Cell Guy pivoted away from me, handed him the tickets, and stalked off.

Son of a bitch. I snapped my mouth shut, deflated. A second late and an admission short. By now the line had shifted forward, and I was only six people from the entrance.

Two more long-ass minutes dragged by, and then it

was go-time. One of the guards, a kid who couldn't have been older than sixteen, approached, wand in hand. My heart jack-hammered. I palmed my badge and pulled it out of my pocket. Before I had a chance to show it, a different guard jogged up. "Hang on," he said.

It took me a second to recognize the guard was Bryan Peterson dressed in a rent-a-cop uniform. He gave me a pointed look and whispered something in the kid's ear. The kid nodded and jerked his thumb at me to enter the auditorium. Peterson melted into the crowd and disappeared.

Whoa. Timing is everything.

The auditorium looked like it held maybe five hundred seats. I slipped into the first empty aisle seat, four rows from the back. The place was filling up fast. I scanned the crowd for any sign of the team, with no luck. They were probably backstage. Plenty of uniforms roamed the room, and I recognized some plainclothes cops. Hordes of others were probably out of sight.

A voice in the back of my head reminded me I was putting my job, and possibly more, on the line. Was it worth it? I thought about the bastard getting up on that podium to wave the flag of equality, while underneath he was nothing more than a deadly snake in expensive clothes. A snake who'd tried to kill Jon, and then Harry and me.

Hell, yes. Taking that son of a bitch down was worth whatever the cost.

The house lights dimmed and people scurried to their seats. I wondered if Campbell had been taken into custody yet.

The crowd quieted in anticipation.

A goateed man in a dark suit approached the podium. "I'm sorry for the delay. Quenton Campbell will be out momentarily. I hope you've all come with open hearts and open wallets to—"

Three thunderous explosions came from backstage. The goateed man looked around in confusion. Someone yelled, "Gunshots!" and that was it. Chaos ensued.

I drew my gun, stepped into the aisle, and surged upstream against a tide of panicked people. The room was a cacophony of shouting. Women's screams reverberated from the rafters. The stampeding crowd pressed toward the exit doors, unmindful of those who weren't moving as fast as they were.

The deluge of hysterical humanity was relentless. I abandoned the aisle and moved deeper into the row, flinging chairs out of my way. I finally hit the front row and vaulted the railing between the seats and the stage. Two more gunshots rang out behind the curtain. I ducked down and charged for the stage stairs. If I could get onto the platform, I could sneak around the curtain shielding the backstage area without totally exposing myself.

I leaped up the set of five steps and grabbed the edge of the black curtain. Before I could complete the action, something crashed into me from the other side. The impact was enough to launch me backward. I sailed over the steps and smashed hard on the unforgiving cement. I felt my head impact the floor, and goddamn, that hurt. The gun was jarred from my hand and slid under the first couple rows of chairs, way out of reach.

My head was spinning, and my eyes didn't want to focus. Welcome to the merry-go-round. I got an elbow under me, and pushed up, only to have it slide out, and down I went again.

With a loud crack, the curtain rod above broke away from its moorings. The fifty-foot bar fell, billowing black cloth, and crashed against the stage. If I hadn't been knocked out of the way, the four-inch diameter rod would've landed right on top of me.

A number of lumps moved under the fallen cloth. A head appeared at one edge, and I recognized a disheveled, wild-eyed Quenton Campbell. He was shouting and struggling with someone who was shielded by the curtain. I desperately tried to pull the subcompact out of my hoodie pocket, but the front sight was snagged on the cloth.

Campbell kicked viciously at whoever was holding him, and they let go. Blood streamed down his face and he looked around wildly. Trying to orient himself?

He clutched a silver pistol in his right hand. He started to rise, then his gaze landed on me. I was still sprawled on my back. Instead of making a dash for freedom he limped to the edge of the stage and looked down at me, hatred burning in his eyes. He pointed his pretty silver widow-maker directly at me.

Suddenly, everything shifted into slow motion. Sound faded. My eyesight tunneled until all I saw was a burst of fire erupt from the end of Campbell's gun. Something hit me. I quit trying to disentangle my gun and shoved the muzzle against the material of my pocket. I pulled the trigger. Once, twice, maybe more.

The impact of at least one of my bullets stopped Campbell's forward motion, but didn't take him down. Campbell's mouth moved. I couldn't hear anything. He swayed. Then Harry, Martinez, and two other men flattened him.

I tried to breathe. Tried again to get to my feet. Made it to my knees before I fell forward. Pain exploded through my nerve endings. I think I cried out. Then Harry was there. He was saying something but I couldn't tell what. His eyes were open wide.

Then I was back. Almost sorry my hearing returned. Harry was shouting; other people shouted back.

Harry tried to roll me over, and it hurt so bad I shrieked. He pressed one hand hard against my side. The other gripped my thigh so tightly I wanted to hit him. I squeezed my eyes shut and told him to stop. Stars floated behind my closed lids.

Then paramedics swarmed me. It was all motion and yelling and bright lights. They strapped me to a gurney in a hurry. Somewhere along the line the darkness took me away.

Chapter 22

Beeping. Regular beep, beep, beeping. So irritating. I tried to swallow. Didn't do much good. My eyes were stuck shut. Tried again, forced one open. White ceiling. I blinked, tilted my head to the side. Alex was sound asleep in a chair.

I dropped into oblivion again.

The next time I surfaced, the beep-beeping was still beeping, but now the low murmur of voices blended into it. Eyes opened easier.

Harry, Rosie, and Alex were huddled at the end of a bed. My bed. This wasn't good. I tried to focus on what was hurting, but still felt too floaty.

"Wha's going...on?"

Alex hustled around the bed, a haunted expression

shadowing her face. "Hey, babe," she whispered and gently brushed her thumb across my forehead.

Harry came up beside her. In an uncharacteristically soft voice, he said, "Think you're gonna get out of hot water playing hurt, do ya?"

Rosie peered around Harry. "She lives." She sounded droll, but even through my stupor I saw concern reflected in her eyes.

I opened my mouth experimentally but nothing more came out.

"Here." Alex grabbed a Pepto-Bismol-colored container and scooped something out of it. She brought a spoon to my lips and tilted it. Pebbly chunks of ice slid into my mouth. I rolled them around my tongue, swallowed, and accepted another scoop.

"Where am I?" My voice sounded like it was coming from the bottom of a rusty bucket.

"HCMC. You were shot at the convention center. Do you remember?"

I closed my eyes. Campbell. My inability to get up. My inability to pull the gun from my pocket. The flash from Campbell's weapon. The split-second decision I made to shoot blind through my jacket.

Everything after that was a big blank. "How bad?"

The muscle in Alex's jaw jumped. "The bullet entered through your right quad, bounced off your femur, nicked your large intestine and right kidney, and exited through your right latissimus dorsi.

Rosie said, "You were in surgery for three hours."

Holy shit. "What day is it?"

"Sunday morning." Harry put his hand on my left knee and gently squeezed.

It was like a switch was flipped. Things went from fuzzy to horrifying. I stiffened and let out a pained hiss. Everything on my right side, from my toes to my shoulder, felt like pulverized beef. I tried to breathe through it, and once the pain receded enough, I consciously worked to relax. The pain faded more. "Jesus."

"Someone needs more pain meds." Harry pushed the nurse's call button while Alex stoically scooped more ice into my mouth. The water slid down my throat, and I concentrated on the cold sensation.

"Harry," I mumbled hoarsely.

"Right here."

"If they don't bring me some fucking good painkillers soon, bring me the bottle I stuck in your trunk."

"The vodka?" he asked.

"Yeah."

"Oops. Thought that was a weird gift from the rental car company. Rosie and I sort of polished it off."

I groaned. "Ass-hat."

He laughed.

"What about Jon?"

Alex put her hand on the top of my head, nowhere near the stitches. "He'll be released tomorrow as long as the doctor cooperates. He's as bad a patient as you are."

I closed my eyes. "I'm a good patient."

A nurse appeared and delivered some magical serum into my IV. She patted my shoulder. "That should take effect very quickly. Call me if you need anything." She whisked out of the room with a smile.

I felt the hit of the drug and my muscles relaxed. Then another thought popped my eyes open. "Campbell?"

Rosie said, "You're one for two. One of your shots missed, but the other caught him in the chest. He'll live. I'm not sure if that's a good thing or not. We got him, though."

"What about," I tried to swallow and accepted another spoonful of ice. Once it melted, I asked, "What about the Soldiers of Christ?"

Rosie gingerly put her hand on my foot. "Martinez will be here in a little bit. We promised him he could tell you about that."

My eyelids were drooping. "S'kay."

I felt lips on my eyebrow, and warm breath rolled across my skin. "Go to sleep, baby," Alex whispered.

I obeyed.

★ ★ ★

When I opened my eyes again Harry and Rosie were gone. Alex was in the chair on my right, and Gin sat on a folding chair on my left. I blinked at Gin.

She glanced up from her magazine and saw my eyes were open. "Look who's awake." She leaned over the edge of the bed. "Hey, sweetheart. You hurting?"

I took a pain inventory. If I didn't move it was okay. I tried out a smile. That worked pretty well. "Okay for now. Sorry to worry you." My voice was less hoarse, and I felt more aware. "Where's Thomas?"

Gin gave me a genuine, from-the-heart smile. "Playing chess with Jon."

"One of these days Jon'll beat him."

"I think," Gin whispered conspiratorially, "Jon lets Thomas win."

A familiar voice called from the doorway, "Safe to visit?"

"Sure," Alex called out.

Director Singleton popped his head around the doorjamb and then came all the way in.

I briefly wondered if I was about to lose my job, but I was too dopey with drugs to get very worked up.

"Alex. Mrs. McKenna." He nodded at Gin. "You've had your hands full with this one, haven't you."

Gin laughed. "That's an understatement."

"I heard the doc says she'll be fixed up in no time." Singleton met my eyes. "I've got good news and bad."

Uh-oh.

"First the bad news. Cailin, you're on mandatory leave." He held up a hand. "Don't you say a word. You are officially suspended, with pay, until the investigation of the Campbell shooting is completed. Then you'll have a meeting with me and Richard Park."

Oh, shit. Park was near the top of the NPIU hierarchy. I was going to kiss my job goodbye. Fuck it. Shooting that son of a bitch was worth it.

"The good news is the investigation into Elisa Knight's death is almost finished, and unless something bizarre happens, I think you'll be cleared of any wrongdoing."

I was so caught up in the "you're cleared" part of Singleton's comment that I hardly heard Gin gasp. "What?" she asked in a bewildered tone. "Eli Knight's dead?"

Oh, God. I croaked out, "Long story."

Singleton glanced from Gin to me. "I'll let Cailin explain later."

Gin sighed.

Alex took my hand and entwined our fingers. I squeezed, and she returned it.

Singleton's kind look slid from his face, and his normal, serious look returned. "Off the record, McKenna, you're a pain in my posterior. Especially when you don't listen. However, I'm extremely happy that you'll be on your feet soon." He gently squeezed my toes. "But, if you ever, *ever* disobey another direct order, I'll publicly tan your hide and send you to a post in Supai, Arizona. Believe me, that's one place you don't want to be for any length of time." He suppressed a smile. "I have to run. Listen to your doctors, do your physical therapy. I want you back ASAP."

Talk about whiplash.

With a polite nod to Alex and Gin, Singleton departed.

Ten minutes later, after being fussed over by a nurse who was delighted that I was awake, the hospital door swung open and Martinez entered. He was decked out in an old leather motorcycle jacket and black jeans. From the look of the shadows below his eyes and the gauntness in his face, he needed a big time-out.

"Mrs. McKenna, Alex." Martinez carefully laid his hand on my left leg. Apparently they'd all been schooled in the fact that my left side was fair game while the right was off limits. "And you. What are we going to do with you, McKenna?"

I stuck my tongue out at him.

Alex laughed, the first real laugh I'd heard out of her since I'd woken. "She's definitely feeling better."

I glanced at Alex, happy to see the furrow between her brows relaxing. The love I felt for her shook me to the core. Then an image of Eli popped into my head. The warm, fuzzy feeling faded.

Martinez said, "Thought you might want an update on the Lorenzo/Campbell case."

"Duh," I muttered.

"Her sarcasm's returning." Alex smiled. "Things are moving in the right direction."

"After the debacle at the convention center," Martinez said, "they reassigned Mike's case to Chad Huber." Chad was an assistant prosecutor who was a fantastic youth advocate. He'd do whatever he could to properly adjudicate Mike and would try to get him the help he needed.

Martinez wearily rubbed his face. "Here's the shit. Looks like Mike's mutt wasn't poisoned by the boys, after all. Appears the next-door neighbor was having radiator problems. Had drained antifreeze into a pan. Left it sitting out while he ate a late dinner. The container was in his garage, but the garage door was open."

"Goddamn," I whispered. My gut clenched and not

from the bullet wound. "How did the dog get out?"

"Turns out Hunter and Billy were in the neighborhood after all, and they opened the gate. They thought it would just be a prank, make Mike hunt for the dog for a while. Bragged to some of their friends about it the next morning."

"Un-fucking-believable." I glanced at Gin, who didn't appreciate the use of cuss words. "Sorry," I said meekly.

"It's all right, sweetheart. Sometimes such language is justified."

What had happened was a losing proposition for everyone. If only the two boys hadn't let the dog out. Would it have mattered if Mike hadn't gotten hold of the hate music? If only the radiator fluid hadn't been left out. If the bullying could have been put to a stop would things have still spiraled out of control? If Mike hadn't managed to get his hands on a gun? If fucking only.

Martinez said, "The school's gung-ho on addressing bullying and actively looking into ways of identifying, confronting, and circumventing it. Problem is, the ultimate answer lies at home, with parents proactively watching for behavior that leads to bullying and then taking action.

"On the bright side, the Twin Cities chapter of the Soldiers of Christ has disbanded, and a few thousand pounds of explosives were found on the property up north. Land belongs to a distant relative of Campbell's. Guess Campbell bribed the relative into letting him use it. At the Minnetonka house, we found notes and floor plans for the Xcel, some handwritten stuff about what they were intending to do. Nice work, McKenna. Because of you and Robinson, Quenton Campbell and his top cronies are going away for a very long time. Talk about a big man fallen."

"You have to get those crazy-as-shit women, too. They were evil personified."

"Oh, yes," Martinez said. "The top cronies I spoke of are a lot of the women. But it's clear that Campbell was the ringleader and the one who incited all of them to violence. Those women wanted his approval."

"I'm glad we got the son of a—" I glanced at Gin. "Jerk. Any news about the body in the mine?" I was not going anywhere near dark, enclosed spaces for a long while.

"Yeah," Martinez said. "Not all the tests are back, and there's still some dirt to dig, but we do know this. Campbell apparently challenged the leader of SOC for the position of the Augustus Primus. What the hell kind of name for a leader is that, anyway?" Martinez shook his head. "Christ. Anyway, the victim was taken to the mine, tied up, and laid across the tracks. Then they ran him over with an ore cart, chopping him into three pieces. Two of the groupies 'fessed up."

Alex's face went pale. "Jesus."

"Angel Saxon," I guessed.

"Bingo," Martinez said. "Makes another count against Campbell. Anyway," he leaned forward and braced his hands on the footboard. "How's Jon?"

Gin said, "Doing well. He'll be out tomorrow. Barring any major setbacks, he'll be fine."

"Excellent. Cailin, you heard from Singleton? How deep in the hole are you?"

"He was in. I'm officially suspended."

"But hey," Alex said, "she gets her pay until the investigation's done."

Martinez said, "She deserves triple time after being shot and branded."

Alex laughed. "My favorite part was when Singleton told her she was a pain his ass." Gin gave her the evil eye. "Whoops, sorry."

"I'll stay on his good side," I said, "so he doesn't send me somewhere that sounded really terrible."

The meds in my IV were suddenly working full power, and I was drifting. The last thing I heard was Martinez saying, "Only you, McKenna."

Chapter 23

Two days later, Alex sat on the bed next to me while we watched the first season of *Greatest American Hero* on an iPad she'd brought from home.

There was a knock at the door. I hit pause and yelled, "Come in." I wondered who would bother knocking. Most everyone I knew simply barged right into the room. We'd been plied with food from the Blue Fin, courtesy of Jada, and Pick had popped in morning and evening on her way to and from work.

A serious-faced Detective Brad Hutchinson came into the room. He was dressed in a fancy suit and his hair was almost waxed into place. He stopped at the end of the bed and shifted from foot to foot.

"Court today?" I asked. He certainly wasn't

dressed up for me.

Hutchinson nodded mournfully. "At two. Worst part of the job."

I laughed. "It can be. What do we owe this pleasure to, Detective? Come to cart me off? It wouldn't look too good for you to cuff me to the bed and wheel me down the hall." I might be stuck on my back, pumped full of fluids and antibiotics and subsisting on a liquid diet, but there was nothing wrong with my mouth.

"Agent McKenna, I heard about your sense of humor," Hutchinson said humorlessly. "I also heard about what happened. I'm glad things went okay and you weren't killed."

Alex slid off the bed. "I can leave..."

Hutchinson glanced at her. "You don't need to."

Alex slowly sat back down.

"I'm here to tell you you're officially off the hook in the Elisa Knight case."

While that was no surprise, a weight lifted off me. "What exactly happened to her?"

Hutchinson slid a hand into his pocket, and I heard the muted clink of coins as he toyed with them. "Turns out Randall Corvik, Miss Knight's assistant, wanted her job a little too badly."

"Randy the Hamster? No way."

"He lured her to the Stone Arch Bridge in the middle of the night on the pretense of giving her some dirt on a rival company. One thing led to another, and they got into an argument about the limits and terms of his position. Things got out of hand, and in a fit of anger, he shoved her over the edge. She whacked her head on an abutment before she hit the water, and that's what killed her. Corvik confessed after we applied pressure. Cracked like an acorn, in fact."

Wow.

"After he saw you come into the office and confront Ms. Knight twice, he figured you were the perfect scapegoat. We've notified your supervisor and told him you're good to go."

"Thanks. This is...thanks." I didn't know what else to say. The whole situation was sad, but I was no longer angry at Eli. Such a shame, a life wasted for greed.

Hutchinson departed.

Alex had just settled beside me when the door opened again.

"What is this," I grumbled, "Grand Central Station?"

Harry walked in with Rosie.

"What's up?" I asked. Both of them had odd looks on their faces. I narrowed my eyes. "What's wrong?"

Instead of chattering at me like she normally did, Rosie glanced at Harry and back at me. "You tell her."

"Chicken?" Humor colored Harry's tone, and I relaxed a fraction.

"Okay, fine." Rosie took a breath. "Harry and I are heading to Hawaii."

"What?" The surprised expression on Alex's face reminded me I hadn't caught her up on their office romance.

Harry cleared his throat. "We'll be back in a couple weeks." He glanced fondly at the top of Rosie's head and then at me. "On a more serious note, we ran into Detective Hutchinson downstairs. He told us what went down with Eli."

"Yeah." I shook my head. "Unbelievable."

"You doing okay?" Rosie asked.

"I am. I need some time to digest the news, but I'm fine."

Harry crossed his arms. "You behave and listen to the good doctor and the nurses. By the time we get back, maybe you'll be out of here."

"Don't worry," Alex said. "I'll keep her on the straight and narrow."

"Good." Harry made for the door and pulled it open.

Rosie hurried after him. "Sorry to run, but we have a plane to catch."

"Harry!" I called.

He turned around.

"Better take good care of her, or else."

His face was surprisingly solemn. "You know it."

After the door shut, Alex gingerly relaxed once again. I grabbed her wrist and planted a kiss on her palm. She curled her hand around my jaw and closed her eyes. "Are you really okay?"

"There's still so much confusion in my brain. Eli. Mike. And Campbell." I sighed. "I know some questions can never be answered." I thought about Quenton Campbell and the hatred he carried. Why? What made someone that way? I didn't have enough energy for that battle at the moment, so I let the thought float away. Alex picked up the remote and slid down the bed so her head was resting more comfortably on the pillow.

"Ready, my Greatest American Hero?"

"Shut up." I carefully shifted into a more comfortable position. Alex rubbed her cheek on my gown-covered shoulder and restarted the show.

I cringed as William Katt crashed in another attempt at flight. "Maybe it's time we took a trip of our own. How does Puerto Rico sound?"

Alex glanced sideways at me. A smile tugged at the corners of her mouth. "You serious?"

"Why not. I have time off. Gives you a chance to see your relatives."

"It's a great thought, but we can't afford it. The flight, the hotel, the time away from work. It's way too expensive."

"No, it's not."

"Yes, baby, it is. I periodically check prices in case something reasonable pops up. It'll take us forever to save for it, and you know how I feel about credit cards."

"I do and I can."

"Can what?"

"Afford it."

"Yeah." She smiled. "Right. You rob the evidence locker at the Fifth Precinct or something?"

"No...but you're cozied up to three quarters of a millionaire."

"What are you talking about?

"The insurance."

Alex stared at me. It was almost funny watching the disbelief ooze over her face. "You get that money? Eli's money?"

"I didn't kill her, so I might. After what she's put us through, we'd deserve it."

"Oh. My God."

"I suppose it'll take a couple of weeks to get the funds, but I have a lot more recovering to do anyway. Once things are squared around, let's do it."

"All right. Let's do it." She stared into space for a moment. "Nice thing about working for your mom. You can guilt her into giving me the time off."

"I'll call her tomorrow and see if we can't find out for sure. It'll give me something to look forward to while those evil PT people put me through my paces." I felt good about giving Alex a chance to see her family and even better about enjoying some sun, sand, and water.

"I love you, Cailin."

The sense of what I'd potentially lost hit me anew. I might have never heard those words again. I caught her chin, pulled her face to mine. My lips hovered a fraction of an inch from hers. I whispered, "I love you, too. So very much." We slowly and gently expressed our love, and I reveled in the promise of what awaited us once I healed. I caught Alex's lower lip between my teeth and lightly bit down before releasing it. "Always forever."

Alex closed her eyes. When she opened them, they sparkled with unshed tears. Her voice cracked as she whispered, "Always forever, baby. Always forever."

Books Available in the
Shay O'Hanlon Caper Series

Bingo Barge Murder
(A Shay O'Hanlon Caper Book 1)
2011, reprint 2014

As co-owner of The Rabbit Hole, a quirky-cool Minneapolis coffee shop, Shay O'Hanlon finds life highly caffeinated but far from dangerous. Until her lifelong friend Coop becomes a murder suspect. Kinky, Coop's former boss and the unsavory owner of The Bingo Barge, a sleazy gambling boat on the Mississippi, is dead. The weapon? Kinky's own supposedly lucky bronzed bingo marker.

While unearthing clues to absolve Coop, Mafia goons, on the hunt for some extremely valuable nuts, threaten Shay's world. Looking for the murderer without help from the cops is a tricky proposition—especially with sparks flying between Shay and the beautiful, yet fierce, Detective JT Bordeaux. When Shay's elderly caretaker and landlady is held for ransom by the mob, all bets are off. Can Shay find the killer before the killer finds her??

2012 Golden Crown Ann Bannon Popular Choice Award winner

Hide and Snake Murder
(A Shay O'Hanlon Caper Book 2)
2012

When Shay O'Hanlon's ill-mannered friend Baz steals a stuffed snake from a wealthy businessman, he wasn't expecting it to be filled with money. Nor was he expecting his aunt Agnes to take it with her on vacation to the Big Easy.

With trigger-happy thugs in hot pursuit, Shay leads her friends on a rowdy rescue mission from Minneapolis to New Orleans and back. Along the way, a bungled burglary puts the gang in a drug cartel's cross hairs, and a beautiful professor offers the only way out. But can Shay and the gang trust her with their lives?

2013 Independent Publisher's Book Award (IPPY) winner
2013 Golden Crown Literary Society Mystery/Thriller Goldie Award winner
2014 USA Book Award finalist

Pickle in the Middle Murder
(A Shay O'Hanlon Caper Book 3)
2013

Shay O'Hanlon never knew the Minnesota Renaissance Festival was such a strange and bawdy event until JT Bordeaux—her badge-wearing, medieval-loving girlfriend—drags her along for a visit. The sixteenth-century faire is full of thrilling jousts, feisty wenches, and pickle vendors showing off their tasty tonsil ticklers, but Shay is distracted by the call of her full bladder. While trying to rein in her newest dog's overactive nose, she finds a dead body with a pickle stuffed in his mouth. A real dead body. In the privy. And before Shay can shout "Huzzah!" JT is arrested for being the porta-potty body's murderer. Together with her quirky crew of caper-solving pals, Shay must scramble for clues to free JT from the clink ...and her troubled past.

2014 USA Book Award finalist

Chip Off the Ice Block Murder
(A Shay O'Hanlon Caper Book 4)
2014

Between back room poker, bloody stiffs, decades-old secrets, smoking guns, and missing fathers, Shay O'Hanlon's beliefs are shaken to the core in *Chip Off the Ice Block Murder*. Love, loyalty, and lies of the past collide in the fourth book of the Shay O'Hanlon Caper series.

2014 USA Book Award Winner

About the Author

Jessie Chandler is a 17-year bingo hall veteran, State Patrol dispatcher, and former police officer. She resides in Minneapolis, Minnesota, with her partner and wife, Betty. Ollie and Fozzy Bear, two frisky canines, graciously allow Jessie and Betty to live with them as long as they receive treats on a regular basis. A former vice president of the Twin Cities Chapter of Sisters In Crime, Jessie is a board member for the Midwest Chapter of Mystery Writers of America. Visit Jessie at jessiechandler.com.

CPSIA information can be obtained
at www.ICGtesting.com
Printed in the USA
FFOW04n0749020315
11373FF

9 781633 048034